Kissing a Killer

David Carter

TrackerDog Media

An Inspector Walter Darriteau Murder Mystery

© David Carter & TrackerDog Media 2017

Follow David on Twitter @TheBookBloke

www.davidcarterbooks.co.uk

First Edition.

Updated July 2021

This book is dedicated to
Adsheads everywhere, and
especially Eric, Colin, Philip
and Hazel (my mother).
Now all gone but still
hugely missed.

By the same author:

The Inspector Walter Darriteau Books:

The Murder Diaries - Seven Times Over
The Sound of Sirens
The Twelfth Apostle
Kissing a Killer
The Legal & the Illicit
The Death Broker
Five Dead Rooks
Old Cold Bones
The Walter Darriteau Box Set – One
The Missing Man
Falling

Other Books:

State Sponsored Terror
The Life and Loves of Gringo Greene
The Inconvenient Unborn
Grist Vergette's Curious Clock
Drift and Badger and the Search for Uncle Mo
Down into the Darkness
The Fish Catcher
The Bunny and the Bear

Chapter One

He was strong. Incredibly strong. She stared up into his dark, unblinking eyes. Nothing there. No pity, no emotion, no feeling, no humanity, nothing but an iciness that chilled her bones.

When you are close to death your whole life flashes before you, so they say, but it was not Eleanor Wright's life that flashed through her tortured brain, but his, the attacker, her killer designate, the cold strong nameless man who held her so.

Why was he doing this? Why did he hate her so much? Why did he hate himself so much? Perhaps he had been abused as a little boy. Perhaps his father had beaten him. Maybe he didn't have a father and had grown up wild. Maybe he'd been beaten by a wicked stepmother, and this was his idea of revenge. All of those things were possible, or none of them at all. Maybe he simply had a screw loose. There are lots of guys wandering about with loose and missing screws, and she knew that well enough, just as most women do.

It was her mother's scolding face that next presented itself to her racing brain. Eleanor recalled the conversation as if she had hours to live, days even. It only took a second.

'You know what you are doing is so wrong!'

'I need the money, mum!'

'Get a bloody job then!'

'What, like you? Serving teas and sandwiches all day to the afternoon coffin dodgers for the minimum wage? I don't think so! Not a chance!'

'At least it's honest…. and respectable.'

'Don't start down that line again!'

'Don't you think God sees what you are doing… every time you do those perverted things?'

1

'God! God? What did your so-called God ever do for you?'

'He gave me you, for a start!'

'Well, you drew the bloody booby prize there!'

'Don't be so wicked! I am blessed. You are blessed, too. On the day of judgement…'

'Yeah, yeah, well I have news for you, mother dear; there's no such thing as a God! Or any crappy day of judgement either. You're in for a big disappointment. I'm off out. Derek said he'd treat me to a curry.'

'And that Derek's a useless article too!'

'Yeah right, and the hot men are queuing up to see you as well.'

'Don't involve me in your sordid business!'

It had been a fairly typical mother/daughter conversation in the Wright family in recent times, but Eleanor's full attention was brought back to the present, to the man in front of her, strangling her.

She wanted to scream, but he was never going to allow that. And anyway, the caravan was remote, at least half a mile to the next one, and being November, that would be vacant anyway. She could hear the rain drumming on the roof. It was getting heavier, too. Screaming would be a total waste of precious energy. She stared up into those dark eyes. If only she could stab him in those cold eyes with her long and strong fingernails; that would make him think twice, but he'd thought of that. He'd come prepared. She recalled his exact words when he had tapped on her caravan door.

'You're open for business, I believe?'

'It's a bit late, ain't it?'

'Never too late for business, bonny lass. Come on, open up, I've plenty of cash, and we have all night.'

'Can't you come back tomorrow? I'm not really in the mood.'

'No! Open up! It's starting to rain,' and he leant on the flimsy door, and she was never going to resist, for one simple reason.

She liked the look of him, and the sound of his calm voice, his neat understated smile, and the thought of plenty of cash.

He was so much better looking than the aging creeps who normally found their way down to her old caravan beside the swirling River Dee. Often violent, often drunk, often in need of a damned good wash, often in filthy smoke-ridden clothes, often out of shape and flabby, the kind of gone-to-seed guys that normal women would run a mile from. That's why they needed her, or someone like her, though they didn't want to pay for it, and often barely had enough cash even for a quick BJ.

Eleanor Wright knew that her name and whereabouts were an open secret in the local pubs. Fact was, that when she had first started doing tricks, she might even have encouraged the landlords to "Send 'em down to see me after you've finished with them!" Though she'd wiped that idiotic chapter from her mind with a big sigh and a shake of the head.

She stood across the caravan from him, weighing him up, as he appeared to be her, as they usually did. It was a little strange. A young, fit, good-looking guy like him having to visit the local whore. You'd think he could find a girl of his own. He'd make a fab boyfriend for someone, and for a moment she allowed herself to daydream.

Maybe he could become her boyfriend. Maybe they could go steady, and who knew where that might lead? He'd sure as hell make a heck of a husband, the kind of guy any girl would love to enter the pub with on his arm. Tall, fit, smart, healthy. But the days when young men like him would look at her seriously had long gone. Whoring's a hard business. It leaves its mark, even on a twenty-something; and there was nowt she could do about that.

She set her newly nail-polished hands on her hips and pouted and said, 'So what is it you want?'

His soft reply seeped through the caravan.

'Bit of rough, bit of slap, lots of sex.'

'All right,' she said, going to the door and flipping over the catch. 'Hundred quid.'

He left out a short, sharp grunt and shook his head.

'Not a chance! Fifty quid, and think yourself lucky,' and he opened his wallet and took out a fifty pound note and tossed it on the plastic topped coffee table.

Eleanor glanced down at it. It was a brand new note, straight from the bank, or the ATM, by the look of it, and fifty quid was fifty quid, and a girl had to eat, and obtain other vital provisions too.

'All right,' she said again. 'But not too rough.'

She thought she detected another slight smile, maybe more of a smirk.

'Come here!' he ordered, and she did as he asked without a second's hesitation.

He took hold of her shoulders and spun her round. He pulled a length of thick cord from his trouser pocket. He'd come prepared, she remembered thinking that, but then they often did, as he wound it round one wrist and then the other, and pulled it tight and knotted it, tying her hands together behind her back.

'Not too tight!'

'Shut it, bitch!'

He was going to be one of those.

An abuser, hopefully more vocal than physical. But she liked him, there was something quite different about this guy, even slightly exciting, and with a little luck she might enjoy what he had in mind. It did happen, occasionally, though not often.

He spun her round again and stared down into her green eyes. She wasn't even scared of him. That would have to change. He slipped his hands around her pretty white neck and squeezed. Not too hard. There was no hurry.

She tried to breathe, but couldn't.

'No!' she said.

'Yes!'

'Why?'

'Needs must.'

'I'll never understand men.'

4

'There's nothing to understand. Just prepare yourself.'

'For what?'

'To meet your maker.'

It was when he'd said that, that she'd recalled that miserable conversation with her overweight mother.

'I don't believe in God,' she gabbled, trying hard to speak.

'Not many people do,' he said, and this time he did smirk. 'Until they are about to meet him, or her, and then everyone does.'

She wanted to stab him in the eye, but that was impossible. She wanted to knee him in the groin, but already her legs were weakening. She thought of spitting in his face, into those dark intense eyes. It would be her final act, to spit in the face of her killer, but was that really how she wanted to sign off from this confusing and cruel world? With anger and spite? Right there, it didn't seem to her to be the right thing to do, and anyway, his grip was tightening. It was unlikely she could find sufficient puff to spit at all. She knew she would find it hard to manage a dribble.

He squeezed again, not fatally, but frighteningly, as if he was enjoying it. Prolonging the play, getting off on building up to a climax. She leant towards him and reached up. He smelt her cheap perfume.

He imagined she was about to bite him, on the throat or nose, lips or cheek.

'Don't you dare bite me, bitch!'

'No,' she said, the tiniest of whispers, or had he relaxed his grip sufficiently to allow her reply?

'Kiss,' she muttered, and standing on tiptoe, she planted a gentle kiss in the centre of his unlined forehead. She pulled away; and saw the lipstick on his fine face.

She tried to smile, but could not.

The dark was coming down fast.

The truth was, she wasn't that bothered. In the previous eighteen months she'd thought about doing it herself many a time. At least this way she would never take with her any guilt.

The perfect suicide.

Have someone else do it for you.

Don't some people pay a lot of money for that in Switzerland these days?

He said nothing further.

Not a word.

His eyes stared down at her, right through her, unblinking.

He was a nice man.

In different circumstances, he could have been a very nice man.

Suffocation.

Panic.

Involuntary struggling.

Even if you want to go, you still struggle. Funny that.

The body overrules the brain.

He was strong. Incredibly strong.

He held her tight and tighter still as she slipped away, and the last thing she remembered before all went black was planting that kiss on the face of her killer.

At least she had gone out with style, grace, and love.

That was something.

In Eleanor Wright's confused world, it was everything.

She was a loving person, was Eleanor, and love is all you need. It really is true. Love is all you need.

Chapter Two

He held her hard and still for a further two minutes. She was limp in his hands, but growing heavier. Her eyes were wide open as if they were about to pop, but it was clear to him they had ceased to see. Another thirty seconds, he thought, and he began counting them down.

Twenty-eight, twenty-nine, thirty, and he grinned to himself and let her go. She fell to the floor in a heap at his feet. He leant down and straightened her out, though he didn't know why he'd done that. Felt for a pulse. There was none. He would have been surprised if there was. He reached across to the coffee table and retrieved the fifty-pound note, and slipped it back in his pocket.

Stood up and went to the door. Unclipped it and went outside. The rain was heavier still, and thick cloud covered the moon and stars. He peered across the fields, back to the twisty unmade up lane that led to the main road. From the caravan doorway he could not see a single light anywhere, and that was as he liked it. There was a plane going over, still quite high, maybe going into Hawarden airport, but the chances of anyone up there seeing him down in the caravan doorway were a million to one.

He skipped outside and went to the end of the caravan, and the group of large old-fashioned blue gas canisters gathered there. They heated the place and provided fuel for the rare bit of cooking Eleanor did to impress an occasional client she deemed worthy of food. An old-fashioned gas canister for an old-fashioned caravan.

He reached behind the first canister, feeling for the red plastic container he had quietly placed there before he'd tapped on the door. The container was wet to the touch, but that didn't matter. It was watertight. Found the handle and grabbed and lifted it and took it inside and closed the door behind him.

7

The dead girl was on her back, staring at the ceiling, exactly where he'd left her. Her mouth was wide open, and that was inviting. He crouched down beside her, unscrewed the top, brought the container carefully to her mouth and gently tipped in liquid, as if she'd asked for a drink of lemonade. The thick clear fluid gurgled down her throat. A smell of petrol filled the small caravan. It was surprising how much went down there. Far more than he'd have guessed.

Then she was full, and overflowing, and petrol began spreading out on the floor, across the old lino that led away to an even older piece of red and green patterned carpet. He stood up and stepped away, and began throwing petrol over the furniture and bedding and old wooden fitments, and back to the girl and that short purple dress with the white frilly trim. He emptied the last of the petrol all over her clothing, soaking her, and set the empty container on the small worktop.

Took another look around.

Had he touched anything?

Not that he could remember, other than the door and the container and the girl, and none of those really mattered, for with a little luck none of those things would exist in another ten minutes. But to be sure he wiped the old metal door catch, inside and out.

He went to the doorway, took one last look, and pursed his lips as if deep in thought.

She was a strange girl.

It was almost as if she had wanted him to do what he had done, and he hadn't expected that. But that didn't matter, for she had made it easier for him. But there was no denying a little more fight, some genuine resistance, might have made things more interesting and more exciting, but hey, there are 3.75 billion females on this planet, give or take, and that number is growing every day, despite the activities of birth control methods and wars and disease, and people like him.

Murderers like him. He thought about the title. It brought another smirk to his clean-cut face. He was a murderer, and that was something; an achievement he never expected to make. Fact was, if he wanted another victim to fight harder, there were plenty of potential candidates to choose from.

He opened the door and stepped outside, and was happy to see the rain dwindling away to nothing. He turned back and looked inside. Took out a box of matches. Held his hands just inside the door to shelter from the wind, and struck one. Lit first time. Tossed it across the room.

BOOF!

Instant blaze.

The purple dress immediately engulfed.

He didn't dare glance at the liquid loaded face.

Pulled the door to and turned about and set off towards the twisty lane.

He was a quick walker and needed to be.

He could feel the heat on his neck and the back of his head.

Stuffed his hands deep in his jacket pockets, hunched his back, and watched his feet working hard to get away. He was leaving footsteps in the mud. That was clear, but it couldn't be helped. Maybe the rain would return and blur his retreat.

BANG!

The first of the gas bottles blew up. He glanced back over his shoulder. The caravan was fully ablaze. Part of the roof was collapsing into the main inferno. Just the metal frame remained, melting and bending and twisting as if in agony, before falling in on itself. Red and yellow and blue flames leapt into the air like a funeral pyre for a goddess.

'The Goddess of pleasure,' he muttered to himself, and smirked again, and already he was half way up that twisty lane on the way back to the main road and his car, and safety and freedom, and then en route back to his demanding day job.

He didn't see or hear a soul all the way back to the car and he wasn't surprised at that, not even a late night dog walker, for he knew not many people used that lane.

As he turned the corner onto the main road, he saw his new silver and black Cayton Cerisa Sports parked up ahead, maybe three hundred yards to the lay-by. By the time he reached the car, one vehicle had passed him coming head on, a large dark SUV. He casually looked away as it passed, while one vehicle had passed him from behind, a small scruffy box wagon, carrying God knows what to God knows where.

Twenty yards from the car, he took out his key fob and bleeped the car open. Orange lights flashed. A tiny bleep filled the heavy November air. He opened the nearside passenger door and reached inside and grabbed the old supermarket plastic bag he'd placed on the seat. He sat on the seat with his feet out on the grass verge and reached down and slipped off the black slip-on shoes. Glad to get them off, for they were a size too big.

He slipped them in the bag and added several large pebbles he'd set carefully in the footwell, and tied the bag tight. He reached across to the driver's seat where he'd left his favourite pair of grey and white trainers. Put them on and tied them up, and they sure felt good, like best quality gloves. Stood out of the car, closed the door, hurried round to the driver's side, opened up, and jumped inside.

Turned on the engine. The clock said 12.42am. November 18th, and a new Saturday was just beginning, and that was cool, for he always had plans aplenty on a Saturday.

It took him less than twenty minutes to drive back to Chester city centre. The traffic was light, and the car was fast and the rain was back, heavy and sustained, and that was cool too. As he approached the Grosvenor Bridge across the cold, dark and deep river, he glanced in the rear mirror. Nothing behind. Nothing at all. Couldn't be better.

He buzzed down the passenger window. Some rain blew in, as he took hold of the heavy plastic bag, and with one confident swing he flung it out of the window like a discus thrower. Over the grey stone parapet it went, as he watched it out of sight, falling down fast, splashing and crashing into the swirling and rain-refreshed water, entering the darkness like an arrow-beaked seabird out hunting, where it sank to the bottom in seconds. Only a few dozing mallard ducks witnessed the missile from above. The wrong sized shoes would never see the light of day again.

Chapter Three

Fred Ross had opened his business in Chester ten years before and had called it the Cuppa Cha Café, a name his first wife suggested, and as he couldn't think of anything better, he went along with it, though he'd often thought of changing it after that.

He was tall and slim with neat black greasy hair that gave him an Italianate appearance, something that he would encourage when referring to himself as the Italian stallion. It would make his predominantly female clientele laugh, and that was good, though there wasn't an Italianate cell in his entire body.

The business had grown steadily, he'd moved to larger premises just the once, and though he would moan and groan that he was working long hours for the benefit of the taxman and the landlord, the business would pay him a decent wage, and show a reasonable return at the year end, profits he ploughed into penny shares, a dangerous world full of sharks that would often bite his ankles, and drain his assets.

The business grew steadily for one solid reason. Attention to detail; and Fred Ross was as good an attention to detail man as you could find. All growing businesses need an attention to detail person, and Fred knew that, and never once took his eye off the ball.

So it wasn't surprising that on Monday morning he noticed Dorothy Wright wasn't quite on top of her game. She'd tried to make at least four calls from her mobile, and they were only the ones he was aware of. It annoyed him for two reasons. First, calls from mobiles were not permitted during work hours, and two, when she was staring at that damned thing she was neglecting the customers, and neglected customers had a frequent habit of seeking pastures new.

It wouldn't do. Competition in the small café world in Chester, just like every developed city on the planet in the twenty-first century, was fierce.

He cornered his manageress, a tall slim well made-up woman named Shirley, who happened to be his second wife.

'What the hell's wrong with Dot today?'

Shirley glanced across at Dot, who was serving and gossiping with a regular, and back at Fred. Shirley possessed many talents, but attention to detail was not one of them, a skill lack that annoyed Fred.

'Nowt that I know of, why?'

'She's been fiddling with that bloody mobile all morning.'

Shirley giggled and said, 'Maybe she's got a new boyfriend,' for Shirley was well aware that Dot was in the market for one.

Fred glanced at Dot's ample figure and doubted that.

'Have a word with her, will you? She's doing my head in!'

Shirley realised that Fred was annoyed about something major and muttered, 'Okay love, leave it with me.'

Fred disappeared into the back rooms to see if the next batch of steak pies were ready, as Shirley moved close to Dot and in a quiet moment whispered, 'Is everything all right, Dot?'

Dorothy pursed her lips and glanced into Shirley's blue eyes.

'Tell you the truth, Shirl, no.'

'What's the matter?'

'It's my Eleanor.'

'What about her?'

'She's fallen in with a bad crowd.'

'In what way?'

'I'd be too embarrassed to tell you, but it's not looking good.'

'Have you spoken to her?'

'I've been trying since Saturday morning. There's no answer, and that's not like our Ellie at all. She always leaves her mobile on for the clients…. her customers, like.'

'Where does she live now?'

'She has a small caravan down by the river. Horrible it is, old and smelly; I've been trying to get her into a decent flat. I can't help thinking she might have fallen over…. or something.'

'Well, you are no good to us like this. Fred's noticed something's wrong. Do you want to go and check?'

'Oh, could I? That would be great! You're fab, Shirl, anyone ever tell you that?' and not waiting a second in case Shirley changed her mind, or Fred came back, she took off her overall, grabbed her grubby raincoat from the hooks, and headed for the door, calling out over her shoulder, 'I'll be back just as soon as I can.'

A minute later, Fred returned and saw Dorothy was missing.

'Where is she?'

'She has a problem with her daughter. I told her to go and sort it out and get back as soon as she can.'

'Brilliant! Just as the lunchtime rush is about to start!'

'Don't fret so. We can manage, Fred!'

'We'll bloody well have to now! I'm stopping her wages!'

'Oh, stop being an old grumblebum, Freddy.'

'I'll grumblebum you in a minute!'

Shirley smirked at Fred and rippled her eyes and muttered, 'Promises promises!' Just as six new customers came in together and began inspecting the day's food offerings in the Cuppa Cha Café.

Dorothy Wright owned the same small modern Ford hatchback car as her daughter, except hers was red and Eleanor's blue. They'd bought them in a BOGOF deal from the local Ford dealer, buy one, get one free, who couldn't believe his luck when he shifted two old part exchange jalopies in one afternoon.

Dorothy was gunning hers round the Chester inner ring road, though in truth the little car was not really a gunning kind of car. It was half an hour later when Dot pulled off the main road and onto the unmade up twisty lane that led down to the river. It

14

must have been at least a mile from the turnoff to the caravan down by the water, but that mile seemed like ten.

Horrendous thoughts crashed through Dot's head. Had Ellie been attacked and injured? Or maybe fallen into the deep river after one vodka cocktail too many. The last twist in the lane revealed Ellie's little car, parked away to the right on a small piece of hard standing. At least she must be in, and that was something.

Earlier, Dot had a premonition that Ellie might have packed her few precious belongings into that car, and headed off to Cornwall or Oban or Wells-next-the-Sea, wherever that was, as she often talked of doing, after a particularly hard week. As far away as possible, she said, as if running away could ever solve deep-seated problems.

Ten more yards and reality hit.

Dot slammed on the brakes, almost banged her forehead on the hard steering wheel. Ellie's caravan was no more. Just a blackened heap of wreckage sitting on the red brick base designed to keep the caravan above the winter floods the Dee produced most years.

Dot's hand went to her mouth and she exhaled loudly.

'Oh, Geez!'

'Oh, bloody hell!'

'No!'

The one sided conversation came to an abrupt close, as Dot booted the car onward and round the last bend and up to the heap of twisted and burnt metal and cinders and ash.

'Kids!' she said, crawling out of the car, for she wasn't sure she wanted to see what there was to see.

'Bloody kids!' she repeated. 'Kids get up to all sorts these days. You'd be surprised,' and Dot thought that maybe Ellie had an outside client, one who preferred "entertaining" in their own home. It happened more and more, so Ellie said one afternoon in one of the local pubs, when she had treated her mother to a Sunday carvery luncheon, a meal that ended in a row after the obvious awkwardness. Two gents, who knew Ellie's trade, had taken to winking and leering at both Ellie, and worse still, her mother too, across the bar, and Dot couldn't wait to get out of there.

That was probably it, thought Dot, as she walked slowly before the face of the wreckage. She'll be working off site. Dot imagined the bricks were still hot, though she may have been wrong. She thought she could smell petrol, though that might have been a leak from the old Ford.

Thinking of which, she went over to Ellie's car and peered through the dirty windows. No one about, no one sleeping inside due to a recent loss of quarters. She tried the door. It opened. Ellie rarely locked it, especially down there where few people, other than Ellie's clients, ventured.

She took out her mobile and rang Ellie's number again, praying for it to ring, praying to hear some simple explanation. Straight to voicemail – *We cannot take your call at this time.*

'Shit!' she said aloud as she wandered back toward the charred remains of Ellie's former home.

The sun came out. A weak watery November sun, though quite bright for all that, and for a second Dot shielded her eyes, so much of a surprise was it. When she took her hand away she spotted something glinting in the sunlight within the wreckage.

'What the hell?'

She stood up uncomfortably on the brick base, set one foot within the charred remains, feeling crunching burnt wreckage giving way beneath her feet, and yes, it was warm too. She bent down and retrieved the sparkle. It was a large diamond, like the one set in Ellie's silver and diamond ring. Her daughter's most prized possession, given to her by her father four years earlier, before the afternoon he abandoned them, walking out, never to return.

Ellie never removed that ring. She'd put on a few pounds since then, and couldn't take it off. It was stuck fast on Ellie's finger, until now.

'Bugger!' said Dot aloud, thinking terrible thoughts as she took out her mobile again and slapped in triple nine.

Chapter Four

Inspector Walter Darriteau was in a great mood. He had a new girlfriend. He'd met her on the Internet. Everyone was doing it, they said, and Walter was no spring chicken, or spring cockerel, to be more accurate, and you only live once, and he'd lived alone for years and years, discounting a few brief dalliances along the way, and now when not far from retirement, he'd decided to take the bull by the horns, so to speak.

He imagined it would be nice to find someone a little more permanent.

Sergeant Karen Greenwood had steered him toward the site. She admitted she'd used it in the past, and that surprised him for Karen Greenwood was young, blonde, slim, blue-eyed, very desirable, and, if it wasn't politically incorrect to think, or say so in the twenty-first century, very pretty too.

'Everyone's doing it,' she'd said, giggling, and she told him the web address, and that was how he'd met the busty Carlene Henderson. Walter began thinking of her, of her heaving bosoms, before the phone rang.

DC Darren Gibbons grabbed it and barked, 'C.I.D'

Dorothy Wright had been passed through from central control.

'I've just discovered my daughter's caravan burnt to the ground. Can you send someone quick? I'm worried she might have been in there.'

'Okay, let's start at the beginning. Your name is?'

Walter stopped thinking of Carlene's assets and glanced across at Gibbons, as did Karen, for there was something immediate in his voice, something that alerted experienced officers like Walter and Karen.

Gibbons was talking again, loud, as was his style.

'Where is the caravan, where was the caravan?'

'By the river.'

'Yes, but where by the river, a postal address.'

'I don't know! She never gets post here, it's too remote. Can you come quick?'

'But where to? We need an address.'

Dot tried hard to remember the name of the twisty lane that led down from the main road but could not.

'I don't know!' she said again, close to tears.

'Keep calm. Which district?' asked Gibbons, maintaining his cool.

'Off the Farndon road.'

'Ah, I get you, hold on a sec,' and he jumped up and ran over to the massive big scale local map that covered half of one wall.

'What's happening?' asked Walter.

'Not sure, Guv, lady says her daughter's caravan has burnt down and she's worried her daughter was inside.'

'Where?' asked Karen, jumping up and joining Gibbons at the wall.

'She says by the river, a twisty lane, off the Farndon road.'

'Don't think there are many lanes off that road,' said Karen, pointing to a possible candidate.

'Yeah, that could be the one,' said Gibbons, hurrying back to the landline.

'Are you still there?'

'Course I'm still here, and twice as bloody worried. I've found a diamond in the wreckage. I think it's from her ring, and she never takes it off, never could take it off. Please hurry!'

'Is it at the bottom of Marigold Lane?'

'It is!! How did you know that?'

'Detective work,' said Gibbons, smirking at Karen. 'Someone will be with you in about twenty minutes.'

'Thank the Lord! See you soon. Don't forget me!'

'We'll not forget, we'll be there soon as we can,' said Gibbons, hanging up. 'Do you want me to go, Guv?'

'No. You hang on here. I want you and Hector to keep going through that CCTV stuff looking for any leads on the drug running op. I'll go. Karen, organise a car, and an unmarked one at that.'

'On my way,' said Karen, jumping up, grabbing her bottle of lemon and lime still water and light waterproof jacket, before heading for the lift.

Walter reached under the desk and put his heavy black shoes back on, and tied them up. Stood up, limped across the office, and tapped on his boss's door.

'Could be something, ma'am,' he muttered. 'Woman reporting her daughter's caravan has burnt down, and she's worried her daughter might have been inside it.'

'Where?' said Mrs West, glancing up and over the top of her new pink spectacles.

'By the river, somewhere down off the Farndon road.'

'Okey-doke. Go and sort it, Walter.'

Walter pursed his lips and nodded and headed back across the office, grabbed his raincoat from the hooks, and headed towards the lift.

'Hope all goes well,' said Gibbons. 'She sounded mighty agitated.'

'Wouldn't we all be agitated at that news?' said Walter, heaving open the double doors.

'Yeah, I guess.'

Karen had heard they were due for a delivery of a new Volvo V40 that day, and lo-and-behold there it was, a beautiful silver-grey hatchback with just seventy-two miles on the clock. She looked like a kid with the best new present on Christmas morning.

'Fab car,' she said.

'Indeed, and an expensive one. Try not to prang it.'

'Me, Guv? When did I ever prang a car?'

20

Walter thought about that. She was a quick driver, and a good one too, and often drove at way above the speed limit, when on operations, but it was true, he could never remember her actually pranging one of the force's best high-powered beasts.

'There's always a first time.'

'Hope not,' said Karen, grinning across at him, as they sped south from Chester heading for Farndon.

Marigold Lane was the last turnoff on the right-hand side before entering the small and cute riverside town of Farndon. Just after lunchtime on a brightish November day, amid light traffic, as Karen turned into Marigold.

For the first hundred yards the road surface was made up in some kind of light coloured concrete, with small detached low build bungalows on either side. But once the bungalows came to an end, so did the made up road. The lane became nothing more than a track, and a pitted, rutted and narrow one at that.

Two distinct blackish tracts where the vehicles' wheels ran, tough grass and weeds in the centre, and no room for passing anywhere, so it was as well nothing came up from the river. Lots of standing water everywhere, evidence of the recent heavy rainfall, and the further down the lane they went, the worse the craters and ravines in the track became.

Despite Karen's careful driving, the new Volvo was bucking and jumping and swaying and creaking all over the place. A big test for a hardy new car, and the Volvo would handle it well, though they both wondered if it was doing the new suspension much good.

'Steady!' said Walter. 'Slower!'

'I am going dead slow now, Guv,' and she was, which meant progress down that long and twisty lane was tortuous, where one mile seemed like twenty.

A moment later, through the spindly trees, they could see a small blue Ford hatchback parked away to the right, and after one more turn to the left, another similar Ford, red this time, with a short buxom woman standing beside it, her hands crossed before her chest, and what looked like a large redbrick barbeque behind her.

'Stop here,' said Walter, and Karen did, and they climbed out and walked over towards Dorothy Wright.

'Thought you weren't coming,' said Dot.

'We're here now,' said Walter as Karen completed the introductions.

The redbrick barbeque was nothing of the kind, but the old foundations where the caravan had once stood. It must have been partly hollow, for the crunched and crashed wreckage had mainly fallen and settled inside.

'Have you touched anything?' asked Walter.

'Just this,' she said, showing them a large diamond, the one she imagined had come from Ellie's precious ring. 'She never took it off, she couldn't take it off.'

'We'll need to take that for examination,' said Karen. 'You'll get it back.'

'Okay,' she said as Walter held out a small plastic bag and Dot dropped it inside. 'I'm really worried about her.'

'Course you are, we'll do everything to find out what's gone on.'

'Ta,' she said, holding back tears.

'Call SOCO,' said Walter, and Karen jumped on her mobile.

'So,' said Walter, 'tell me about your daughter.'

'What do you want to know?'

'Everything.'

'It's a bit embarrassing.'

'In what way?'

'She wasn't always a very good girl.'

'The more you tell us the better, let's go and sit in the car,' and they did, in the front of her little Ford. Karen stayed outside, walking round the redbrick base, peering inside, sniffing, a slight but definite aroma of spirit, petrol or paraffin, wondering what had really happened. Dorothy Wright poured her heart out to Walter in the car, about how Ellie had gone off the rails when her dad had left, never to be seen or heard of since. Of how she'd flunked college, hated menial shop serving jobs, had fallen in with the wrong crowd, had taken up drinking and dabbling in drugs, and to pay for it, well, she'd started doing tricks for men; and women too, if the demand was there. Anything to earn a handful of gold.

It wasn't a pretty story, though not an unusual one in twenty-first century Britain, where a certain segment of society appeared to slip through the gaps in the floor, and into hard times. But that was nothing new either, as Walter was all too aware. It had been going on since Victorian days, and probably long before that, and always would. There were always plenty of hopeless case people who couldn't cope, and he doubted if that would ever change.

'What's your husband's name?'

'Tommy, Tommy Wright.'

'And you don't know where he is now?'

'Not a clue, not a frigging idea. Sorry, Inspector. Could be anywhere.'

'And did Ellie have a boyfriend, someone special?'

'Not really. She knocked around with a guy called Derek Nesbitt, but he's a useless article. All talk and style but no substance. Vacuous Derek, I used to think.'

'Do you know where he lives?'

Dot nodded and coughed up the address.

'Look, try not to worry, we don't know anything definite yet.'

'But the diamond?'

'Maybe it fell out. They do that sometimes. Maybe she had burglars, could be anything,' but the look on Dot's suddenly lined face betrayed her innermost thoughts.

'Come on,' said Walter, 'let's go and join Karen.'

Back at the burnt out wreckage Karen said, 'Petrol fumes,' pointing at the blackened debris.

'I thought that,' said Dot.

Walter sniffed and nodded his head. He glanced at Karen.

'Can you go and tape off the area from the bottom of the lane? We don't want loads of people and vehicles contaminating the area.'

Karen nodded and retreated to the Volvo. Walter had wanted to say "crime scene", but there was no crime. Not yet.

Five minutes later SOCO arrived, all young and keen, white suited and booted within minutes, three of them in all, two young women and a slightly older man. Walter filled them in and they nodded and stepped to it.

'Why don't you go and sit in the car with Karen and tell her all about Ellie,' suggested Walter.

'I thought I told you everything.'

'I'm sure there's plenty more,' and Walter nodded at Karen and over toward the little Ford. She received the message and took Dot Wright's arm and led her away, saying, 'Tell me all about Ellie, what's her star sign?'

Walter wanted Dot well away, for his suspected awkward discoveries would not be long in coming. In the meantime he checked out the ground. Lots of blurred footprints, fuzzed up by the rain, and quite a few tyre tracks too. Looked like Ellie Wright had been busy, a popular girl, and that might make his job all the harder, if harm had come to her, if she had a wide circle of clients.

He ambled back towards the wreckage. Lights had been set up, and a large white almost medieval looking canopy had been erected to keep any further rain off the site. Photographing was going on from every which way. The SOCO people didn't seem to harbour any doubt, and ten minutes later the guy came over and opened his white-gloved balled fist and revealed a large tooth.

'Female?' said Walter.

'Almost certainly.'

'How can you tell?'

'Size mainly, I'd bet my pension on it. And I'd say it's the tooth of a young woman. It's in good nick. And there's more.'

'Like what?'

24

'Looks like a full skeleton. As you know, human bones are made of material akin to metal. They rarely burn away in a house fire.'

'Oh, dear. We'd better get a doctor down here fast.'

'Thought you'd have done that already.'

Walter shrugged and gave the guy a look, and took out his mobile and rang Doc Grayling.

Chapter Five

Dorothy Wright never went back to work at the Cuppa Cha Café. She couldn't pluck up the courage to face Shirley and Fred Ross again. She might have felt a little guilty about that, but surely they would understand.

Instead, she took to drink. Dot had always enjoyed alcohol, but it became her sole release, and for a year she drank as if she'd just staggered from the Gobi desert.

The morning after the events at the foot of Marigold Lane the Chester CID team were in situ in the office, waiting for Walter to start. Everyone was there. Karen Greenwood and Darren Gibbons, Hector Browne, Jenny Thompson, now a full-time member of the CID team, and a new guy called Nicky Barr, a short slight bloke, and recently promoted from uniform. He harboured dreams of becoming the best detective Chester had ever seen. That could become annoying.

He'd replaced Jan the Pole, who had experienced a Paul on the road to Damascus moment, when suddenly changing career, from detective, to studying for the priesthood.

Jan the Pole was missed by everyone, but particularly by Jenny, for they'd briefly become an item, and though the rumour was she was still seeing him, even though he'd moved across the country to Lincoln, there didn't seem much future in it, with Jan being determined to become a Catholic priest. It didn't affect Jenny's work, leastways that was what she said, but the powers that be were keeping a close eye on things.

Mrs West came out of her office and sat in a chair at the end and pursed her lips and nodded at Walter, and he did the same to Karen, and she opened the meet.

'Ellie (Eleanor) Wright,' and a recent image of Ellie Wright wearing a purple white trimmed dress a little too short for her, came on the screen. 'Met her end in an old caravan at the foot of Marigold Lane by the River Dee, near Farndon. She was a prostitute with a wide client base.'

'Lots of clients, lots of suspects,' muttered Gibbons.

'Maybe,' said Walter, 'but let's hear the MO first.'

Gibbons pulled a face and nodded.

'Accelerant was used to burn down the caravan. Probably petrol. The reports are in, but we cannot be sure if Ellie was already dead before the caravan went up. It was a fierce blaze and not a lot was left.'

'Might she have done it herself?' asked Hector Browne.

'Fair point, Hector,' said Walter. 'Her mother was evasive to say the least, when we asked her about Ellie's possible suicidal tendencies.'

Hector nodded and scribbled notes, as was his wont.

'Did she have a boyfriend?' asked Nicky.

'Lots of them,' smirked Darren. 'I would think.'

'There's a big difference between boyfriends and clients,' said Walter. 'But they all have to be eliminated.'

'Just coming to the boyfriend thing,' continued Karen. 'There was someone, or is someone, a guy called Derek Nesbitt. The mother didn't think much of him.'

'Remind us of the address?' said Walter.

'Flat 3B, 56 Easton Road,' said Karen, glancing down at her notes.

'Pay him a visit!' snapped Mrs West.

Walter nodded and mumbled, 'On it, ma'am.'

Karen again. 'The location of the caravan was remote, ideal from the perp's point of view. A few bungalows at the top of the lane, but nothing close by, other than one or two other empty and disused shacks and caravans.'

Walter took up the thread. 'Jenny and Nick, I want you to interview all the people who live in those bungalows. See if anyone saw or heard anything unusual. If you get nothing there, try further away.'

'Sure, Guv,' said Jenny.

Nicky grinned across at her and said, 'Me and you, Jen, cool.'

Jenny looked anything but impressed.

'Because of the remoteness there is no CCTV anywhere near the incident site,' said Karen.

'Saves us all day looking through it,' said a relieved Gibbons, for more and more of his time was taken up gazing at blurry CCTV images. Why the hell couldn't they be better quality pics with twenty-first century technology?

'We don't yet know if this is a murder case, but it looks like it could be, hence our intense interest until proved otherwise,' said Mrs West.

'And with that in mind,' said Walter, 'I want Hector to go through all recent prison releases, see if there are any possible candidates we need to be checking on.'

Hector nodded and said, 'Sure, Guv. Going back how long?'

'Three months to start, but longer if you have to, and all the usual suspects, Manchester, Liverpool, Shrewsbury, and the newer prisons too like Wrexham.'

Hector nodded and scribbled notes, but didn't look that impressed.

'Shall I go and check on Patsy the mouth?' asked Gibbons.

'I was just going to ask you to do that,' said Walter.

Patsy the mouth was the local street snout who kept his eyes and ears to the ground, and occasionally came up with intel that proved useful in exchange for the odd banknote and an easy life, when it came to his minor misdemeanours, or so he imagined.

'Do that,' said Walter, 'and after you've done that, go and speak to the local pub landlords closest to Marigold Lane. And don't take any flannel from them. Ellie was known to frequent those pubs, probably picked up customers there, maybe even the odd member of staff too, so lean on them, and hard if you have to.'

'Be delighted,' said Gibbons.

'Any questions?' asked Karen.

'If this is murder, what's the motive?' asked Nicky, glad to be the centre of attention again.

'Could be anything,' said Walter. 'Robbery, vengeance, jealousy, dissatisfaction, unwanted competition, there's five to be going on with, and by the way, Ellie was known to use drugs too, though not that seriously, according to her mother, so you can factor that in as an element as well. Where there's illegal drugs violence is never far away, as you know.'

'Gotcha, Guv,' said Nicky, looking mighty pleased with himself.

'It's now a quarter to ten, I want you all back here by 5pm with your full reports. Clear?' said Walter, looking at each of them in turn.

Karen added, 'And keep Guv informed if there are any developments throughout the day.'

'That's it, get to it,' said Walter, and everyone stood up and collected their coats, except Hector, who would remain behind, and begin trawling through prison records and recent releases, though thankfully a great deal of that info could now be accessed at the touch of a few buttons, courtesy of Police and Home Office computers.

'Good luck, team,' said Mrs West in her shrill voice, before she stood and hurried back to her office, for she had revision to do for a promotion exam, and though it wasn't recommended to do it while at work, sometimes needs must.

Ten minutes later, Walter and Karen were driving the short distance toward Easton Road.

'What do you make of the new guy?' asked Karen.

'Over-keen, as per normal, but better that than the other way round. He'll soon learn.'

'Jen doesn't like him much.'

'I think anyone could see that!' said Walter, as Karen pulled the Ford saloon to a halt outside 56 Easton Road. Walter stood out of the car and pulled his raincoat around him and buttoned up. It was dry but overcast, and getting a bit nippy, a warning of winter to come. He gazed up at the grey stone house, Victorian by the look of it, or maybe early Edwardian. A huge semi-detached property with vast and tall windows set on three floors, four if you included the spacious basement, a property converted into flats.

The front garden had been half-heartedly converted into a car park, little more than someone had thrown down a few bags of gravel on the old front lawn. There were plenty of tyre marks, but only the one car, a smart yellow Cayton Cerisa. Most of the flat inhabitants were either out, or non-drivers.

Walter and Karen ambled up the grey stone path and tried the huge front door. It opened without a problem. No such thing as security locks at number 56.

'3B you say?' said Walter, looking at doors and numbers.

'Yep, first floor by the look of it.'

Walter nodded and grabbed the handrail above the elaborate wrought-iron balustrade, and followed Karen up the old stone stairs, their footsteps echoing through the building.

On the first floor landing 3B was facing them. Walter went to the door and in the absence of any obvious bell he banged on the black glossed timber.

No one came. Walter listened at the door. No music inside, no telly on, no people talking, no dog barking, no children home alone.

'Try again,' said Karen, and he did that with the same result.

'Maybe he's at work,' said Karen.

'Looks that way. Damn! If only we knew where he worked.'

The door to 3A opened and a smart woman in a yellow suit and wide-brimmed hat stood out. She looked at the strangers, half smiled and said, 'Can I help you?'

'We are looking for Derek.'

'He'll be at work now.'

'You wouldn't happen to know where he works?' asked Karen.

'Sure. He's a floor manager at First Image.'

'Gents outfitters,' clarified Karen.

'I know that!' said Walter. 'I am a gent, and I do buy outfits.'

'Yeah, sure, course, sorry, Guv.'

'You're police aren't you?' said the woman, smirking.

'Yes, how did you know?' said Walter.

'Oh every woman knows you now, Walter, you're quite famous around Chester these days.'

Karen grinned.

'Really?' said Walter, unable to keep a smile from his face.

'Oh, yes,' she said. 'No one would ever forget a man with an image like yours.'

Karen smiled and gave her boss the once over as if she had never really examined him before. Maybe the woman was right. A big black man with a head of unkempt grey hair, even in twenty-first century Britain there would not be too many Walter Darriteau look-a-likes strolling round Chester, that was for sure.

'He's not in any trouble, is he?'

'No, nothing like that, just routine enquiries.'

'Ah, that's what you always say, "routine enquiries". If I know you, he's probably mixed up in some gruesome murder.'

'I don't think so,' said Karen, picking up on Walter's body language that suggested he wanted the chatter to end.

But Walter surprised her by continuing the chat.

'That your car downstairs?'

'It is. How did you know?'

'Only one there, and it's yellow. Colour coordinated,' and Walter glanced pointedly at the yellow suit and hat.

The woman laughed.

'We try. Once a detective, always a detective, eh?'

'Something like that. New is it, the car?'

'Six months.'

'Do you like it?'

'Best car I've ever had.'

'Great,' said Walter. 'What's your name, by the way?'

'Mary Warner, I'm not a suspect too, am I?'

'No. Course not, just….'

'Yes, I know, "routine enquiries".'

Walter nodded and grinned.

'Can't stand about here all day,' she said. 'Nice to have met you. Good luck with whatever it is you are looking into.'

'And you too,' said Walter, as they followed her down the stairs and out into the gloomy November day.

Sitting in the car, they watched her back the Cayton out and smile and wave and drive off.

'What was that all about?' asked Karen.

'I have no idea. Nice woman, though.'

'You fancied her?'

'I wouldn't say that exactly. And anyway….'

'Anyway what?'

'I have a new lady friend now.'

'Do you? Since when?'

'Didn't I tell you?'

'No, you did not.'

'Met her on the Internet.'

'Did you now?'

'Yes.'

'On the site I mentioned?'

'The very same.'

'What's her name? What's she like?'

'Not now, let's get on with the job. I'll maybe tell you later.'

Karen grinned and made a mental note to come back to that.

'Where to? First Image?'

Walter nodded and growled, 'Yep,' and then he added, 'how old do you think she was, yellow Mary?'

Karen pulled a face and said, 'Hard to tell, forty, maybe forty-five.'

'She was well preserved for that.'

'You think so? I hope I look like her when I am forty-five. Forty-five is positively ancient.'

'Forty-five is young, but that's another issue, come on, I want to talk to this vacuous man, Nesbitt, as Dot described him.'

'Me too,' said Karen. 'Can't wait.'

Chapter Six

The general manager at First Image wasn't keen on having an important member of his sales staff dragged off the floor during peak time selling, and even less impressed when the police commandeered his office to speak to Nesbitt. Derek came to the open door and knocked.

'You wanted to see me?'

'Yes,' said Karen, doing the introductions.

'No trouble is there?' said a nervous Derek, as he sat down in front of the desk.

'Just routine,' said Walter, trying to put the guy at ease.

Walter glanced across as the man. What was he? Mid to late thirties, probably six feet, slim to medium build, short neatly parted brown hair, dark eyes, and neatly and smartly dressed, which was almost certainly a requirement in his profession. Walter kicked things off.

'Correct me if I'm wrong, but are you Ellie Wright's boyfriend?'

'Ellie? No, why? I know her but she isn't my girlfriend, no way, never.'

'Really?' said Karen. 'But Ellie's mother told us that you went to Spain on holiday with her.'

'Well yes, we did, but just as mates, not as a couple, we're not bed sharers, or anything like that.'

'But you knew her well?' asked Walter.

'Yeah, I guess, look what is this all about? What's Ellie been up to now? What's she been saying?'

Walter and Karen ignored the questions for both wanted to ask the same thing. Walter got there first. 'When did you last see her?'

'Ooh, let me think, last week sometime.'

'When last week?' persisted Karen.

'Let me think, Friday, we went for a curry together, no, hang on, Thursday night it was, Friday I was out playing darts.'

Walter clarified. 'You last saw her on Thursday night?'

Derek nodded and looked confident. 'Yeah, Thursday it was, look, do you mind telling me what this is all about?'

Again the officers ignored his question.

Walter asked, 'Do you know where she lives?'

'Yeah, course, she's staying in a dilapidated old caravan down by the river, at the end of Marigold Lane, pretty rank it is too. I've been trying to persuade her to get a decent flat.'

'Do you do drugs, Derek?' asked Karen.

'Me? Certainly not. I'm clean.'

'But you knew that Ellie did?' said Walter.

Derek pulled a face and said, 'Yeah, she's messed about with it, but nothing too serious. At least I don't think so.'

'Do you deal drugs?' asked Karen.

'Me! No! Course not! What do you take me for? Look, what is this all about?'

'What else do you know about Ellie Wright?' asked Walter.

'How do you mean?'

'You know what we mean!' said Karen.

Derek breathed out heavy and fidgeted in his seat. Looked as if he needed a cigarette.

'Come on Derek,' said Walter. 'What else?'

'You mean the men?'

Walter nodded.

'The men?' said Karen.

'Yeah. You know, she did tricks for men, for cash like, now and again.'

'Down at the caravan?' said Walter.

'Yeah, there, and other places too.'

'What other places?' asked Karen.

'She went to their gaffs sometimes, so she said, even in hotel rooms, on occasion.'

'And you approved of that?' asked Walter.

35

'Course not!'

'Are you her pimp, Derek?' asked Karen.

'What! No! Don't be ridiculous!'

'But you didn't try to stop her?'

'Course I did! She didn't want to know. To tell you the truth, I think she quite enjoyed her way of earning a living.'

'Is there anyone special in her life?' asked Walter.

'How do you mean?'

'It's a straightforward question,' said Karen. 'Are any of the men special to her?'

'Not that I know of.'

'Did she mention any names?' asked Walter.

'Not that I remember, and by the way, it wasn't just men.'

Walter ignored that for he knew it already, and asked, 'Where did she meet these men?'

'She was well known around the local pubs.'

'Which pubs?' asked Karen, and Derek reeled off four different drinking establishments.

'Did she have any close friends?' asked Walter.

'Not really. There was one girl, a mate. Jani Jefferson, Janice, they'd go out drinking and clubbing sometimes, she's the only one I know of.'

'Where does she live?' asked Karen.

'She has a little flat near the railway station. Over one of the shops. Over a cycle shop, it is, can't remember the address exactly.'

Karen and Walter shared a look and Karen said, 'I know the shop, Guv.'

'Look! What's going on here? What's she been up to?'

'On Friday night Ellie's caravan burnt down,' said Walter.

'No! Is she alright?'

'We believe she was inside it at the time,' said Karen.

'What! You mean she's dead?'

'It looks that way,' said Walter.

Derek leant forward, put his hands on his knees, pursed his lips and breathed out heavy. 'Shit!' he said. 'I can't get my head around this.'

'Which pub were you playing darts in, Derek?'

'Eh? Oh, the Red Lion.'

'What time did you leave?' asked Walter.

'About eleven, why? Hey, hang on a minute. Was this fire started deliberately?'

'Was it Derek?' asked Walter.

'Eh? How the hell would I know? Look, what the hell's going on here? Are you trying to say she was murdered? Do you think I had something to do with it?'

'Did you?' asked Karen.

'Of course I bloody didn't! Ellie was a good friend to me.'

'So far, we don't think anything, Derek. We are just trying to find out what happened down there,' said Walter. 'In the meantime can you please not leave the city without telling us first, and if you think of anything further that may help us with our enquiries, we'd appreciate a call,' and Walter held his card out across the desk.

Derek took it, glanced at it, and nodded and slipped it behind the red handkerchief in his breast pocket.

'Do you own a car, Derek?' asked Karen.

'Sure. A silver Cayton.'

'And did you ever drive down Marigold Lane?'

'Once or twice.'

'Recently?'

'Yeah, on that Thursday night.'

'The last time you saw her?'

'Correct.'

Walter nodded and glanced at Karen.

Derek jumped into the momentary silence.

'Is that it? Can I go now?'

'Yes,' said Walter, 'and thank you for your assistance.'

Derek nodded and didn't need a second chance to flee the room. A moment later the manager reappeared and stood in the open doorway.

'Everything all right here?'

'Yes,' said Walter. 'It would seem that one of Derek's friends has recently died. He's obviously a little shaken up.'

'Oh, fair enough, that's a relief, I thought he was in some kind of trouble there for a moment…. sorry that didn't come out quite right,' said the manager, looking uncomfortable.

'Do you know any of Derek's friends?' asked Karen.

'Me? No! Certainly not, we don't socialise at all, purely a boss and employee relationship.'

'Quite,' said Walter. 'And your name again is?'

'Kenneth Boyce.'

'Well, thank you, Mr Boyce, you have been most helpful, sorry to have interrupted your day.'

'Glad to assist,' he said, as the officers left the room and hurried from the building and back to the car.

Walter scratched his nose and sat back in his seat. Karen took a quick swig of blackcurrant still water and said, 'What did you make of Derek?'

'He didn't come across as particularly vacuous.'

'No, I thought that.'

'But if he left the Red Lion at eleven, he could have driven straight to Marigold Lane. He knew where it was, and he probably knew she would be there. And if there are tyre tracks of his, he's covered that by saying he was there on Thursday.'

'Does he come across as a murderer?' asked Karen.

'Not especially, but who knows what went on down there? Maybe he visited her and things got out of hand. Anything could have happened.'

'He's the best we've got.'

'So far….'

'Maybe we should take a look at his car.'

'He's already admitted he's been down there. We'd expect to find Marigold Lane mud on his vehicle. Doesn't prove a thing.'

'Guess you're right. Where now? Jani's?'

'You got it.'

It didn't take them long to find the cycle shop, and the flat above, but Janice Jefferson wasn't there. In Madeira, so the helpful young bloke in the cycle shop said, enjoying a little early winter sunshine, back in a couple of days, he said. Walter wrote a brief note on a card to get in touch, and slipped it through the letterbox. Any input from Jani would have to wait.

Everyone was back and ready and keen to get started by half-past four. There was no point in delaying. Walter called the evening meet to order.

Karen kicked things off by sharing the data about Derek Nesbitt and Janice Jefferson. Next up was Hector Browne, and he had real things to contribute.

'There were three possible runners in the recent prison releases.' Everyone glanced at the screen. 'All of them are out on licence so we have full recent records as to where they are residing, and they all have to report in at varying intervals, and up till now they all have.'

'Go on,' said Walter, eager to get to the meat.

'I think we can rule this one out. Housebound. He's got a broken leg.'

'How did that happen?' asked Karen.

'Playing football, apparently.'

'And the others?' said Walter.

'Number two is James "Jimmy" Crocker. Aged thirty-six.'

They all stared up at the balding hard-faced figure that insolently stared back through cold eyes.

'Tell us more,' said Walter; trying hard to remember if he'd ever met the guy.

'Long time career criminal, but mainly low key stuff, but then for some reason he imagined he was a hard man and began battering people, sometimes for money, sometimes because he enjoyed it. He'd racked up a big score of assaults before he was finally sent down.'

'I remember him,' said Gibbons. 'A right prick!'

'Passed me by,' said Walter.

'Me too,' added Karen.

'Anyway,' continued Hector, 'he got ten years for GBH, and was released after five.'

'When was that?' asked Karen.

'Three weeks ago.'

'Got an address?' asked Walter.

'Sure,' said Hector. 'He's back with his mother at Saltney Ferry. 20 Laburnum Gardens.'

Walter grunted and said, 'One for you Gibbons, I think. Take Nick with you first thing in the morning. Find out where Crocker was on Friday, and thoroughly check out any alibi.'

'Thanks a lot, Guv,' said Gibbons, not really wanting to meet Jimmy Crocker again.

'And the third one?' said Walter.

'The most interesting and promising one, in my opinion,' said Hector, looking pleased with himself.

'Let's hear it.'

'Michael, Mickey Flanagan. Aged thirty-nine. Went to prison for twelve years for the manslaughter of his wife. Released after seven on licence for good behaviour.'

Everyone looked up at the new picture gazing down on them. Long straggly greasy dark hair parted in the middle. Looked like some refugee from a metal rock band. Hard looking eyes; but weren't they always when they were photographed under stress in a police station.

'He has one son who was taken into care. He'll be twelve now. So far, Michael Flanagan has not been permitted to see his son, and indeed the boy has expressed a wish not to see his father.'

'When was he released?'

'Twenty-six days ago,' said Hector without hesitation.

'Where's he living?'

'Christleton.'

'Address?'

Hector coughed it up. Walter memorised it.

Jenny said, 'Do you want me to check him out, Guv?'

'Won't be necessary, Jen, I want to see this guy myself.'

'That it, Hector?' asked Karen.

'Yep, for now.'

'How did you get on?' asked Walter, glancing at Jen and Nick.

'Not a lot, in truth,' said Jenny. 'We interviewed everyone who was available in Marigold Lane. Two families are away, one on holiday, one away working. Of the others no one heard or saw a thing except for a Mr Duffield.'

Nick Barr took up the story.

'Mr Duffield is not allowed to smoke in his bungalow.'

Slight tittering filled the briefing room.

'All right,' said Walter. 'Settle down. And?'

Nick grinned and began again.

'His wife won't permit it in the house; so just before he went to bed he stepped outside the back of his property onto a large flagged patio and enjoyed a late night fag. While he was doing that he noticed a glow in the sky from the direction of the caravan, but put it down to kids who had been known to go down there at the weekends, and make a fire and drink, and stuff. He didn't think it unusual. He says he didn't hear or see anything else, and after his ciggie was done he stepped back inside, not least because it was raining, and thought nothing more of it.'

'Did he see anyone driving up the lane later on?' asked Karen.

'Nope. Their room is at the back, so they couldn't have seen a thing.'

'Pity,' said Walter.

'If someone set fire to the caravan, they could have walked up the lane,' suggested Jenny.

'Possible,' said Walter. 'But why would you?'

'Avoid tyre tracks, maybe.'

'Or maybe a local person?' added Gibbons.

'Possibly,' said Walter.

'Or perhaps,' said Jenny, 'they didn't want Ellie to hear their arrival by car, so they crept down there on foot instead.'

'And left the car, if they had one, back up on the main road,' said Karen.

'All possible, but we want something more concrete than that,' said Walter.

'There is a lay-by on the main road, maybe a couple of hundred yards along from Marigold,' added Gibbons.

'Someone might have seen it if a car were left there,' suggested Nick.

'Again, it's possible,' said Walter. 'Did you turn up anything else, Jen?'

'No, we tried lots of other further away properties, maybe thirty or forty, but no one saw or heard anything unusual.'

'That just leaves you, Gibbons,' said Walter, and everyone turned and stared at Darren. 'What did you turn up in the pubs?'

'Plenty of tittle-tattle and interest. Lots of the punters knew Ellie Wright, though none of them were brave enough to admit to visiting her at home, so to speak.'

'So there's quite a few liars in the pubs then?' said Karen.

'Clearly,' said Mrs West. 'And there's no point in testing them for DNA because we have nothing left at the possible crime scene to compare it with, and there's nothing left in the wreckage of the caravan to incriminate anyone. No juicy diary or business records, or appreciative gifts. That would have been nice.'

'Someone in those pubs must know something,' said Walter. 'I think we need to have another go at them.'

'Is that it for now?' asked Mrs West, anxious to get on with other work.

'Looks that way,' said Walter.

'Is it a visit to Mickey Flanagan first thing tomorrow?' asked Karen.

Walter glanced at his watch.

'It's only five to six,' he said. 'Let's go and do it now. Never put off till tomorrow, and all that.'

One or two of them smirked at Karen's annoyance for they knew she had a hot date. She hid it well; you had to give her that.

Chapter Seven

They had expected Michael Flanagan's address to be some kind of down-at-heel boarding house, or an unloved renter, but they could not have been more wrong. He was living in a brand new townhouse, one of three, in a small cul-de-sac off the main A41, south and east of Chester.

There were small square gardens at the front, different coloured front doors, red sandstone porches built in the local stone, and they looked a nice place to live.

'Crime must pay,' muttered Karen, opening the small white front gate, and wondering why she could not afford a little house like it.

'Looks that way,' said Walter, as they headed for the red door and rang the doorbell set to the right.

No one came.

Walter peered through the partly frosted glass panel and squinted inside. Couldn't see any action. Tried the bell again.

Movement inside. A shadowy figure coming down the stairs, and in the next moment a tall neat man opened the door. He didn't look happy.

'We're looking for Michael Flanagan,' said Walter.

'And you are?' said the guy, though his instinct told him these people were police.

Karen did the introductions.

'I'm Michael Flanagan,' he said. 'What do you want?' Which was something of a surprise for he didn't look anything like his photo. He'd cut his hair, short and neat; he was well dressed too, neatly shaved, smelt nice, and looked more like a businessman than a rough killer.

'Can we come in for a minute?' said Walter. 'We need your help on something.'

'I'm busy right now.'

44

'So are we,' said Karen, as Walter eased the door open, and they both stepped inside, and followed Michael into a small but neat front sitting room. The new theme continued. New large TV, new music system, new sofa, nice pictures on the wall, good beige carpet on the floor, all clean and tidy, all good to go. The three of them stood in the centre of the room and checked each other out.

'Nice place,' said Walter.

'I know what you're thinking.'

'What are we thinking?' asked Karen.

'You're thinking, how come a jailbird like me has such a nice gaff as this?'

'It might have crossed my mind,' said Walter. 'So how do you?'

Flanagan breathed out heavy as if he was sick to the back teeth of justifying things, but he would anyway.

'Thankfully, there are some well-meaning charitable societies and trusts and housing associations out there that look after people just out of prison, people like me. Make an effort to give us a fresh start, and just to be clear about it, I only get this house for eighteen months max. After that I have to find my own place, and just to be clear also, it was an accident, what happened to my wife.'

'Oh?' said Karen.

'She came at me with a poker. I'd caught her playing around. She could have killed me. I had no choice. I gave her a slap, just the one, nothing really; she fell over and banged her head on the corner of the marble fireplace. It could have happened to anyone. Manslaughter, they said, it was an accident for Pete's sake, but you know all this, no point in going over it again. I'm working hard, and trying to get my life back together, so give me a break and get off my case, eh?'

'It's not your case we are looking at,' said Walter.

'Oh? So what do you want?'

'Where were you last Friday night?'

'Friday? Here of course. I'm tagged, don't they tell you anything?' and he pulled up his trouser leg and revealed the white

45

electronic tag on his ankle. 'Seven till seven curfew. Always knew the bloody thing would come in useful sometime, and now it has,' and he grinned. 'You can check.'

'So you didn't go out at all that night?'

'Course not. Said so, didn't I.'

'What do you do for a living?' asked Walter, but before Flanagan could answer, a loud bump came to the ceiling above.

'We are not alone here?' said Walter, glancing skywards.

'Nope. Not a crime is it?'

'You didn't think to say?' said Karen.

'You didn't ask.'

'Who's upstairs?' asked Walter.

Michael shrugged his shoulders and looked shifty.

'A friend, my girlfriend, if you must know.'

'I'll check it out, Guv,' said Karen, going to the stairs and running up them.

The door to the front bedroom was wide open. A naked young woman lay on the new double bed, smirking. Maybe twenties, maybe a little younger.

'What's your name?' asked Karen.

'Misty,' she said, propping herself up on her elbows.

'No it's not!' said Karen. 'I know you, don't I?'

'Do you? I don't know you, lady.'

'I think you do. What's your real name?'

'You never leave people alone, do you?'

'Real name!'

'For god's sake! Tracey Day, if you must know.'

'Ah yes, I remember now. Tracey Day, you've been done several times for prostitution, if memory serves. Which reminds me, do you know a girl called Ellie Wright?'

'Nope, who's she?'

'No matter, just someone we are interested in. Anyway, get yourself dressed, right now! There'll be no business done here today, I'll expect you downstairs in five.'

46

'Oh, for heaven's sake! People can do what they like in their own homes!'

'No they can't! Not when they are out on licence. Get dressed! I won't tell you again.'

Tracey sulkily slid from the bed and headed toward her clothes bunched up on a low dressing table. Karen nodded and went downstairs.

'Well?' said Walter.

'Tracey Day, a known Tom, about to do business by the look of things.'

Walter glanced at Michael and pulled a questioning face.

'I can do what I like in my own place.'

'Do you think the charitable trust would approve of that?'

'Oh, don't tell them, for God's sake, I'm just getting back on my feet.'

'I'll think about it,' said Walter. 'So long as you cooperate.'

Michael scowled, as a sheepish looking Tracey in a very short skirt appeared and stood in the doorway. 'Can I go now?'

'You can,' said Walter, as Tracey headed toward the front door.

'Give me a ring!' shouted Michael.

'You will not be ringing here, will you Tracey?' growled Walter.

'No mister black-man-police-man,' she shouted back, giggling at her own little joke, as she let herself out, and hurried away down the path before they thought to search in her handbag.

'Where were we?' muttered Walter.

'You wanted to know what I was doing for a living.'

'Ah yes, and what is that?'

'Cab driver, if you must know.'

'But only from seven till seven,' said Karen.

'Correct.'

'Don't you have to have a CRB check to drive cabs?' said Karen.

'No! Not with all the firms, and anyway, you're out of date with that, young woman. It's a DBS check now, Disclosure and Barring Service.'

47

Karen glanced at Walter for confirmation. What Michael said was true, the old Criminal Records Bureau checks had been replaced by the DBS, and it was true too that not all cab drivers were checked out.

'Just what we need,' muttered Walter. 'Convicted criminals, even killers, driving around our vulnerable young women at the dead of night.'

'And young men,' added Karen.

'Yeah, that too.'

'I'm not a killer! I'm working hard. I'm trying to get my life back together, get back on my feet. I want to see my son again. What would you have me do, sit on my backside all day, picking up the dole money? And besides, I'm not driving round young women and young men, rarely anyway. More likely ferrying all the old biddies home from the supermarket, or pensioners to the station, going off on their holidays to Benidorm, or to and from the local bingo hall.'

'Do you know where Marigold Lane is?' asked Walter.

'Course I do. I am a cab driver; we have to learn all the roads. Part of the job.'

'Have you been down there?' asked Karen.

'Once or twice.'

'Recently?' said Karen.

'Last week sometime.'

'When last week?' asked Walter.

'Wednesday or Thursday I think it was.'

'How far down Marigold Lane did you go?' asked Karen.

'All the way.'

'To the caravan, by the river?' asked Walter.

Michael nodded and looked uncomfortable.

'Who did you take down there?' asked Karen.

'Some guy. Didn't give me his name. Customers tend not to.'

'Did you wait for him?' asked Walter.

'Nope. Just left him there.'

'What time was this?'

'Got there about six, I couldn't wait on, tag time coming up, and all that.'

'Did you see the person who lives there?' asked Karen.

'No. Not a soul.'

'Did you know the young woman who lives there?'

Flanagan shook his head.

'Did you know she was a prostitute?' asked Walter.

'Certainly not! Look, what is this?'

'Can you describe the guy you took down there?' asked Karen.

'Yeah, probably, though after a while all the punters tend to look the same.'

'Try,' said Walter.

'Thirties, maybe, businessman type guy, suit shirt and tie, that kind of thing, didn't say much, didn't tip much either.'

'Height?'

'Six feet maybe, about my height.'

'Hair?' said Karen.

'Dark, black or brown.'

'Is Tracey Day a friend of Ellie Wright?'

'Who's Ellie Wright?'

'The woman who lived in the caravan,' said Karen.

'I have no idea. You'd have to ask her.'

'Did you set fire to Ellie Wright's caravan?' asked Walter.

Before he could answer Karen waded in with, 'Did you kill Ellie Wright?'

Mickey Flanagan pulled a face and said, 'Leave it out. Why would I do that?'

'Maybe she didn't want to know you,' suggested Karen.

'Maybe she turned you down flat,' added Walter. 'You're in the market for an available young woman, we know that.'

'Don't be crazy.'

Karen wasn't to be so easily put off.

'Maybe you hit her because she wouldn't give you what you wanted, and maybe she fell over and banged her head. Sound familiar?'

'Now you're just being stupid.'

'Don't think so,' said Walter. 'We are trying to find out how Ellie Wright died.'

'She's really dead?' said Flanagan, sitting heavily in the sofa, looking surprised, either that or he was a damned good actor.

'She is dead,' confirmed Walter. 'Do you know anything about that?'

'I do not, I wish I did.'

Walter glanced at his watch.

'It's seven o'clock,' he said aloud.

'It is,' said Michael. 'And I am tag-tied to this house for another day, and night.'

'Save you getting into any more trouble, Michael,' said Karen, smirking.

'We'd better be off,' said Walter. 'If you think of anything else about Ellie and her little caravan I'd appreciate it if you'd let us know,' and he set a card on the small hall cupboard.

'Okay, I will, but I'd appreciate it if you'd not tell the charitable trust about, well, you know, Tracey and that.'

'That could be arranged,' said Walter. 'But do yourself a favour and stay away from on-hire girls, get you into trouble every time.'

Michael nodded and muttered something about men having certain needs, and it was damned difficult meeting anyone when you had to be home by 7pm every night.

In the car outside Karen said, 'Back to base, Guv?'

'Yes. What did you make of that?'

'Michael Flanagan?'

'The same.'

'He's certainly smartened himself up.'

'Yes, looked a different man, didn't he? Wonder when he did that.'

'Dunno, but I think he's a more likely candidate than Derek Nesbitt. Flanagan's got form, killed a woman, for heaven's sake,

50

and we know he went to the caravan, and frankly, I didn't believe that he didn't meet Ellie. He looked real cut up when you said she was dead.'

'Yes he did. Check if he's broken the seven to seven curfew, and get hold of the papers from his original case. See if there's anything in there about the wife's background.'

'You mean you think she might have been a prostitute too?'

'Who knows? No reason to think it, but he said she was messing around. Be interesting to know what *messing around* actually means.'

'He's been in prison for manslaughter, he patronises prostitutes, he admitted he'd visited the caravan site, and we both thought he knew Ellie, that's pretty powerful stuff.'

'Yes, it is, but entirely circumstantial. We'd need a lot more than that.'

'True, Guv. I wonder who the guy was he took down Marigold Lane.'

'Could be anyone.'

'If he took anyone at all. That could all be so much smoke-screening.'

'Possibly, though I thought he sounded quite convincing.'

'So we've now three in the frame, Derek Nesbitt, Michael Flanagan, and the guy Flanagan took down there.'

'And don't forget Jimmy Crocker too. He's no angel.'

Karen pulled a face and muttered, 'True, Guv,' and shook her head and drove back to the station, fast. She was always a quick driver, but this was different.

'You in a hurry?'

'Got a date, Guv.'

'Sorry if I've detained you.'

'Not a prob.'

'With your pal, Greg?'

'Nope. I'm not seeing Greg anymore. Thought you knew.'

'Sorry to hear that.'

'Don't be. His complete lack of an adult sense of humour finally wore me down.'

'Dare I ask who?'

'Tell you another time, Guv,' she said, as they left the car in the underground car park beneath the main police station. Karen dashed off for the lift, for she wanted to get upstairs and finish things off, and get away and not be too late.

Chapter Eight

The first rumble of thunder could be heard across the old city at just gone seven. Heavy clouds had been rolling in from Snowdonia all day, the forecast was dire, and for once the forecasters were on the money.

The rain began falling at half-past seven, heavy bursts that lasted ten or fifteen minutes, and then abated for a similar time, before returning, only heavier.

Belinda Cooper arrived home at just after half-past seven. She pushed the old front door open with her foot and dropped two big bags of Bestdas groceries onto the hall floor, shook the umbrella outside, dropped her handbag onto the *Welcome* mat, glanced up at the dark and angry sky, just as a jab of fork lightning smashed to ground not five hundred yards away.

Belinda jumped.

She'd always been terrified of lightning.

Wasn't everyone?

She stumbled into the hall and closed the door behind her, happy and grateful to be home, sopping wet, but safe and sound in her old and happy house. The heating was on, but not too high, came on with a timer at 6.30pm, and it was getting colder with each passing day, or so it seemed, and it would stay on until at least 10pm, big gas bill or not.

Bel, as all her friends called her, slipped off her beige Mac, shook it hard and hung it on the hooks above the hall radiator where it would dry before the morning. She kicked off her boots and sprinted, as best she could, up the stairs. Good exercise; and she didn't get so much of that. But at thirty-six she was in her prime, everyone said so. Just a pity she was living her prime all alone, though she would tell her friends she was happy and content, and to an extent, she was.

She was off men, she said, whenever any of her friends asked her about it, or even worse, tried to fix her up with someone new. To date she had enjoyed five serious boyfriends, or were they now menfriends? Like so many others she was confused as to when precisely in life boyfriends became menfriends, but in the end, all five had disappointed her.

Two had turned out to be married. (Why did men lie so much?) While another, Marcus, had revealed one night in the Flying Horse after one too many gin and tonics, that he'd enjoyed several gay affairs in the past, something that Bel could never live with. While a fourth gentleman, Iain, with two "i's" as he was always keen to point out, well, maybe in Iain's case she was responsible for the break-up there, because she'd become besotted with Gareth, a city solicitor who worked across the road from their shop. He was one of the married men, and after that upheaval and trauma she needed a damned good break from men altogether, and affairs of the heart, and everything that went with it. It was just too much hassle and effort.

Five lovers and five failures, not a pretty record, though only Bel was aware of that stat. Besides, compared to some women she was almost a nun. Nevertheless, she was definitely off men, and for the foreseeable future that would remain the case.

Dinner consisted of a pork chop, tinned peas, instant gravy, and mashed potatoes, something her mother and father would have happily served up twenty years before. But as they were both now residing in the central Chester graveyard, there was rarely a need to cook for more than one. Sometimes she didn't bother cooking at all, just made a sandwich and gnawed on an apple or a punnet of pears, and that lack of heavy dinners helped to keep her fit and trim.

TV that night was even worse than usual, the more channels there were, the worse it gets, or so it seems, and that boredom was only broken when one of her friends, Lena, rang. Bel knew her from the travel company where they both worked. They were planning another trip abroad, and Lena had read all about the Baltic States. 'They're fab,' she'd said, though Bel remained to be convinced, and they could not agree on a destination.

Bel wasn't happy with the TV being on at all, what with the continuing thunder and lightning, and recalled how her mother always insisted that not only was the TV turned off at the first sight and sound of thunder, but that the mains plug was pulled out of the wall, and the aerial disconnected.

Often they would do that, and the storm would pass over, and they would reconnect everything, only for the lightning to return ten minutes later, much to everyone's annoyance.

She smiled to herself and thought of her old mum and dad. How nice it would have been if they were there with her again, but how awkward too, for they would never have accepted her drinking alcohol, and having affairs, and they wouldn't have been happy with her sleeping in that king-size bed in the main front bedroom either, their room, that Bel rarely entered as a child and teenager.

Maybe it was just as well they were gone. After all, they'd had their innings, and a pretty good one at that, seeing as they never once lived alone in their whole lives, and never endured loneliness, something that didn't worry Bel overmuch. Though she was aware that it could creep up on single people with no warning at all. 'Watch those creeping years, watch that creeping loneliness,' one of her friends was fond of saying, though Bel couldn't recall which one.

She shrugged her shoulders and rewarded herself with a hot herbal bath, and a cold bottle of Pinot Grigio, which she set on an old wooden tray her father had made in the shed at the foot of the garden, and duly varnished, she remembered him presenting it to her mother as if it were made of gold, and the big kiss that was planted on his five o'clock shadow cheek, as his reward. Happy days, but days long gone, days of yore, days that would never return. She shook her head and tried to think of happier things, for if she didn't she knew she'd shed a tear.

Twenty minutes later, with the latest American bloodthirsty crime novel jammed under her arm, tray and bottle and wine glass before her, she was happy to prance up those dancers, as her mother always referred to the thirteen stairs that took her to the first floor.

Ten precious minutes slipped away, and she was in bed, book in one hand, glass of chilled wine in the other, happy and content, seeking her place in four hundred pages, for she had forgotten to run down the corner, something she knew was frowned on by many, but a simple trick that did the job. Who cared anyway?

It was a particularly violent and bloody book, one of those blockbuster female American novelists who specialised in gory details, and ample murders and autopsies, and handsome men, and mentally damaged wicked murderers, and precisely the kind of thing she went for every time. She adored it, for it gave her a real thrill, and there were not too many of those in Belinda Cooper's life.

She wasn't the first woman to imagine the world inside books was a lot more exciting and fulfilling than the real one in which she found herself; and she wouldn't be the last. Come to think of it, she wasn't imagining it at all, it was a cold hard fact, and there was no doubt about it.

She slurped another mouthful of fine wine, and was surprised to find her overlarge glass already empty. Not a problem, she reached across and topped it up. The bottle was nearly empty too, though that didn't matter, for she always kept ample supplies in the old pantry just off the kitchen. Those damned supermarkets gave a ten percent discount if you bought a box of six, an offer she could never refuse. Though she didn't want to leave her cosy bed and go downstairs for another.

She had no mortgage. She'd never had such a thing, courtesy of her ma and pa. In fact she'd never taken out a loan of any kind in her entire life, and being an only child there had never been any thought or possibility of sharing her inheritance with anyone else. She possessed a decent job, was good at what she did, so it was unlikely she would ever be fired, and she didn't smoke, or spend too much cash on fancy clothes.

Bel never bought expensive designer items unless she happened to come across something decent in a charity shop, so in Bel's happy world, there was precious little to spend her money on, other than holidays, and drink.

A huge flash filled the room.

Bel jumped in her bed.

Three seconds later and a thunderclap almost deafened her, so powerful was it she could have sworn the white wine waved and vibrated in the glass like a mini tide coming in and going out.

Another hefty gang of bangs came out of nowhere.

Boom – Bang! Bang! Tumbledown-Bang!

The old wooden floorboards vibrated.

Bel swore at the storm, as if that might chase it away.

There would be no point in settling down and trying to sleep, for that would be impossible to find, and anyway, the young doctor in the book, had just found a severed woman's arm in a barrel, loosely covered in hay, at the back of the barn, and there was a chestnut horse loose in the lane. Bel shivered and sucked her lips and couldn't possibly stop reading. Whatever had happened to the poor girl? Dreadful! And was she already dead when the arm was severed? Or was she mutilated whilst still being alive? Bel shuddered at the thought.

Another huge thunderbolt tore down the street and the thick curtains danced and fell still.

Bel grimaced, and considered running downstairs for another bottle, but thought better of it, and then it happened.

She heard the sound of breaking glass.

Chapter Nine

Karen hurried home to run a bath. She tossed some perfumed herbal relaxant oil into the water, tested it wasn't too hot. Slipped from her day clothes, blouse and tight slacks, and stepped in and let the water run as hot as she could bear, until the bath was full to the overflow, leant back and closed her eyes.

Why did she enjoy hot baths so much? She had no idea, but knew she always had, for as long as she could remember.

She had been thinking about what to wear. Over a hurried light lunch she'd read a woman's mag. Dress to impress, was the definite advice for new or recently met dates, and with that in mind she'd settled on the tried and tested LBD. David hadn't seen it before, and Gregory had always been excited by that little black dress, and couldn't keep his hands off her, and if it had the same impression on Dave, though he didn't like to be called that, the time was fast approaching where their relationship needed to be consummated.

'Maybe tonight,' she said aloud, and followed that with a wicked giggle. 'If you are very lucky, Mr Baker.'

She wondered where they might go for dinner. She hoped it would be somewhere smart. She was sure it would be somewhere good for David had a good job, and earned far more than she did. He wasn't stingy, or that was the impression he gave in the four dates they had enjoyed.

He was a good kisser too.

And that was incredibly important, as it is to most women. A better kisser than Greg ever was, though his body wasn't in Greg's league. Oh, he was fit right enough, David that is, slim and toned, or so she imagined beneath his tight-fitting clothes, but not a muscular hunk like Gregory, but David was six feet and that was all good. But neither of them were as funny and amusing as Rodney had been. Because Rodney was the most amusing and desirable man she had ever met, and she sighed hard, though that was all over, and always would be.

She had taken to fantasising about him, David that is, and it took a lot to remove Rodney from the position of Fantasy Man Number One. But he had, and that had to mean something.

And that was another thing about hot baths. They really did relax her and lull her into a place that few other things did, and the passage of time meant little to her. It flew by, and it was only the significant cooling of the water that brought her back to the present.

'Shit!' she said aloud. Standing up and reaching for the fresh white towel, and realising she was going to be late. She dried herself and went through to the bedroom and opened the wardrobe and took out the dress. It still looked cool, and new too. She'd only worn it two or three times, and was confident in its magic. She slipped it on, zipped up the back, looked at herself in the long mirror, front, side, and back, and rubbed her palm down her slim taut body, smoothing out a couple of tiny creases.

Yes! She would do. Damned right she would do. If Davey boy didn't fancy the backside off her in this, there must be something wrong with the man. She brushed her straight blonde hair, added a little make-up, though not a lot for she never needed it. Grabbed the expensive American perfume her father had brought back from New York, and sprayed a little, and a little more. Returned to the wardrobe, took out the black patent leather heels and slipped them on.

One last look in the mirror, and that produced a satisfied smile. She was a lucky girl, and she knew it. She had everything in life, a nice apartment, good car, a great job that she really enjoyed, good looks, great health, but no steady boyfriend, or husband, and definitely no children, so maybe not quite everything.

Her mobile was on the small dining table in the living room. It sang that old-fashioned jangly double ringing tone.

She ran through and picked up.

It was David. Karen smiled.

'Haven't you left yet?' she said.

'I have a little problem at this end.'

'Oh, what?'

'Something's come up.'

'What's come up?'

'Work issues.'

'What kind of bloody work issues?'

'The boss wants me to go down and see someone in Malpas.'

'What? Now?'

'Yep, sorry. Right away. He was going to go himself, but he's had a fall at home and sprained his ankle, or so he says.'

'Typical! Can't it be rescheduled?'

'No. The contract has to be signed tonight, or we'll lose it to the competition.'

'How long are you going to be?'

'All night. You know what these corn millers are like. Staying power of long-distance runners. It'll go on long past midnight. I'm really sorry, Karen. Can we do it tomorrow night instead?'

'I can't do tomorrow!' said Karen in a rush.

'Well, we'll talk about it tomorrow night and sort something out.'

'If you want.'

'Course I want. Look, I'll have to go, ring you, yeah.'

'Yeah,' but by then he'd already gone.

Karen tossed the phone back on the table with a clunk.

'Shit!' she said aloud, and returned to the bedroom, kicked off her shoes, and removed the dress and slipped on some loose jeans. Returned to the kitchen and took a vegetable cannelloni from the freezer and set it in the microwave with a bang.

Why did so many men have to be such complete and absolute dorks? It always seemed to come with the territory. She wouldn't fantasise about David bloody Baker that night, or any other night, come to that, or if she did, it would only be in his gruesome

60

bloody murder. She glanced at her watch. A quarter to nine. Another wasted evening spent alone with nothing to show for it.

Maybe Internet men were just too much trouble. It was beginning to look that way. The microwave pinged. She took the meal out. It didn't look great. She ate half and left the rest. Went to the fridge. Took out a big pack of fresh raspberries. Saw a half drunk bottle of chardonnay there. Took that out too and poured a large glass. Sat in front of the rubbish telly and sipped the wine and pigged out on the berries. They were good. Best thing of the whole evening. By miles.

A huge flash of lightning lit up the flat. That seemed to sum things up. All flash and no bang.

Walter had done what he always said he wouldn't do, he had made far too much spaghetti Bolognese, but when do you ever see half size jars of that delicious but fattening sauce? Answer: Never, so what are you meant to do, throw half of it away? He wasn't a throw food away kind of guy, and promised himself that he would only eat half, and maybe save the rest for tomorrow.

But it was so tasty, and he hadn't eaten much all day, and he didn't fancy eating the same thing tomorrow, and he'd let temptation get the better of him, and returned to the pot and taken a little more, and then there was only a little left, and there was no point in keeping a smidgeon, so he had eaten the damned lot.

Not long ago, weren't spaghetti Bolognese sauce manufacturers forced to admit it was bad for you to eat too much of the blessed stuff? Maybe once a week tops, they recommended, and he comforted himself that he would indeed only eat such a thing the once that week, conveniently overlooking the tiny fact he had eaten enough for three or four people.

'Bugger!' he said aloud, and followed that with a hefty burp that he wouldn't have released if there had been anyone else in the house.

The old landline phone in the hall rang.

Walter's mood lifted for it would be one of three things. Work, and he always delighted in such things; it could never be too late for that. He glanced at his large watch. Just gone nine. It could also be those fools in India who pestered him occasionally. Usually to assure him that his computer operating system was not working properly, and they could fix it right there, right then, for less than three hundred pounds, which was bloody ridiculous, because he did not possess a computer at home. Go away! Clowns!

But it could be the lovely Carlene Henderson, and thinking about it he knew which he'd prefer, though secretly he'd have to admit his preferred caller would still be a close call between work and Carlene.

Walter grabbed the old phone and set it to his ear.

'Darriteau towers,' he said, his rich earthy voice winging its way down the line and out into the night.

'Indeed? And how is Mr Darriteau today?'

She possessed quite a deep voice herself, did Carlene.

'I am fine thank you, and how is Mrs Henderson?'

'Oh, please don't call me that, I haven't been a Mrs in ages.'

'So what can I do for you, Miss Henderson?'

Carlene giggled at the thought of being a "miss".

'Actually I thought I might be able to do something for you.'

'Really? Go on.'

'The thing is, I've done barbequed chicken, and of course I have done far too much for one, as you do, and I was wondering if you might like to come round and partake.'

For a second Walter thought of juicy barbequed chicken, one of his all-time favourites, and he tapped his full tum and wondered if by the time he went round there, maybe he might be able to fit some in. But no, there comes a time when even he had to say "no thanks".

'It's the best offer I have had all day, but sad to say, I have already eaten too much, if truth be told.'

'Ah, well. That's a pity. Never mind, it'll keep. What did you have?'

'Spagbol.'

'Nice, but fattening.'

'Yes, but so is barbequed chicken.'

'Not in moderation.'

'My trouble is the "moderation" word.'

Carlene laughed her earthy laugh again.

'You and me both.'

There was something endearing about it, that voice of hers, like an old-fashioned Hollywood film star from the fifties or sixties. No Hollywood stars laughed like that these days. Though come to think of it, the starlets in the twenty-first century came and went without ever making much of a lasting impression on the world. That was how Walter saw things.

Carlene's deep voice was talking again.

'You could come round for a glass of wine anyway, if you fancy it, stay over even…. if you want.'

Wow, thought Walter. He hadn't expected that.

'What time?'

'Any time you like.'

'You got it. Be with you around ten.'

'Lovely,' she said. 'See you later, WD.'

'Yes,' he said. 'I'll be there,' setting the phone gently down.

A thunderbolt rained down on the district.

Walter laughed aloud.

'Thor's at it again,' he said. 'Maybe it's a good omen,' and he headed for the shower, and the fragrant shower gel he was intent on soaking himself in.

Chapter Ten

Belinda Cooper stepped silently from the bed and slipped on her soft white slippers. Behind the bedroom door was an old wooden baseball bat. It had been there for almost thirty years.

Her father had picked it up in a local house clearance auction place, and had described it as a burglar deterrent, and all the while it had stood there, it had worked. They had never once been troubled by burglars and thieves.

Bel didn't think she was being troubled by burglars, but one couldn't be too careful. She bent down and picked up the heavy timber bat without making a sound. Tried to silently open the bedroom door, but knew that was impossible because the closing mechanism creaked when being opened and closed. Luckily, another thunderclap blanketed the sound.

She stood on the landing and listened.

Not a sound, other than the heavy rain on the stained glass window at the far end of the landing, and the distant sound of wind in the leafless trees across the road.

In films and TV programmes whenever someone was alone in a house, and that person thinks someone else might be downstairs, they always go to the top of the stairs and call out, 'Hello, is there anyone there?'

How ludicrous is that?

If you thought there might be someone in the house, a thief or attacker or murderer, even, the last thing you would do is yell something, giving yourself away, and alerting the invader that you are coming for them. Belinda wasn't stupid. She remained silent, and still.

She crept to the top of the stairs. The only light shining was the little coming from her pulled-to bedroom door. Switching on the landing light would only alert whoever it was downstairs, that someone was awake and moving. She wouldn't switch anything on.

She listened hard. Nothing new, nothing detected, nothing to indicate there was a person or persons in her house. She thought of retreating to her bedroom, getting her mobile, and ringing for help. Maybe ring Lena, maybe even ring the police. But didn't that sound too ridiculous for words. To ring the police, and say what exactly? 'Excuse me, but I think I heard a noise downstairs,' and all that during a fearsome electrical storm. Of course you can hear a noise downstairs, you stupid neurotic bitch, was how she imagined the station sergeant might reply, or at the very least imagine, even if he was too polite to say.

She set her foot on the top stair and, catlike, began descending those thirteen precious dancers.

Belinda's house had been built in 1925, and was loosely described as Edwardian, even though George the Fifth was parked on the throne at the time, when he was not getting up to all sorts. It was a typical smallish detached house of its day, three bedrooms, two reception rooms downstairs, front lounge, and rear sitting room that Bel's mother grandly liked to call, the drawing-room.

Bel crept down the stairs, knowing full well the second to last one creaked. It always had. She stepped over the creaking step and was safely on the ground floor, standing still in the carpeted hallway. It was pitch dark, other than occasional lightning flashes, but thankfully the lightning had changed from forked to flash, and everyone knows that flash lightning can't hurt you, can it? Bel shivered. There was a distinct draught blowing through the ground floor, and a cold one, at that.

It was coming from the drawing-room door. In the blackness, she felt for the door. It was open. That was odd because she was certain she had closed all the downstairs doors before she went to bed, though she couldn't be sure. After all, she had been carrying a lot of stuff, so maybe she had forgotten and left it open.

She eased it open.

Flash lightning filled the room.

There was no one in there. But there were shards of glass on the maroon carpet, momentarily lit up like huge precious stones. She had a moment to glance at the French doors before the light vanished. One of the small panes of glass, close to the lock, maybe seven inches by five inches, was broken, hence the glass on the floor. Once broken, anyone outside could reach in and turn the lock and open the door.

She had thought many times to have it replaced with a new double glazed unit with super locks that would forever keep her safe, but she could not, for silly sentimental reasons. Her dad had fitted those doors almost thirty years before, with his own hands. It would take something real and tangible away from the building, from the home, if they were removed and dumped, and sterile white plastic replacements fitted. Stupid, she thought right there, but understandable.

She went to the door and found it unlocked. Someone had either been in the house, or had attempted entry, or they were still inside. That thought made her mind up. She would call the police. Stupidly, she had left her mobile upstairs. She would use the landline, and that was in the kitchen on the other side of the hall.

She locked the door and turned round and peered into the darkness across the drawing-room.

A huge flash filled the room, dazzling the eyes.

She put her hand to her face and in that split second saw, or imagined she saw, a man, a tall slim man, standing in the internal doorway, a man who leapt from view the moment the flash appeared.

Bel's heart raced.

What to do?

Scream? Seemed fairly pointless.

66

Retreat to the French door, let herself out, and go and find help. But the thought of running down the road in the pouring rain in her dressing gown and fluffy white slip-on slippers, amidst thunder and lightning and rain sodden streets, didn't fill her with confidence. Besides, she was armed, with the heavy bat, and she was young-ish and fit-ish.

She attended the gym occasionally, though right there she reprimanded herself for not going often enough. But she was strong and courageous, and no damned man was going to chase her from her own home, the same sturdy house that had been the home of the Cooper family for more than forty years.

She would go after him, and hunt him down, and woe betide him when she found him, for she would hit him with all the anger she possessed, and there was a lot of that inside her after five failed relationships, with all that entailed. She was off men, for the foreseeable, no question about it, and if she happened to whack one hard, then so much the better.

And hadn't the government recently announced that homeowners defending their own homes had the right to attack and injure invaders? She seemed to recall such a thing. She raised the bat ready above her right shoulder and crept across the room toward the door. She paused and waited and listened. She was ready. Couldn't hear a thing. No man breathing, no man smell, no man's clothes rustling, no man's feet on the stairs, or crossing the stone kitchen floor. But he was there all right. Wasn't he?

Flash!

The hallway lit up better than daylight.

No one there, either. No one visible. No fleeting movement.

Tricks on the eyes? Could have been.

The door to the kitchen was open.

Again, she couldn't remember if she had left it open or not.

Blackness again, and just the noise of wind and heavy rain.

She crept into the hallway, intent on heading to the kitchen, and the landline telephone there, a tried and tested piece of old technology that never needed charging, that never kept users waiting to get a signal, that never got lost, that rarely if ever let you down, and never got stolen. That's the thing about old stuff, and old tech. It was built to last. It kept on going.

She felt the cold stone floor beneath her feet, as she tiptoed across the silent and still kitchen. Fumbled for the old grey telephone, the same phone her parents had used, and a phone she had stubbornly refused to upgrade for that very reason. It was another direct connection to her only flesh and blood. She picked up the handset and felt for the number pad, trying to remember where the 9 was, readying to poke in three 9's, practising her whispered lines. It was only then she realised the handset was no longer connected to anything else. Someone had cut it free. Sometimes old tech didn't work.

Final proof positive that a stranger had been in her house, or worse than that, was still in the building. A thought raced through her head in a millisecond. What should I do now? Go upstairs and get the mobile. Put all the lights on. Open all the windows and doors and scream the place down. Or get out of there and run for your life.

In the darkness, Belinda was frightened. Terrified even, but there was something else there too. Shear enjoyment. The thrill and excitement of it. It was better than her favourite novel. Her heart raced. She was relishing the hunt. She wasn't and never had been a pathetic damsel in distress. Her mind flashed back to being a young teenager. That time her pushy mother bought her a decent horse, with one aim in mind.

For her to join the hunting set, and mix with the great and good of the county. Perhaps even one day to land a wealthy and titled husband, and to everyone's amazement she found that she enjoyed it immensely, the hunting lark, and couldn't wait for the next one, and the bloodier it was, the more she enjoyed it.

Back then it was legal to kill foxes, and occasionally other creatures too, when not too many nosey parker people with big mouths and big morals and small minds were about, and Bel remembered it as if it were yesterday. The first time, the day she was on hand when that big old insolent fox, Reynard, was torn to shreds before her eyes, and right afterwards the leader of the hunt had grabbed a still warm bloody piece of fresh fox flesh, and had wiped it across Belinda's brow, the blood dripping into her eyes, seeping down into her pink mouth, knowing full well that she was a hunting kill virgin, and tradition was tradition, going back centuries. Everyone had to go through the initiation ceremony the first time; that was the way of things, and how bloody exciting it was too.

Truth was, it was the most exciting thing that had ever happened to her, the most exhilarating day of her entire life, and five failed relationships with five failed men had never come close to matching that day in any way.

In the darkness she smiled a cold smile. Flexed her muscles around the bat handle, and thought to herself, okay, mister fox, mister invader, mister burglar, mister man, mister tiny mind, you, my friend, have invaded my territory. You've bitten off more than you can chew, and now you must pay the price.

Belinda Cooper is gunning for you, or to be more precise, batting for you, for your life, and before the daylight returned, blood was sure to be spilt. It was simply a question of whose? The hunt was on.

Chapter Eleven

Walter arrived at Carlene Henderson's smart, modern flat at a quarter past ten. He rang the intercom and turned around and squinted up at the hostile sky. The storm has been rumbling for several hours and showed no sign of abating. Flash lightning lit up the heavens as Carlene's deep voice floated from the square metal box beside the door.

'Is that you, Walter?'

'Were you expecting someone else?'

'No, Mr Darriteau. You'd better come in out of the rain,' and the half glazed security door sprang open.

Carlene's neat flat was on the second floor. No lift, so Walter took the stairs gently, not wishing to arrive breathless. The door was open, and she was standing just inside. Walter smiled and entered and closed the door behind him.

'Thought you might like a top up for your wine cellar,' he said, passing over the bottle of white she liked, hurriedly acquired in Abdul's off licence before he closed.

'Ooh, thanks,' she said, taking it and setting it temporarily on the small but tall hall table.

'Let me take your coat,' she said. 'You're soaking, what a wild night it is,' as Walter slipped off his raincoat and hung it on the 60s style coat stand. She held her arms wide. She was a particularly tactile woman, was Carlene, one of the reasons he liked her so, and in the next moment they enjoyed a huge hug.

She'd slipped on a dark blue figure hugging satin dress. She'd had it ages, but it was an expensive thing. It rustled when it was squeezed, and it rustled there, and that was nice too, as Walter kissed her ample lips.

'Thank you for coming,' she whispered.

'Thank you for asking me.'

She grabbed his huge hand and led him through into the kitchen cum sitting room. The aroma of barbequed chicken was unmissable. On the kitchen bar lay a large white plate, and on the plate, numerous pieces of succulent fare unashamedly displayed themselves.

'Sure I can't tempt you?' she said, nodding at the still warm goodies.

'Maybe later.'

'I'll slip them back in the oven to keep warm,' she said, going about her business. 'You sit down. Fancy a beer? Or wine?'

Walter sat in the black leather sofa and muttered, 'A beer would be great. Heavy one if you've got it.'

Carlene was well aware he liked stout and had bought in supplies specially. She squished open a can, carefully tipped it into a tall glass, and went over and handed it to him. He took it and sipped it, as she collected a large glass of white wine and sat beside him and linked his arm.

'How did you get here?'

'Taxi,' which was true, though he'd been careful which taxi firm he used for Carrie the Cab, who always did the late duty, was a former girlfriend, and he didn't want to meet her.

'Why don't you get a car, Walter?'

'I have a driver who drives me around all day. I get the bus to work. It's only ten minutes, and it's a good service. I don't need a car, or the worry of maintaining such a thing. I can always get a car if I need one.'

'Nice to have, though, especially on a night like tonight.'

'You have a car, don't you?'

'Course I do.'

'There you are then. If we need a car you can always take me out.'

She smiled and kissed him again, just a quick peck. She quite liked the "we" part he mentioned.

'So,' she said. 'Are you going to stay over?'

'No, can't do that.'

'But you'll stay for a while?'

'Oh, yes, I'll stay for a while.'

'How long.'

'Till two, if you want.'

'Oh yes, Walter, I want.'

They both laughed and sipped their drinks before Carlene said, 'Bloody marvellous invention, the Internet, don't you think?'

'Yes, I suppose it is, though it's not without its faults. What made you say that?'

Carlene smiled that warm smile again and said, 'But for the Internet, I would never have met you, would I?'

'Ah, I see. Yes, it has its uses, that's for sure.'

Walter's glass was empty.

'Do you want another?'

'Later. Much later.'

Across town, Karen stayed up late. Till midnight to be precise, channel surfing the TV, waiting for David Baker to make a contrite phone call, as he made his way home, apologising for standing her up after she'd gone to so much effort.

But the dork didn't ring.

She wondered where he was and what he was doing.

She wondered if he had been truthful with her. Did he really go and see a corn miller to sort out some complicated contract? It didn't seem likely to her. Maybe that was just a smokescreen, when in reality he'd double booked his dates, and was at that very moment jazzing it up with another woman. That made sense, and that was one thing she would not tolerate, him two-timing her.

She was a detective, and a damned good one. She knew how to extract the truth from people, often without them knowing it. She had been on enough courses to learn how to do precisely that, though in truth, she had always possessed that particular knack.

Much of the technique centred on asking the same set of questions twice, on two different occasions, fitted into seemingly ordinary conversation. Where the answers differed, there were the lies. If he were lying to her, she would find out. If he were lying to her, he wouldn't see her for dust. Toast, he'd be. Burnt toast.

She crawled into bed at twenty past twelve, miserable and confused, for there had been no late night telephone call. It would be a fitful, unsatisfying sleep and she wondered why that was. Yet she knew the reason why. She liked him. It was obvious. She liked him a lot, though she tried hard not to show it, yet images of David cavorting with other women were never far from her mind.

In another apartment in another part of town, Walter was in bed by twenty past twelve, and had been for quite some time. He'd stay there until half-past one, when hot barbequed chicken would be served up in the kitchen, alongside fresh coffee and warm buttered rolls, by a happy looking curvy lady.

Chapter Twelve

Belinda Cooper retreated to the hallway. The lightning had finally abated. She thought again about switching on the lights, but that was a double-edge sword. She might be able to see him, but he would be able to see her.

In her mind, she was now the hunter. Hunters live off stealth and surprise. She didn't want him to be able to see her. She didn't want him to know where she was.

She didn't want him to detect the heavy blow she'd issue when the opportunity arose. She imagined the strike raining down on his fragile head. No human skull is a match for a heavy baseball bat. That's why drug dealers keep them in their cars and flats and houses, as she had read in those thrillers countless times. Silent but deadly. It was just a case of setting up the opportunity. The lights would stay off. If it were necessary, she would kill him. She was ready for that. But where was he? He wasn't in the kitchen. He wasn't in the hall. He wasn't in the drawing-room. That only left the front lounge, or failing that, upstairs.

The silent power of touch told her the door to the front lounge was closed. She tried to recall when it was last open. Could he and would he have gone in there? Had he opened the door and stepped inside and closed it again? It seemed unlikely. And what was he doing in her house, anyway? What was the motive for his late-night visit? What was he after? Robbery? Rape? A violent thrill? Simply to scare her, or terrify her? Or something worse, like murder? And why was he playing stupid games? Like disappearing and reappearing. What was that about? Perhaps he was toying with her as a cat does with a mouse, before killing and devouring it.

A noise came from upstairs. Not a crashing breaking noise, but a slight bumping sound, as if he had knocked something off her dressing table, or disturbed something in the bathroom. He wasn't in the front lounge; that was certain. He was upstairs, doing God knows what. But was he luring her into a trap? There was only one thing to do. Go and find out. Her hands deposited sweat on the varnished bat handle, as she stepped over the telltale stair, and started up the flight.

In total dark towards the top, she stopped and paused. Wondered if he was there, waiting for her, planning on striking her before she struck him. Where would he, and could he be hiding on a darkened landing? When his only hiding place was the darkness itself?

But he wasn't on the landing. She knew that for sure, because she could smell him. Three distinct masculine odours, and the stink was coming, without any doubt, from her bedroom, where someone had turned off the light.

She crept toward the door, her soft slippers enabling silent running, and breathed in through her nose, just once. Not a sniff, not a noise inducing action, but gentle inhalation... of man, and invader, in her house, in her bedroom, for God's sake.

Deodorant. The first odour. That high profile under arm and all-over brand advertised on the TV and in men's magazines. The one that was supposed to have women drooling in numbers and falling at men's feet, the one that men supposedly couldn't live without, the one that bestowed on all men a magnetic attraction, no matter how ugly, no matter how old, no matter how fat, no matter how cold.

It didn't attract her. Not one bit.

Aftershave. Odour number two. Another big brand that came at a hefty price. The same brand Gareth the solicitor soaked himself in, imagining that it made him more attractive to women, and in a way it did, for no woman wants a sour smelling man. But you can have too much of a good thing, and in common with many men, he always used far too much of it.

Bel stood stock still outside her bedroom door. She reached out to touch it, but it wasn't there, not where it would have been if it were anywhere near closed. It was open, at least half way open, and that was as she expected.

The third odour was there too.

The stink of a nervous man.

Not body odour per se, but that indefinable reek that a jumpy male exudes. They probably don't even know they are exuding, their pores busy expelling surplus natural perfume. He almost certainly didn't, and that aroma of man hadn't been present in her bedroom since Gareth had done damned things in there he probably shouldn't, and if that wasn't enough proof for her, there was the icing on the cake.

She could hear him breathing.

Even though he was trying hard to hold his breath, even though he was standing stock still, even though he was doing his best to keep his heart rate under control, and his body functions neutral, she could hear him operating in the darkness, like the complicated and amazing machine that he was.

Bits moving in and out. Air flowing through the gears. Liquid rushing around the pipes. Electricity running through the brain. Fuel digesting in the fires of his stomach, bones readying to move, like some giant locomotive. They all made noise, no matter how soft or how stunted, no matter how disguised or cloaked. She could hear his systems working hard, on slowdown maybe, but there, nonetheless, excited, readying themselves. The only thing her hyper senses didn't tell her was where precisely in the bedroom he was.

The door was hinged on the left-hand side. It was a new door, one of the few things that she had allowed to be tampered with, for the original high waisted doors had buckled over time, and would no longer close properly. She had replaced all four of them a year before with modern, white panelled models.

She put herself in his position. Where would she be? Where would she hide? Where would she place herself for maximum safety and protection, and the greatest surprise? It had to be behind the door. Where else would anyone wait in ambush?

She flared her nostrils and allowed clean air to circulate in. The same three odours were still present, one-two-three, all quite separate, distinct and unique, yet all combined into one positive trail, telling her that her quarry was not moving, not coiled and about to spring out, but waiting for an opportune moment, biding his time, waiting for her to make her move, waiting for her to enter the room when he could attack. Or bolt for freedom, like a startled fox driven from its lair.

Bel nodded to herself in the sureness of her logic, and envisaged what was about to happen. She made her move. She gently pulled the bat back the last few inches to the top of the back swing, as the golf coaches say, the highest point, the point of no return, the zenith, the point from where all future movement and momentum and force is directed down, and across, and forwards, and on, smashing into the target.

In the blackness she crept into her bedroom and unleashed a single blow, the likes of which would have brought down a lion. The trajectory went around the edge of the door, and behind the door, and struck viciously to precisely where she saw in her mind he was cowering, striking down the triple-odoured man who had invaded her home, her space, her bedroom, and her quiet life.

The bat kept on going, Bel clinging onto the handle, though it almost slipped from her grasp. It slammed into the primrose painted plaster, making a large indentation, a fingerprint from the bat itself, onto and into the wall. He had not been cowering behind the door. In that millisecond of recognition she realised she was in deep trouble, for she'd given her position away, enabling the man to pounce.

He was immediately on her, behind her. Grabbing the bat at both ends through gloved hands. He was clever, that was clear. He'd done his envisaging well. He'd out thought her this time, and he was incredibly strong.

'What the hell are you doing?' she screamed.

It was a waste of breath and vital energy, and worse still, thinking time. He didn't reply, not a word, but pulled the bat back, hard and true, against her slim throat, pinning her to him, her back to his toned chest. She tried to get her hands and arms up between the bat and her throat, but had missed her opportunity.

She was young-ish and fit-ish and would not go down without a fight. She tried to kick him with her heels, but soft slip-on slippers were never going to bother him. Where were her stilettos when she needed them? If only she had slipped them on, the ones with the tall slimline metal heels. They could have done real damage. She tried to wriggle free, feinting one way to the left, only to switch all her strength and energy back immediately to the right, but again he appeared to read her every move. He held her fast.

She tried to turn her head around to face him in the darkness, from where she could perhaps reach up and bite him, and if nothing else, the restraining wood of the timber would be less of a threat on the back of her neck than on her naked throat, but again he sensed her line of thinking. He held her still. Looking away from him though she could not see a thing. It was as if the hunting cat playing with the mouse had enjoyed its fun, and it was time for the denouement. He snapped the baseball bat back towards him with all the strength he possessed.

It was way more than enough.

He broke two vertebrae as if they were seasoned twigs. He'd broken her neck. Human beings rarely survive a broken neck without immediate and knowledgeable assistance. Thirty-six-year-old Belinda Cooper would receive neither.

The invader sniffed and tossed the timber bat onto the double bed. He thought of turning on the light, but didn't wish to imprint on his brain the scene that he alone had created. He clapped his gloved hands together as if in triumph, and left the room. Ambled down the stairs and into the drawing-room. Went to the double French doors, opened them, and stepped outside. It wasn't raining. He turned around and locked the doors, and tossed the key through the broken pane, and across the room. It fell to the carpet with the tiniest of thuds, bouncing once.

He grinned to himself. Walked around the side of the house. Opened and closed the tall timber side gate. Ambled out onto the pavement as if he owned the place. Glanced at his watch. The neon hands told him it was twenty to one. Peered up and down the road and glanced at the sky. The thick clouds were breaking up. A hint of moonlight filled the sky. There was no one about. No late night dog walkers, no courting couples, no moving cars in the road, no revellers making their way home after a night on the town, not even a shifty burglar looking for an easy and unguarded and unprotected home.

He made his way to the end of the road. The streetlights were popping out. Chester Council cost-cutting measures darkening the area. He smiled to himself. It had been an exciting evening. Better than last time, and it was finished. He'd never do anything like that again. That was something. That was the plan. He walked for ten minutes through suburbia, back to the Cayton Cerisa that was obediently waiting for him, parked up by the canal.

He opened the car and removed the two large pebbles he had carefully set on the front passenger seat. Took off the gloves, inserted a pebble in each, crossed the road to the canal, bent down as if to tie his shoes, and gently dropped both heavy gloves into the murky water. A nearby coot cooed three times at being disturbed. The gloves sank to the bottom and nestled into the cold mud, taking ample DNA with them. No one would ever search for them. No one would ever think of it. He re-crossed the road, jumped in the car, started the quiet and silky engine, and purred away on the fifteen-minute trip home.

What a stupid woman she was, he thought, on reflection, to imagine that she could outfox him, and out-fight him. It had come as something of a surprise, her resistance. Courageous though, you had to give her that. He shook his head and banished all thoughts of the evening from his mind. He would try never to think of it, and of her, ever again. He was strong, very strong, in mind and body, and he knew it too, in the prime of his life, and it would carry him through.

Chapter Thirteen

Karen usually slept soundly, but that night sleep would not come. She tossed and turned and glanced at the clock several times as if to check it was time to rise and dress. By 6am she'd had enough.

She slipped from the bed and went into the shower. Let the water run very hot and then icy cold. Dried and dressed, slacks and blouse, light jacket, and through to the kitchen.

She rarely ate breakfast. Went to the fridge and took out a bottle of flavoured water. Opened it and swigged a little, grabbed a large green apple from the overflowing fruit bowl, collected her keys and let herself out.

Her car was sleeping in the garage. The up and over metal door creaked and banged as she opened it, alerting her neighbours she was up and out early. She drove into the old city and parked in the big car park across the road from the central police station, behind the law courts, down by the river. She'd bought a parking season ticket there, and it was expensive, and was intent on getting her money's worth.

She was the first of the regular team in the office. She logged into the computer, bit into the apple, and began reading the overnight crime reports and notes. It was still before 7am. Walter came in twenty minutes later, looking jaunty and content. She noted that.

'Morning, Greenwood,' he said. 'You're in early. Couldn't sleep?'

'Yeah, something like that.'

Walter limped to the coffee machine and came back with a steaming drink. 'Anything happening?'

'Nothing new.'

Jenny Thompson came in next and smiled and nodded at the over-nighters, and she was followed by Hector Browne and Darren Gibbons.

'Err, excuse me, but aren't you and Nick supposed to be seeing Jimmy Crocker first thing this morning?' said Walter, glugging on the coffee and gazing at Darren.

'Couldn't, Guv. Nicky's going to his grandma's funeral today, he rang me last night.'

'Did he now? He kept that to himself.'

Walter made a mental note to check if that were true, for in the past they had once had a clever dick of a PC who had attended at least five grandmother's funerals over the years, taking the piss, he was, and Walter couldn't abide being lied to.

'It still has to be done, take Hector with you, get down there now. It's still early, you know the thinking, visit early before they get out of bed, before they have woken up, before they have gone to work, or whatever they get up to.'

Gibbons nodded and looked at Hector, who had heard everything and had gone for his jacket. Walter was talking again.

'And after you've seen him, go and see those bloody publicans again. You might like to drop a hint that the hierarchy here might not be so happy to approve the renewal of their alcohol licences next time round, if they can't be more cooperative and helpful in our enquiries into the affairs of the late Eleanor Wright.'

Gibbons grinned and said, 'Sure Guv,' and the two guys shrugged and left the building.

Walter glanced across the desk at Karen. She looked a little tired; maybe she'd enjoyed an exciting night.

'How did the date go?'

'Don't ask,' she said, throwing the apple core in the metal bin with a clang. 'Terrible.'

So he didn't ask, it was none of his business, and he knew that she would tell him in her own good time, if she wished to, and if she didn't, that was cool. He couldn't stop a grin crossing his heavy face. His unplanned date had gone fantastically well, though he'd keep that nugget to himself.

Hector drove the unmarked car to Saltney Ferry and 20 Laburnum Gardens. It was a small redbrick townhouse, two floors, one of five linked houses, one of the middle ones. It looked older than its ten years, but that was down to a lack of care and maintenance. The paint on the white window frames was peeling in places, and the small front garden hadn't been weeded in at least a year, and it showed. As they made their way up the small path toward the front door, Hector began whistling.

'Give it a rest, Heck,' said Gibbons, as he rang the bell.

The bell inside rang, and the big dog barked.

'Shit!' said Hector. 'That's all we need, a damn big dog.'

Gibbons grinned and muttered, 'Probably a pussy.'

They both heard a guy inside yell, 'Ma! Some bastard's at the front door.'

'I'm going, ya lazy tyke,' and in the next second a big woman appeared wearing a cavernous blue dressing gown. She pulled the door open, while holding back an ugly looking brown beast that was keen to get better acquainted. The woman glared knowingly at them, for she could smell the law at two hundred paces, as did the dog.

Hector did the introductions as the woman turned and yelled up the stairs, 'Jimmy! Get your arse out of that bed. The coppers are here for you.'

They heard him say, 'Oh, what the hell do they want now?'

'Come and find out! I'll put the dog in the kitchen,' and she turned around and did just that.

A minute later Jimmy Crocker appeared in the hallway, having thrown on a grubby white T-shirt and a pair of old jeans. He eyed up Gibbons for a second, for he'd come across him in battle before.

'Come inside,' he said. 'I don't want the whole damned world knowing my business.'

Darren and Hector stepped into the small and crowded hallway. It smelt of big brown dog.

'We are making enquiries about a young woman named Eleanor Wright,' said Hector.

'No comment,' said Jimmy C, out of habit.

'We can do this here, or we can do it down the station,' said Darren, 'and that could easily take all day, and half the night.'

Jimmy pulled a face and shook his head and said, 'Eleanor who?'

'Eleanor Wright.'

'Don't know anyone of that name.'

'Are you sure?' asked Darren.

'Positive. Who is she?'

Hector ignored Jimmy's question and asked, 'Where were you on Friday night?'

Jimmy sniffed and turned away and shouted into the lounge, 'Ma! Where was I on Friday night?'

'He was here, with me, all night,' came back the yelled and predictable reply.

'Anyone else here?' asked Darren.

'Only Bozo.'

'Who's Bozo?' asked Hector.

'The dog.'

'Did you go anywhere near the river on Friday?' asked Darren.

'Course I did. The river winds through the city, it's hard not to.'

He had a point there.

'Did you visit a young woman in a caravan down by the river?' persisted Gibbons.

'No, worse luck. Why? Was she a goer?' and Crocker smirked.

'The young woman in question is dead,' said Darren, staring into the back of Crocker's beady eyes.

Crocker pursed his lips. His bottom lip came out, and he said, 'It happens. We all die sometime.'

'She was burned to death, in her caravan,' said Gibbons.

'So?'

'Do you smoke?' asked Hector.

'Yeah, now and again, not a crime, is it?'

'So you have matches on you, maybe a lighter?'

'Now hang on a minute!'

'Do you own a car?' asked Gibbons.

'No. Use me mam's, when I need to.'

'Where is it now?' asked Hector.

Crocker opened the front door and nodded across the road to a small car park where five cars were gathered together, side by side.

'It's the old red Vauxhall, buggered it is,' said Crocker. 'Hope to get my own soon.'

They all looked out and there it was, second from the end.

'And you've never met Eleanor Wright?' asked Hector.

'No I haven't, said so, didn't I?'

Hector and Darren shared a look and nodded, and couldn't think of anything else to ask. Darren muttered something about thanking him for his time, and in the next second they were walking away across the road to examine the car.

'What do you think?' asked Darren.

'Could be him,' said Hector. 'Slippery git.'

'He is that,' and Darren took a small plastic bag from his pocket and slipped on a pair of wafer thin plastic gloves and bent down and looked at the tyres. There were some small pieces of mud there, and muddy marks on the edges of the tyres too, but that meant nothing, for with that storm last night and the rain before that, and the wet and muddy roads, almost every car in the city would be sporting muddy marks that morning. He peeled several small lumps from the rubber and slipped them in the bag, sealed it, and placed it in his jacket pocket.

Hector nodded and said, 'Where to now?'

'The pubs, of course, Heck, the pubs.'

Chapter Fourteen

At smack on ten o'clock, Walter received a telephone call. It was from Janice Jefferson. Walter told Karen to listen in. 'Inspector Darriteau?'

'That's me.'

'You slipped a card through my door. I suppose it's about poor Ellie. Terrible isn't it? I'm still in shock.'

'So you've heard?'

'Yeah, when I saw your card I rang Ellie out of habit, we shared most things, bezzie pals you might say, and when I couldn't get her, I rang her mother. She told me the news, I still can't believe it.'

'When did you last see her?'

'The day before I went to Madeira.'

'How was she?'

'To tell you the truth, Inspector, she was a little on edge.'

'Why? What was causing that?'

'Not sure exactly, but there were men in her life. Some of them she liked, and some of them she didn't. She was no angel, that's for sure, but maybe you know that already.'

'We are not here to judge anyone. All we want to do is find out what happened to her.'

'Well Inspector, she told me things.'

'What kind of things?'

'Terrible things.'

'Can you be more specific?'

'I'd rather not, not right now.'

'Can we come and have a chat?'

'I guess.'

'When's suitable for you?'

'You can come now if you like. I'm not working at pres, I'm between jobs, I'm at my sister's for the day.'

'Where's that?'

'Portobello Towers. It's....'

'I know where it is.'

'Thought you might. Number 35. Second top floor, but you're in luck. The lift's working, for a change.'

'See you in half an hour, Janice, and thanks for calling.'

'You're welcome, I just feel so sorry for Ellie; she had a filthy life.'

Walter rang off and glanced at Karen.

'Car?' she said.

'Sure, I'll have a quick word with Mrs West. See you downstairs in ten.'

At that hour of the day all the good cars had been grabbed, and the best Karen could do was an aging Ford saloon with a smell all of its own. Strangely, Karen quite liked it for it had a big engine and was quick, but a throaty gas-guzzler. The kind of vehicle being phased out because of high running costs. Petrol, car tax, and insurance were all penalising, and someone in budgets was bound to spot that, and kill it before long.

Portobello Towers was a sixties tower block on the Beacon estate, the kind of place where people stayed because they could not find or afford anywhere better. The kind of place where people lived until they moved on, and moved up. The kind of place where immigrants, illegal and otherwise, were found accommodation, the kind of place where long-term residents grew old before their time, and then could never move out, and the kind of place where kids, and not so young kids, set up and ran illegal pirate radio stations.

The tower blocks were ideal places to erect aerials high in the sky, where Ofcom radio aerial inspectors could be spotted from half a mile away, the broadcasting equipment dismantled, and taken down and hidden before the authorities arrived. It was an ongoing irritant that was never quite solved because the people charged with doing so were overworked, and always had something better or more urgent to occupy their time.

Janice was right. The lifts were working, and that was a relief. Number 35 was on the eighth floor. Karen knocked softly on the light blue door.

A young woman, presumably Janice, came to the door and let them in. There was a radio on, broadcasting the latest pop. The song finished and a station jingle came on. *Dee-Bee-Cee – Deva Broadcasting Company – The Happy Sound of Free Pirate Radio for Chester and the North West.*

That pirate radio station again, cocky, cocksure, and confident with it, with seemingly not a care in the world about prosecution. Both Walter and Karen noticed that. Janice rushed to the set and switched it off.

Another almost identical young woman was sitting in an old sofa in the smart lounge. She grinned at the visitors. She had a toddler of a little boy on her knee who clearly was about to fall asleep.

Both of the young women boasted deep tans, fake or real, pondered Walter. Possibly real, maybe they had been to Madeira together.

'This is Chantelle, my younger sister, and he's Benny, aren't you, Ben?' said Janice.

Right on cue Benny's eyelids fell closed, and Chantelle stood up and took him into a bedroom to put down for a couple of quiet hours.

'Sit down, will ya?' said Janice, and they did.

'You've been to Madeira?' said Walter.

'Yeah. Great it was. I didn't want to come back.'

'And you're not working?' asked Karen.

'No,' said Janice, immediately going on the defensive. 'It's not a crime, is it? No work and going on holiday. I'll soon get another job.'

'Course you will,' said Walter.

'What do you do when you work?' asked Karen.

'Oh, all sorts, shop work, office work, waitressing, stacking the shelves in Bestdas, anything that pays well. I'm a hard worker, me. Hey, hang on a minute, you don't think I do, we do, me and Chantelle, the same thing as Ellie, do ya?'

'No, course not,' said Walter. 'We are just filling in the background.'

Janice pursed her lips and did not look happy.

'Did Chantelle go with you?' asked Walter.

'Yeah, but the baby was well looked after, he's not abandoned or anything like that. Mum took him, she adores the kid.'

'I'll bet she does. You've both got the same tans,' said Walter.

'Ah, yes, I see, yeah well, it was so bloody hot there. We were so surprised, at this time of year, and all.'

'You said Ellie told you things?' said Walter.

'Yeah.'

'Go on,' said Karen.

'I don't think she had anyone else she could talk to. Not really. Derek's a wet weekend of a man, and I don't think she talked to her mum at all, so she kind of confided in me.'

'Anything you can tell us,' said Walter, 'will help us a great deal.'

'Was she murdered?'

'We think that's possible,' said Karen.

'That's why anything you can tell us could be vitally important,' added Walter.

Janice pointed hard at the window and said, 'Those men, those bloody men out there, some of those men were, and are, quite disgusting. And do you know the worst of it; many of the bastards are married. Can you imagine being married to a man like that, who goes out doing all sorts at all hours, and comes home as if the grass doesn't grow?' Janice looked hard at Karen and said, 'Can you imagine being married to a man who carried on like that?'

89

For a moment Karen imagined being married to David Baker, and wondered what he would be like as a husband. Would he ever, and had he ever, patronised young women like Ellie Wright and Tracey Day? Maybe he still did. It didn't bear thinking about.

Walter said, 'Was there anyone in particular you had in mind, when talking about *Those Men?*'

Janice breathed out hard and spat out words, 'There were hundreds of them! Literally. Sometimes she told me she did ten of them in a single day, or night. Can you imagine? Geez! I find one of them hard enough work to deal with, but ten... Or more. No thank you! And of course she had a habit too.'

'Drugs?' said Walter.

Janice nodded. 'Nothing too serious, but it gets a grip of you, so I believe, and even a small habit can cost a pretty penny. That's why she kept on working.'

'Coke?' asked Karen.

Janice nodded and said, 'Yeah.'

'Where did she get it?' asked Karen.

'Oh, don't ask, you can get it anywhere if you look hard enough.'

'Not from Derek?' asked Karen.

'No, course not, he's never going to get involved in anything like that.'

'Did any of them ever threaten her?' asked Karen.

'Course they did! All the time. She lived in fear of it. But I guess it comes with the territory in that line of business.'

'Was there anyone she told you about who worried her or pestered her the most?' asked Walter.

Janice nodded. 'There was one bloke. To begin with, she really liked him. He was dead good-looking and very generous. Tell you the truth, I think she fell a little in love with him, which was something she said she would never do, not with the punters. That was forbidden territory.'

'Do you have a name?' asked Walter.

'No. But he's foreign.'

90

'What do you mean, foreign?' asked Walter. 'Black, like me?'

'No, no! Not like you at all, Inspector. You're nice. No, this guy speaks with an accent. Good English but with a definite accent.'

'German, French, what?' asked Karen.

'No. More eastern European, I would think.'

'What? Polish?' asked Karen.

Janice pulled face and shook her head, and said, 'No, Bulgarian or Romanian, I think, she did say once, but I can't remember now. Latvian maybe, one of them lot.'

'Did she describe him at all?' asked Walter.

'Nope, but she didn't need to.'

'Why's that?' asked Karen.

''Cos I saw them together once.'

'You saw him?' said Walter. 'Where and when?'

'In the Crazy Cow steakhouse. A couple of months ago.'

'He took her for a meal?' asked Karen.

Janice nodded.

'To begin with he was always taking her out, and he wasn't short of money either, that's when I think she got some fancy ideas about him. She even went away with him to Ross-on-Wye for a whole weekend once, stayed in some fancy hotel. Got up to all sorts. He came well equipped, she said. She was made up with that trip, I can tell you. But the dinners and the treats gradually became less and less, and the other thing became worse and worse.'

'What other thing?' asked Karen.

'You know. The services she provided, and the ones he wanted.'

'Go on,' said Karen.

'Do I have to?'

'A little way,' soothed Walter.

'Look! I thought I knew about life, I thought I knew what men were like, but some of the stories she told me made my hair curl, I can tell you, and I've never had a curl in my life. And some of those men often wanted her to do things their wives would never dream of doing, or tolerate doing either. Not ever. It was gradually getting out of hand.'

'With the eastern European?' clarified Walter.

'Yeah, among others.'

'Do you know what he did for a living?' asked Karen.

'Yeah, course I do. Didn't I say?'

'Go on,' said Walter.

'He's a banker,' and Janice laughed aloud.

'What's so funny?' asked Karen.

'She always called him "my wanker of a banker", and she said he always paid good too, but he wanted his money's worth, that was the problem.'

'Can you describe him?'

'Course I can.'

'Go on.'

'Good looking, six foot, slim, fit, nice dark hair, neatly parted, brown eyes I think, well dressed, perfect husband material, really.'

Karen thought of David Baker again. *Perfect husband material, really.* But for the foreign accent her description fitted him to a tee.

'If they were sitting down having dinner how do you know he was six foot tall?' asked Walter.

'Because when they had finished the meal they got up and walked out. She linked his arm, and he seemed happy enough with that, not awkward at all. He was a six footer all right, maybe slightly more, I'm not pulling your plonker, if that's what you think.'

'We don't think that,' assured Walter.

'Anything else?' asked Karen.

'Like what?'

'Do you know where he worked? Do you know where he lived?' asked Walter.

'Nope and nope. Though I think he worked here in Chester, though I don't know why I think that, just do.'

'And she never said his name? In all your chats?'

Janice shook her head, but then smiled broadly.

'Mirror! That's what she said his name was, only the once, I remember now. She said his name was Mirror, and she could see her own fate in it, the mirror, like, I'd forgotten all about that, strange really.'

'Mirror?' queried Karen, spelling it out. 'M-I-R-R-O-R?'

Janice nodded firmly. 'That's what she said, deffo.'

'How often did she see him?' asked Walter.

'No idea, but a lot, and he paid her well too, I told you that, so she said. But he didn't like her seeing other men, I know that much, but she could never stop doing that.'

'Was there anyone else specific besides this Mirror character?' asked Walter.

'Loads of others, lots of weirdo's too, I mean dozens, but not another one who sticks out. Not like him.'

'You've been very helpful,' said Walter.

'I hope I have.'

'If you think of anything else, no matter how tiny or insubstantial it might seem to you, will you give me another call?'

'Course I will. Can I call you Walter?'

'Course you can,' said Walter, and he smiled his best friendly uncle smile and hoped that it didn't come out too creepy.

Chantelle came back into the room and grinned.

Pound to a penny she'd been listening at the door.

'Your sister's been very helpful,' said Walter.

'That's good,' she said, nodding and sitting down.

Walter asked, 'Did Ellie ever mention a girl called Tracey Day?'

'Not a name I know of. Why?'

'No reason, just another name that's cropped up in our inquiry.'

'You didn't ever meet any of these guys, did you?' asked Karen.

'Course not! What do you take me for? Got more sense than to get mixed up in all that!'

'Sure, course you have,' said Walter.

'You collect glass paperweights?' said Karen, nodding at a display case full of round glass paperweights, turquoise, green and blue, that was pushed in against the far wall.

'Yeah,' said Chantelle, chuffed that the coppers had noticed her prized collection. 'Always loved them, and do you know what they are really good for?'

'What?' said Karen and Walter as one.

'Hurling at burglars! Stop 'em stone dead, they would,' and both the sisters laughed together.

Walter and Karen grinned and stood up, and the girls stood too, and the toddler started crying, and Chantelle let slip the F word.

'Will you call me? If there's any news?' asked Janice.

'Sure,' said Walter. 'And you'll call me if anything else turns up here.'

Janice grinned and nodded and went to the radio and turned it back on.

Dee-Bee-Cee! The Continuing Sound of Free Radio.

It was time to go, Janice opened the front door, and a second later the coppers were through it and out of there and gone.

94

Chapter Fifteen

Everyone was back in the office by half-past three, as the update briefing got under way. Mrs West kicked things off by saying, 'Are we making any progress, or are we wasting our time?'

Which seemed an odd thing to say to most of her captive audience. Though no doubt she was under pressure again on costing and time management issues, and the like.

'We have a new lead, ma'am,' said Walter.

'Go on.'

'Ellie Wright's best friend, maybe her only friend, is a girl called Janice Jefferson. Janice told us that Ellie was real frightened of one particular client. He's reported to be some kind of foreign banker, or a banker with a foreign accent, and we have a good description because Janice saw the man. He's six footish, IC1, clean cut, dark hair and eyes, and speaks good English with a foreign, possibly eastern European, maybe Bulgarian, Romanian accent, that sort of thing.'

'Do we have a name for this guy?'

'Janice said his name was Mirror.'

'Mirror, as in looking glass?'

'That's what Janice said.'

'Odd name.'

'It is, ma'am, and it's not a name listed in any names directory. Jenny, I want you to ring round all the local banking institutions and ask if they have anyone of that name.'

Jenny nodded and said, 'Sure, Guv. Is that a Christian name or surname?'

'Could be either.'

'What about getting this Janice girl in to compile a photofit?' suggested Mrs West.

'If you think it's worthwhile,' said Walter.

'While we are spending so much time on this, we might as well have something to show for it.'

Walter nodded and said he'd organise it.

'What happened to the names Hector threw in the ring?' asked Mrs West, sniffling into a neat hankie.

'We went to see Crocker,' said Gibbons. 'Heck and me. Crocker has an alibi for Friday night, his huge mother. She said he was in the house all night, but I'd say that's about as reliable as rice paper in a storm. He denied ever knowing Ellie, denied ever visiting any girl in a caravan down by the river. We took a sample of mud from the tyres of his mother's car, he doesn't have his own wheels, so he said, and that's gone to the lab to see if it matches with the stuff at the foot of Marigold Lane.'

'Good. What was your gut feeling?' asked Walter.

'I'd say he's capable of it, there's a temper on him, for sure, and violence in him too, we know that. But unless the mud comes back positive we have nothing to connect him with Ellie Wright at all.'

'You agree, Hector?'

'Yes, Guv, I didn't like the guy one bit, but he didn't give me any reason to think he'd murdered someone in the last few days.'

'What about Michael Flanagan?' asked Mrs West, glancing at her watch.

'Guv and I had the pleasure,' said Karen.

'And was it?' said Mrs West. 'A pleasure?'

'Not really, though he's certainly changed his image.'

'In what way?'

'Big haircut, now short and smart. Looked more like a businessman about town than a heavy metal rock guy.'

Walter added, 'When we visited he was entertaining company.'

'Who?' said Mrs West.

'A little local Tom called Tracey Day.'

'I wonder if Tracey Day knew Ellie Wright,' said Mrs West, thinking out loud.

'I asked Janice that. She didn't know the name,' said Walter.

Karen added, 'And I asked Tracey, and she denied knowing Ellie as well.'

'But there is a definite connection between Flanagan and Ellie Wright,' said Walter.

'What kind of connection?' said Mrs West.

'Flanagan's a cab driver. He said he recently took a man down Marigold Lane on more than one occasion, a man who visited Ellie. Gave us a description, and it's close to the one Janice gave of this Mirror man.'

'Could be something,' said Mrs West.

'It could,' agreed Walter. 'We just need to find him to eliminate him from our enquiries.'

'Going back to Flanagan for a second,' said Hector. 'Doesn't he fit the description too?'

'He does now, pretty much, with his new smart image,' said Karen.

Hector continued. 'This guy Flanagan has just come out of prison after murdering someone, correction, causing the death of a woman, namely his wife. We know he consorts with prostitutes, and we know he's visited Marigold Lane, he's admitted that. That's powerful enough, isn't it?'

'It is,' said Jenny, 'but he's tagged, remember? Seven till seven curfew, and I've checked with the tagging people and they say there have been no irregularities reported in the last ten days, and we know the caravan went up in flames around midnight, so said our witness Mr Duffield, so how could Flanagan possibly have been there then?'

Hector scowled and said, 'How reliable are these bloody tags?'

'Very!' said Mrs West.

'They are indeed reliable,' confirmed Karen, 'but like all modern technology they can have occasional blips and glitches. No modern tech is ever a hundred percent.'

'I'm happy with them,' said Mrs West, thinking back years to when she'd first recommended them, and pondering on how much money they had saved in the intervening time, as against keeping low-grade criminals longer in custody. For people like her, and all administrators and accountants, they were a godsend.

'There is one other gent we should not yet discount,' floated Gibbons.

'Derek Nesbitt?' said Karen.

'The same. We know he also visited Marigold Lane. He wanted Ellie to give up her profession, we know that too. Maybe he had some crazy idea of shacking up with her if she'd stop working. Maybe they argued, and it got out of hand. It happens. It's all possible, and he also happens to vaguely fit the description of the man who dined with Ellie, and the man who visited Ellie in Flanagan's cab.'

'But he doesn't have a foreign accent, or the need to use cabs because he has his own car,' said Walter.

'True, just thinking aloud, Guv.'

'How did you get on with the publicans?' asked Walter.

Gibbons glanced at some notes and said, 'Better, Guv. They gave us a list of twenty possible clients. They weren't too happy at being threatened, mind.'

'Not threatened, Gibbons,' said Walter, unable to keep a smile from his face. 'Persuaded, I would say.'

'Yeah, right.'

'You and Hector can crack on with that for the foreseeable, checking them all out.'

'What about Nick?'

'Ah yes, I'd almost forgotten him, I want a word with that young man when he returns, but yes, he can help you on that too.'

'So?' said Mrs West. 'Do we have a prime suspect?'

'Mirror for me,' said Karen.

'Flanagan for me,' said Hector. 'Definitely.'

'And it's Nesbitt for me,' said Gibbons. 'Just have a feeling about it.'

'Feelings don't solve cases,' said Walter, 'evidence does.'

'So who do you think?' asked Mrs West.

'I don't think any of them yet, ma'am, though like the rest of us, I'd sure like to interview the Mirror man.'

Mrs West clapped her small cold hands together. She'd heard enough. 'Right! Let's get on with it, you know what you have to do,' and she jumped up and hurried back to her office and the meeting broke up, and the detectives returned to checking and re-checking all known facts in an effort to push the inquiry forward. Was there a murderer on their patch? And was he still active? Probably and possibly, were the best guesses, but they needed much more than that.

In the travel agents in the city, Lena Freeman rang Belinda for a third time. Left another message. Both she and her boss were surprised, and not a little concerned that she hadn't reported in to work, nor had returned any of their calls.

Lena was particularly on edge because Bel had seemed so upbeat and healthy when they'd spoken the previous night. Lena was still confident she could convince Bel the Baltic States should be the destination for their next holiday jaunt. It wasn't like Bel at all, for she was such a steady and reliable woman. Lena would try again that evening and give it to the morning at the latest. If Belinda wasn't back by then, alarm bells would ring.

Chapter Sixteen

At five o'clock the team began drifting away. It had been a hard day and progress had been slow. 'You've been quiet,' said Walter.

Karen forced a smile and said, 'You never miss much, do you?'

'Comes with the job. Man trouble, is it?'

'No, not really, they always disappoint you, don't they?'

'Do they?'

'Mine seem to.'

'Do you want to tell me about it?'

Karen sat back in her chair and breathed out heavy, in two minds whether to say anything, and then she thought, what the hell? And proceeded to tell Walter about her date that never was, and of how much she had been looking forward to it, and now she was wondering whether he was two-timing her, and maybe she was wasting her time.

'I hope it wasn't because I kept you late,' said Walter.

'Course not, Guv. He was late anyway, it must have been around nine before he called.'

'That's all right then. So what are you going to do?'

'See him again, I guess, see if I can find out if he's genuine, or simply a liar.'

'You're training should help you decide that.'

'You'd think so, Guv. But somehow when it's so close to home, everything gets cloudy, and I always seem to end up giving them the benefit of the doubt.'

'I'd back your judgment any day. You know the score. Get more info. Evaluate the intelligence. Act accordingly.'

'Yeah,' she said, seemingly miles away, and then she said, 'Never mind me, what about you?'

Walter was unable to keep a broad smile crossing his face.

'I had a fantastic date.'

'Really?'

'Yep, one of the best,' and he told her all about the late night barbequed chicken, and threw in a few hints of what had gone on before.

'Lucky you!'

'And of course it's all down to you.'

'Really? How so?'

'Putting me on to that Internet dating site in the first place.'

'She came from there?'

'She certainly did.'

'Does she know what you do?'

'No, not yet, though I don't suppose it will make any difference.'

Karen didn't comment on that. But in her experience it wasn't unusual for members of the team to lose their new partner once a full job description had been discussed, and tossed around.

'When are you seeing her again?'

'Don't know yet. Might ring her tonight.'

'You do that, Guv. Wanna lift home?'

'That would be fab, Greenwood, I'll just go and say ta-ta to the boss lady.'

'She's already gone, Guv.'

'I didn't hear her go.'

'Think you were in the bog at the time.'

Walter grunted and bent under the desk and put his shoes back on, and did up the laces.

Twenty minutes later, Karen pulled the car to a standstill outside Walter's three-bedroom Edwardian detached house. It was already full dark and particularly dismal, the streetlights straining to penetrate the murk.

'Have a good night,' he said, heaving himself out of the car.

'You too, Guv,' and twenty minutes after that he was setting the surplus barbequed chicken pieces Carlene had insisted he take home, in the oven and turning it on blitz. He didn't even bother looking inside the silver foil. It didn't matter about re-heating chicken, did it? No health issues there, were there? He was hungry, and he was going to eat the damned lot, along with a little crusty bread left over from the spagbol.

Karen hurried home and sat on the sofa and considered making something to eat, though she wasn't in the least bit hungry. She thought about Eleanor Wright, and what drove her to take up such a hazardous profession. Lack of cash, probably, she concluded, what else could it have been? And she thought about Tracey Day too, venturing down the same precarious road, and wondering if she had any real idea how dangerous it could be.

There were no stats, to Karen's knowledge, as to the percentage of women under say thirty, who were murdered while practising the same grubby business, but Karen's guess would be a big number. But what could you do? Make it legal? That opened a whole new can of worms, like making drugs legal. Where do you stop? Where do you draw the line?

She thought of something else. What about the Guv, eh? Wasn't he just the lucky one, hitting the jackpot, by all accounts, when it came to Internet dating, though she didn't begrudge him his obvious happiness. He'd lived alone for such a long time, but hey, where was her happiness coming from, and she let herself feel sorry for herself for all of twenty seconds, and right there, right then, her phone rang.

She picked it up and glanced at the screen.

David Baker.

Her first thought was to turn it off, blank him, but she didn't. She'd hear what he had to say.

'Hi, there,' she said, as indifferently as she could muster.

'Am I still in the doghouse?'

'I don't know. Are you?'

'Not at this end.'

'What can I do for you, Mr Baker?'

'Wondered if you'd like to go out for a drink later.'

'Nope. Can't.'

'Why?'

'I'm busy.'

'Doing what?'

'Work stuff.'

'You're still angry with me, aren't you?'

'What gave you that idea?'

'I can tell.'

Karen sighed over-loudly and said, 'I did think you might have called me last night on your way home, or something.'

'I didn't get home till nearly two, and didn't think you'd appreciate me calling at that unholy hour.'

She wouldn't tell him she'd waited up late.

'And did it go well?'

'Yeah. Pretty much. Contract all signed and sealed.'

'Really?'

'Yeah. Do you want to see it, or something? Inspect the evidence?'

'No, I don't.'

'Don't be like that.'

'Don't be like what?'

'You know, offhand with me. I am trying to make it up to you here.'

Karen sighed again. 'I don't get the feeling that I am the most important thing in your life, and if we're to go forward as a couple, I bloody well should be.'

'Course you are!'

'It doesn't feel that way.'

'What have I got to do to make it up to you?' and in the way he spoke she could tell he was grinning, and feeling super confident about things.

'Try harder.'

It wasn't the answer he had expected.

'Sorry? What did you say?'

'You heard me.'

'I am trying. Dinner tonight. Good place, nice wine, my treat.'

'No, I'm busy, gotta go,' and she cut him off.

Afterwards, she remained on the sofa and replayed the conversation in her head. Did she regret giving him a hard time? No, not a chance. Did she think she'd put him off? No, but if she had, he wasn't worth much anyway. Did she feel better about things? Yes! A hundred percent, he could experience a brush off and a cancelled or missed date for a change. See how he liked it. She grinned to herself. Her appetite had returned. There were some low fat vegetable burgers in the freezer, and she'd grill those and serve them up with a little fromage frais, rocket lettuce, and crisp bread biscuits.

Walter gnawed the last of the chicken off the bones and set them haphazardly on the plate. He licked his lips and wiped his fingers and mouth on the pieces of paper towel he had brought with him from the kitchen.

He'd have to ask her for the recipe, for they were gorgeous. He stood up and took the plate back to the kitchen and made his way down the hall to the landline phone. Picked it up, dabbed in Carlene's easy to remember local number that resembled a taxi rank number. 08080.

She answered pretty much straight away.

'And how is Mrs Henderson tonight?'

'I am fine, and how is Mr Darriteau?'

'I'm great. I've just finished the chicken, it was fab, you must give me the recipe.'

'I'll dig it out.'

'Actually, that's not why I rang.'

'Oh?'

'I just wanted to say how much I enjoyed last night.'

'I thought you did, I'm so glad, I did too.'

'And I wondered if you'd like to go out for a drink later?'

Carlene sighed and said, 'Ah.'

That didn't sound so good, thought Walter, so he said, 'Or maybe tomorrow?'

'This is a little awkward, Walter.'

'What is?'

'I've had an email, a couple of hours ago.'

'From?'

'My husband.'

'I thought you said you were separated.'

'I am. We are. He lives in New Zealand, and you can't get much more separated than that.'

'So?'

'He's coming back next week.'

'But when you said separated, I thought you meant it was all over and done with between you two.'

'It is… in a way. I haven't seen him for six months.'

'But you're not completely separated, are you?'

'We are! It's difficult, Walter, awkward, I told you, I'll have to see him, I can't just refuse to speak to him, or see him.'

'I see. So where does that leave…'

'Leave us? I don't know. We'll just have to talk again, when things are clearer, when he's been and gone. He's not staying long. Look, I'm really sorry, Walter, we'll speak again soon, yeah? I'll have to go now, I've things I must sort out, bye-eee,' and she put the phone down.

Walter glared at the old wallpaper.

'Bugger,' he snarled, setting the phone down, and he sighed and returned to the lounge where he put his shoes back on. He didn't feel like sitting in the house all alone all night brooding on that news. He'd amble down to the local pub where there were a good gang of fellas who welcomed him into their company, not least since he had become something of a minor celeb locally, been on local news TV quite a few times.

He'd sink a few glasses of the black stuff, and no doubt would have to withstand the same old joke: Thick black stuff for a thick black man, and listen to a few other jokes too, some at his expense, some not, hopefully a few of them might even be funny, maybe even tell a few too, and he'd do his damnedest to forget all about Carlene bloody Henderson for the day, and night. Sounded like a plan, and a good one at that.

Chapter Seventeen

Karen was first at work in the morning, looking refreshed and much happier than the day before. Walter came in ten minutes later looking a little worse for wear. He'd cut himself shaving too, on the left side of the chin, and though the trace of blood had hardened up, it looked a mess.

Nicky Barr arrived next and said a happy good morning, and as he passed Walter's desk, Walter growled, 'I want a word with you.'

'Sure, Guv. What's going down?'

'You were off yesterday.'

'Yeah, I told Gibbons.'

'You didn't tell me, or any senior officer.'

'Sorry, Guv. Didn't think.'

'This job is all about thinking, DC Barr. It's what we do. If you can't think, you are of little use to me. Understand?'

Nicky looked at Walter quizzically, thinking he'd got away with it, and said, 'Yeah sure, Guv, sorry,' and went to walk away.

'I haven't finished with you yet! Funeral, was it?'

Nicky stopped still and said, 'Yeah, something like that.'

'Well, was it a funeral or wasn't it?'

'It was.'

'And whose funeral was it?'

'My old gran's. I told Gibbons.'

Walter scratched his chin, taking care to avoid the cut, and said, 'What was your grandmother's name?'

'Pardon, Guv.'

'Please don't make me repeat everything, DC Barr. You heard me the first time.'

'Dorothy Barr. Why? What's up?'

'And where was this funeral?'

'At the crem.'

'And what time was it?'

'Eh? In the morning. Eleven o'clock.'

'So if I rang the crem now and asked them who was cooking at eleven o'clock yesterday morning they'd tell me it was Dorothy Barr, would they?'

'Well, I wouldn't have quite put it like that, but yeah, they should do.'

Walter pursed his lips and said nothing.

'Is that it, Guv?'

'Let's see, shall we? Let's ring,' and Walter picked up the phone and spoke to the main switchboard operator, and asked them to get the crematorium on the line.

Nicky Barr looked nervous and scratched his chin.

Walter stared at the phone, waiting.

Nicky said, 'Actually, Guv…'

'Actually, what?'

'There wasn't a funeral yesterday.'

'There was no Barr family funeral yesterday? What? Not at all?'

'No, Guv. Sorry.'

The phone rang and the switchboard operator said, 'I have the crem on the line.'

'Thanks, but I don't need them any longer. Sorry to have wasted your time.'

'No problem,' came back the singsong happy voice.

Walter glared at Nicky and said, 'So you lied to Gibbons, and you lied to me. In fact you lied to me several times.'

'Sorry, Guv, it's just that the girlfriend…'

'I don't want to know anything about your girlfriend!'

Nicky nodded hard and said nothing, which right there was just about the best thing he could have done.

'This office,' said Walter, wafting his big hand around, 'spends a great deal of time tracking down liars, tripping up liars, tying them up in their own webs of lies and deceit. So how do you think it looks when one of our own, right here, one of my team, thinks it's okay to casually tell one lie after another?'

'Not good, Guv.'

'You're right, DC Barr. Not good! Not good at all. I give everyone who joins this precious band one chance. You've just had yours. If I ever catch you lying to me or anyone else in this room again, I'll kick your backside all the way to Rhyl and back. You'll be returned to traffic duty before you could say Llan-bloody-dudno. Is that clear?'

Nicky nodded slowly and looked suitably contrite, and muttered, 'Really sorry, Guv.'

'Go away! See Gibbons, he has important work for you.'

Nicky nodded fast and hurried off.

Karen glanced at the departing guy and back at Walter and said, 'Silly boy.'

'He ruddy well is, but he won't do it again. I hope.'

'How did you know?'

'I have met my share of Smart Alec's over the years and I can sus them out at fifty paces. It wasn't that difficult.'

Karen swigged her water and was keen to change the conversation. He seemed in a real bad mood over something.

'I'll ring Janice, see if I can get her in today.'

'You do that,' said Walter, settling down to study the crime reports.

An hour later a beaming Jenny came over to Walter's desk and said, 'I think I've got something, Guv.'

Karen glanced up from the old Michael Flanagan case notes.

'Mirror man?' mumbled Walter.

Jenny nodded.

'I can't find anyone going by the name of Mirror, but I have found a local banker who works for the Anglo-Slavic National Bank. The ASNB, they are based here in Chester, and this guy's

109

name is Miroslav Rekatic, though he prefers the shortened version of Miro.'

'How old is he? Do you know?' asked Walter.

'He's thirty-seven.'

'And what are the chances he's six feet tall, speaks with an eastern European accent, and has dark hair and eyes, and is vaguely good looking?' said Karen.

'I can't comment on the height, but the rest fits like a glove. I've cribbed his picture from their website. Here he is, our Miroslav,' and she set a good colour photo down in front of them.

'I know this ASNB outfit,' said Karen. 'It's one of the new generation of banks that are pushing hard to get a foothold in the UK market.'

'They are,' confirmed Jenny. 'Putting new ATMs all over the place.'

'Address?' said Walter.

'Chester Business Park.'

'Car?' said Karen.

'Please, unmarked.'

'Shall I see you downstairs?' asked Karen.

'Be there in a sec, just going to keep Mrs W up to speed.'

Jenny said, 'I'll keep looking, see if I can find anyone else.'

'Do that, Jen. And well done.'

The huge sprawling and modern Chester Business Park was located on the southern side of the city, strategically placed for easy access to the road system, with the nearby A55 and A483 dual carriageways funnelling traffic east west and south, and onto the M53, and the national motorway system beyond.

The modern landscaped site was not far short of 200 acres and was a pleasant place to work, boasting green spaces and lakes and woodland, and it was no surprise that plenty of British, American and European Finance houses and banks had been tempted to set up shop there.

In the short car ride south Karen said, 'So it looks like Janice misheard Ellie say Mirror when she actually said Miro, you reckon?'

'Looks that way, let's hope so anyway, and it would be an easy mistake to make,' and in less than ten minutes they were pulling off the main road and entering the impressive looking park.

The ASNB building was much larger than expected, and resembled something of a modern glass fronted sports stadium, but oddly fronted with white Romanesque columns flanking the entrance.

'Banking must pay awfully well,' said Karen, bringing the car to a halt in the large car park, as she glanced up at the vast glass facade.

'We all know that,' said Walter, thinking of the whacking monthly interest addition on his credit card statement, 'and yet, it's constantly a mystery to me as to how they manage to lose so much money, every now and again.'

'Incompetence, do you think?' said Karen, unable to keep a smile from her fair face, at the thought of it.

'Probably. Maybe the Mirror man will be able to throw some light on that,' said Walter.

'How are we going to play this, Guv? Interview him here, or back at the station.'

'What would you do?'

'Here to start with, and if we don't like what we are hearing, back at our place.'

'Got it in one! And don't mention that Ellie's dead,' Walter said, getting out of the car, and doing up his coat and limping away.

Inside, the modern hi-tech look was everywhere. Ahead of them was a shiny black reception desk with the obligatory bright young thing on parade, eager and willing and waiting to field their enquiries. Walter and Karen hustled over to the desk and Karen flashed ID and completed the introductions.

'Please show us through to see Mr Rekatic right away,' said Walter, staring round at the huge pieces of blue, yellow and white modern art adorning the walls.

'Do you have an appointment?'

'No, we don't, and we don't need one,' said Karen.

'It's a little unusual.'

'Yes,' said Walter. 'It is. Mr Rekatic please... now, chop chop.'

The young woman pulled a face and stared at Walter and realised he wasn't a man to mess with, and pointed to her right at a modern half-glazed door and said, 'Through there, fourth on the right.'

'A thousand thank you's,' said Walter, turning away and limping toward the door that took them through to a wide and long corridor. They could both hear a modern phone burbling away somewhere up ahead, and both imagined it was the young woman alerting her boss the law was on the way.

The fourth door on the right was wide open, and inside, a smart man was talking on a phone. He was looking at the doorway as if expecting visitors, and sure enough there they were, walking straight in, Karen's ID on full display.

'Mr Rekatic?' she said. 'Mr Miroslav Rekatic.'

The dark-haired man nodded and said, 'That's me, and you are?'

Karen completed the intros, and Rekatic set the phone down without comment, and came out from behind his desk and closed the office door.

'Take a seat,' he said. 'What can I do for you? I can give you ten minutes. Lots on the go today, you know how it is.'

Walter sat in one of the grey and black comfortable visitors' chairs, probably cost a fair fortune, as Karen sat down beside him.

'It'll take more than ten minutes,' said Walter. 'Much more.'

'Maybe you should have made an appointment.'

Maybe you shouldn't be consorting with young for-sale girls, and I'll bet you're a happily married man too, thought Karen, though she kept those colourful thoughts to herself.

'It can be here and now for as long as it takes, or at the station right now, for as long as it takes, I'm not really that bothered,' said Walter, looking across and into the back of the man's dark eyes. What was he? Six foot, clean cut, dark hair and eyes, and a noticeable eastern European accent. What a surprise.

Rekatic sat back in his chair, sighed hard, and realised he was in no position to argue.

'Okay. Let's get to it,' he said.

'Your name is Miroslav Rekatic?' asked Karen.

'It is.'

'And you're sometimes known as Miro?'

'Yes, to my friends and acquaintances.'

'Are you also known as Mirror?' asked Walter.

Rekatic pulled a face and shook his head. 'Miro yes, Mirror, no, never. Why? What can I do for you?'

'We want to talk to you about a young woman by the name of Ellie Wright,' said Karen, as Walter never took his eyes from the guy.

'Ellie? What about her?' said Rekatic.

'You do know Ellie?' asked Karen.

'Yes, I know Ellie. Why? What's this all about?'

Walter leant forward and said softly, 'What is your relationship with Ellie Wright?'

Rekatic grimaced and shifted in his chair.

'She's a nice kid. Great company.'

'Good company?' clarified Karen.

Rekatic nodded, didn't say anything, though it was clear he was thinking of saying something else. The officers remained silent, awaiting further comment. Karen nodded, encouraging the man.

When he did speak, he said, 'It's a little difficult.'

'Yes?' said Walter. 'Is it? What is?' for he was in no mood to make it any easier for the guy.

'If you know Ellie you probably know she's something of a good-time girl.'

113

'A good-time girl?' said Karen, speaking slowly, each word coming out almost as single short sentence.

'Do I have to spell it out?'

'You do to me,' said Karen.

'You mean to say, she's a prostitute?' said Walter.

Rekatic nodded. 'Something like that.'

'We might as well use terms we all understand. The thing I find difficult,' said Walter, 'is why a successful businessman like yourself, with a beautiful wife and family,' and he reached across and picked up the silver-plated photo frame that adorned the desk, and glanced at the picture of the attractive blonde woman, and two even more beautiful blonde haired girls, 'why a man such as yourself should be consorting with street girls at all. Why is that exactly, Miro?'

Rekatic clicked his tongue and shook his head and said, 'You know how it is, you're a man of the world.'

It was Walter's turn to shake his head.

'No!' he said decisively. 'If I were married to a woman like that,' nodding at the photograph he set back on the desk, 'I wouldn't look at a street girl in a million years.'

Rekatic went silent and sat back in his chair. He took a moment out, thinking hard. What the hell was this about? And why was he bothering to answer the English police officers' questions? He'd humour them a little while longer.

'It's the old thing,' he said, allowing a crooked smile to invade his fox-like Slavic face. 'Sometimes when a man doesn't get what he wants at home, he has to look elsewhere.'

His eyes switched from the overweight black man to the underweight English blonde, checking to see if he'd shocked her. He hadn't. Not such a surprise. In her line of work she must see all sorts.

'You mean your wife doesn't like sex,' said Walter, mischievously. 'I would never have guessed that from her photograph. That does surprise me.'

'Of course my wife likes sex!' he said in a hurry, 'not that it is any business of yours,' thinking he may have revealed more than he intended.

'But not kinky sex?' said a stone-faced Karen.

Rekatic grimaced and put out his hand, palm down over the desk, and twisted it as if to say, close, but not quite right.

'Rough sex?' said Walter, and Rekatic smiled a cold smile and pointed at Walter as if to say, there's a man after my own heart, a man who knows what's what.

'How rough?' asked Karen, not giving him a second to think.

'Well, you know…'

'No, we don't know,' said Walter. 'Not at all. Answer the question.'

'I'm not sure how one would grade these things.'

'On a scale from one to ten, how would you rate your meetings with Ellie Wright?'

'God! I don't know.'

'Well, I certainly don't,' said Karen.

'On a scale from one to ten?' repeated Walter, keen to not let the guy off the hook.

Rekatic sighed hard and muttered, 'Maybe seven or eight.'

'Seven or eight,' said Walter thoughtfully, pondering on where that took them in the pantheon of rough antics.

'Yeah, about that,' Miro said, a hint of cockiness entering his voice.

Walter spoke again: 'And would that include heat… and burning?'

'What the hell are you talking about?'

'I think you know well enough, Miro. Clamps. Hot needles? Electric shocks. Cigarette burns, stubbed out on the skin? Sound familiar?'

'Don't be ridiculous!'

'Ridiculous, is it?' said Karen.

'All we are trying to do is fill in the blanks,' said Walter. 'Get a clearer picture of what precisely you are talking about, of what exactly Ellie Wright was expected to accept, and endure, things that your good wife was unwilling to do, and I have to say, that so far, you haven't shed tons of light.'

Rekatic had heard enough.

'I don't know where you are going with this, but I am not answering any more questions until you tell me what this is all about.'

'What is your wife's name?' asked Karen.

That was an easier one.

'Grizelda, everyone calls her Grizzy. She's German. Why?'

'And what nationality would you be?' asked Walter.

'Serb. Why? What's that got to do with anything?'

'It goes without saying that you have the necessary work permits?' asked Walter.

'Course I have! Is this what this is all about?'

'No, not really,' said Walter.

'Do you want to get to the point?'

'When did you last visit Ellie Wright at the foot of Marigold Lane?'

'Eh?'

'You heard the Inspector,' said Karen.

It looked like Miro needed thinking time on that one, and he got it too, for his phone rang, the landline on the desk before him. Miro grabbed it and yelled, 'What?'

'Your next appointment is here for you now, Mr Rekatic.'

It was a good phone system. Crystal clear. Walter and Karen heard every word.

'Cancel it!'

'But I can't, they have come all the way from Leeds!'

'I said, cancel it!' bawled Rekatic, as he set the phone down hard. 'Sorry about that. Work issues. I did tell you I was busy today.'

'So you did,' said Walter. 'Now where were we? Ah yes, you were about to tell us when you last visited Ellie, and what you got up to down by the river.'

116

Chapter Eighteen

In the travel agents in the city centre, Lena glanced at her watch. It was coming up lunchtime. She'd rung Bel three times that morning, still without success. Her boss came back from the bank and glanced across at an obviously worried Lena, and said, 'Any news?'

'Not a thing. Still no answer. It isn't like Belinda. You know that, don't you?'

The boss man pulled a face and looked up at the wall clock. It was true it had never happened before. On the very rare occasions when Belinda Cooper had fallen ill, bad flu, badly sprained ankle, that kind of thing, she had always without exception kept them fully informed.

'Do you want to go and see if she's alright?'

Lena nodded, and said, 'It would put my mind at rest.'

The boss nodded too, and said, 'Fair enough, it's almost your lunch hour, why don't you take an early lunch and go and check it out?'

An incredibly generous offer, thought Lena, sarcastically, and she said, 'I'll do that, I'll get back as soon as I can.'

The boss man nodded again and began opening new cardboard boxes full of fresh brochures to restock the shelves.

'Keep me informed,' he muttered, as Lena collected her things together and slipped on her beige raincoat, and headed for the door.

It took her no more than twenty minutes to arrive outside Bel's nice little detached house. All looked quiet and in order from the front. Lena skipped up the short garden path and rang the bell. She heard it clearly enough, but no one came. She stooped and pushed open the old green metal letterbox, and looked inside. She couldn't see much. There was another internal door maybe four feet away, that led to the hall.

'Bel!' she yelled. 'It's Lena. Are you okay?'

No sound. No reply. No nothing.

Lena took a step back and glanced up at the bedroom windows. The curtains were drawn. That was a little odd for the middle of the day. She headed round to the side of the house and the side gate. Over the small wall to next door a man came out and began fiddling about with the refuse wheelie bin.

He peeked over the wall and saw Lena there. He thought he'd seen her once or twice before, and he had.

Lena caught his eye and said, 'Have you seen Bel at all? She's not been at work, and she's not answering her phone.'

The man scratched his chin as if thinking, and said, 'Come to think of it, I haven't seen her for a few days.'

'Can I get round the back?' said Lena, trying the side gate that opened easily enough.

'Do you want me to come with you?' said the man.

Lena nodded and muttered, 'Please do,' and they made their way around the side of the house.

Several puddles of rainwater covered the small paved patio that lay outside the French windows, but it wasn't the puddles that grabbed Lena's and the neighbour's immediate attention, but the broken pane of glass.

'I don't like the look of this,' said Lena, pointing to shards of glass inside on the carpet.

'You and me both.'

The neighbour tried the door. Locked fast.

'Look!' said Lena, 'the key,' and they both stared through the glass at the key, nestling in the centre of the carpet, more than half way across the room.

'Bel!' yelled Lena. 'It's Lena, from work, are you in there, are you okay?'

No reply, nothing at all, other than a wailing and working bin lorry somewhere in the distance, as it approached the road.

'I could get my fishing rod,' suggested the neighbour. 'That'll do the trick.'

'Do that!' said Lena, and the guy hurried back to his house to collect his angling gear. He was back within five minutes, but by the time he'd returned, Lena had changed her mind.

'I don't think we should go in,' she said. 'I don't like this at all. I think we should call the police.'

'I agree, it is more than a little odd. Have you got a phone?'

Lena nodded and pulled out her phone and carefully prodded in 999.

Walter gawped at Miroslav Rekatic and rippled his eyebrows as a little reminder that he was awaiting a reply.

'Sorry,' said Rekatic. 'What did you say?'

'I said, when did you last visit Ellie?'

'Err,' Rekatic scratched his chin, trying hard to remember, or was that a charade he was putting on to gain thinking time. 'Last week, sometime.'

'When last week?' shot back Karen.

'Friday, yes, I think it was Friday.'

'Come on, Miro, you can do better than that. You weren't visiting her to drop off a letter, or say hello, or pass the time of day, or take a leisurely country walk together, none of those things were true. You were visiting her for a rough sex session, and in that moment it was the most important and exciting thing in your entire life, and therefore you would remember to the very second what time you got there. You'd probably been looking forward to it all day, all week maybe, and you would know, to the day, to the hour and minute.'

Miro grimaced and said, 'It was Friday, about six o'clock.'

'A little teatime excitement session, was it?' asked Karen.

'If you want to put it that way. We're very busy with all the expansion plans at the moment. It's a very stressful business, top-line banking, we all need some form of release and relaxation. Some people drink, others do drugs, I like female company, and there's no law against it. Lots of bankers have mistresses.'

'I'll bet they do,' said Walter. 'How did you get down there? To Marigold Lane?'

'Cab.'

'And what time did you leave the caravan?' asked Karen.

'About eight.'

'Cab again?' said Walter.

Miro nodded and said, 'Same firm, different driver, you can check,' and that all matched with Michael Flanagan's statements.

'Tell me what happened at Ross-on-Wye?' said Walter, ever eager to flummox interviewees with a sharp change in direction.

'What?'

'You heard the Inspector.'

'You mean with Ellie?'

'That's who we are talking about,' said Walter.

'I took her away for the weekend once or twice. Sometimes we went to Ross. What's your point?'

'And presumably Grizzy wasn't aware of that?' asked Karen.

'Course not,' said Miro. 'What do you think?'

'Just filling in background,' smirked Karen.

'Correct me if I'm wrong,' said Miro, 'but it's not a crime in this country to have both a wife and a mistress, is it?'

'No. Not a crime,' said Karen, 'just deceitful, despicable, disrespectful, and I'm sure your wife might even say, disgusting.'

'But Ellie Wright wasn't your mistress at all, was she?' said Walter. 'She was a paid whore, servicing any number of clients.'

Miro pulled a face as if to say, whatever, is there a difference? before he said, 'It's much easier this way, than to have an actual mistress. You can turn it on and off, as and when you please.'

Walter repeated the words aloud. 'Turn it on and off, as and when you please,' and that said a lot about the guy.

120

Didn't he have any idea how cold, uncaring, and cowardly he sounded, thought Karen.

'What went on in Ross?' repeated Walter.

Miro pulled another surprised face and said, 'Really Inspector, do you want chapter and verse? I didn't film it, if that's what you think.'

'I heard you went "well equipped",' said Walter. 'Care to elaborate on that?'

'Did Ellie say that? Stupid girl? You know how it is, just a few little sex toys, to spice things up. Nothing outrageous.'

'Sex toys?' said Karen.

'What kind of toys?' asked Walter. 'You mean clamps, electric shock inducers, lighters, candles, what exactly?'

'Certainly not! You seem to have an obsession there, my friend.'

'I'm not your friend,' said Walter, 'and I'm still waiting for an answer to my question.'

Miro took a deep breath, breathed out heavy, and acted like he was getting tired with the whole thing, and grinned and gurned and said, 'She liked to be incapacitated.'

'Incapacitated?' said Karen.

'Explain,' said Walter.

'It's just a little piece of equipment I picked up in Hamburg.'

'Go on,' said Walter.

'There's not much to it, really,' just a metal bar that goes behind her neck, her hands go over the top, black leather straps, she can't really move, not at all, get the picture?'

'Isn't the truth of it, that you liked to incapacitate her, when she had no choice in the matter, and that you enjoyed inflicting pain on Ellie Wright,' said Walter, 'and she didn't want to participate in that sordid business at all?'

'Course she did! She's a whore, remember; she does things for money, anything you want, and was paid bloody well for it. She told me I was one of her best clients. Even gave me a birthday card, for god's sake. Said I was her banker banker.'

Or wanker of a banker, thought Karen.

'Do you still have the card?' asked Walter.

'Nope. Got rid of it, just in case…'

'In case Grizzy found it,' said Karen.

'Yeah. Something like that.'

'Have you tried this incapacitator on Grizzy?' asked Karen, suspecting she knew the answer.

'Course not, don't be ridiculous!'

'Ellie told her best friend she was frightened of you because you hurt her, care to comment on that?' asked Walter.

'What! Don't be crazy. She enjoyed a bit of pain. It was all part of the whole business.'

'Isn't the truth of it that you enjoyed inflicting pain on Ellie Wright,' said Karen. 'That you got off on it, got a high out of it, because your wife wouldn't entertain such a thing, and Ellie couldn't do anything about it, because you had incapacitated her, totally, completely, and utterly.'

'No! That's not how it was at all. It was just a bit of harmless fun between friends. Look! If you don't believe me, ask Ellie, she'll set you straight. She's not a fool.'

'We can't,' said Walter, 'she's dead.'

In the station, Gibbons took Lena's call. Recognised the worry and distress in the caller's voice straight away, and promised someone would be there within twenty minutes. He ran across and told Mrs West about the report of a possible break in, and a possible missing person too. She told him to take Hector with him and go and check it out PDQ. She also instructed Gibbons to tell Jenny Thompson to ring Karen and keep Walter abreast of the situation.

In the palatial ASNB office Walter's revelation that Eleanor Wright was deceased took the wind out of Miroslav Rekatic's sails, or that was the impression he gave. Neither of the officers were convinced of his performance.

'So,' said Walter, 'as it stands, you are the last person to see Ellie Wright alive.'

Miro breathed out heavy and shook his head.

'How did she die?'

'You tell us,' said Karen.

'How the hell would I know?'

'Come on, Miro,' said Walter. 'It's time to clean the slate. What exactly went on down at the foot of Marigold Lane last Friday?'

Before he could answer, Karen's mobile rang. She glanced at the screen. Saw who it was.

'Can you talk?' asked Jenny.

'Just a sec,' and she glanced at Walter and muttered, 'I have to take this.'

Walter nodded and Karen stepped outside.

Jenny said, 'Ma'am told me to advise you and the Guv that we have a reported burglary in Chester where a missing thirty-six-year-old woman resides. Very concerned workmates and friends and neighbours, by all accounts. Could be something. I'll let you know when I hear more.'

'Okay, Jen. Keep us up to speed.'

While Karen was outside, Walter said, 'Did you argue about something?'

'No.'

'So, what did you do?'

'What do you think?'

'I don't know, I am waiting for you to tell me.'

'I went to the caravan for sex.'

'Rough sex?'

Miro shrugged and glanced at the bear-like black man, and thought he'd better elaborate.

'I gave her a good spanking.'

'Spanking?'

Karen came back in and exchanged eye contact with Walter and muttered, 'Could be something, could be nothing.'

Walter turned back to Miro and said, 'And was the incapacitator used?'

'No.'

'Why not?'

'I forgot to take it.'

Karen said, 'Where does it reside, this item of torture of yours, when not in use. At your home?'

'No, course not. There's a cupboard here at work, I have the only key.'

'I want to see it before we go,' said Karen.

'I want to seize it as evidence,' said Walter.

'What?'

'You heard me. So, after the spanking session, what happened then?'

'What do you think?'

'I don't know. You were the only one who was there who's still alive. You tell us.'

'We had… You know.'

'Sex?' said Karen.

'Rough sex?' said Walter.

'Yeah, you could say that.'

'How much did you pay for that?' asked Karen.

'Two hundred quid.'

'Is that the going rate for incapacitation, and torture?' asked Karen.

'I guess. She seemed happy enough.'

'What happened next?'

'Not much. I got dressed. She got dressed too. I gave her a decent tip. Said I'd see her again next Friday.'

'A regular appointment, is it?' said Karen.

'Not a fixed one, but pretty regular, yeah. I have a big libido.'

'You tell a lot of lies as well,' said Karen.

Miro shrugged as if they were little white lies, and no more.

124

'What happened then?' asked Walter.

'I rang for a cab.'

'On your mobile,' said Walter.

Miro nodded.

'Show me your phone.'

Miro took his phone from his trouser pocket and set it on the desk.

'You rang the cab company on this phone?'

'Yes.'

'Bag, Karen,' and she produced a small clear evidence bag, and Walter dropped it in.

'What are you doing?'

'I am seizing this phone as potential evidence to a murder inquiry.'

'You can't do that!'

'I've already done it,' and the bag and phone disappeared into Walter's cavernous coat pocket.

'Was she really murdered?'

'You tell us,' said Karen.

'She was alive and well and as happy as I had seen her in weeks when I left her.'

'And you left her at what time?'

'About eight, I told you, the cab company will confirm it.'

Karen asked, 'Did she say if she had any further appointments that night?'

'Not to me.'

'Did she say anything about going out to get something to eat?' asked Walter.

'No. She had a little kitchen thing there, and a camping style gas stove. I got the impression she was going to cook something, though I could be wrong.'

'She didn't offer you anything to eat?'

'No, course not. She wanted me out of there, and I wanted to get out of there too. I wanted to get home and see the wife and kids, before they went to bed.'

'That's noble of you,' said Walter.

'I'm not saying it was an ideal arrangement.'

'Well, that's a fact,' said Karen.

'So you left her around 8pm, and she was fit and well at that time?'

Miro nodded.

'Pity you can't prove that,' said Karen.

'And you can't prove that wasn't the case,' said Miro, trying to be a little too clever.

'We will,' said Walter. 'If we have to.'

'Is that it?'

'For now.'

'When can I have my phone back?'

'When we have finished with it,' said Karen. 'Maybe.'

'Just one other thing,' said Walter.

'What?'

'Did you, or do you, visit other good-time girls, as you call them?'

'In Hamburg a few times, but not here.'

'Never?'

'Never!'

'Incapacitator?' said Karen. 'Show us.'

Chapter Nineteen

DCs Darren Gibbons and Hector Browne arrived outside Belinda Cooper's house in quick time. Gibbons assumed the senior role through length of service, though

Hector was far better qualified academically, having been fast-tracked from Uni. Lena Freeman and a man, the neighbour, were standing on the pavement outside.

Hector flashed ID and did the introductions, as Lena said, 'There's no reply when we knock, she's not answering her phone, and there's a broken pane of glass in the French windows at the back.'

'What's the lady's name?' asked Gibbons.

'Belinda Cooper.'

'Show us the broken glass,' said Hector, and they hustled round the side of the house to the back, and onto the grey patio.

There was no glass on the patio, but plenty of broken glass on the carpet inside.

'The key's there, look,' said Lena, pointing across the room, and they all looked and nodded.

'I brought my fishing rod,' said the neighbour. 'I could hook the key, no problem.'

'Fish away,' said Gibbons, 'but try not to touch the doors or the glass.'

The neighbour bobbed his head and slipped his long rod through the door. It was lengthy enough to reach the key, and in the next second he'd slipped the end of the rod through the key ring, and with a little juggling, it was raising up, easing back towards the doors.

'Careful!' said Hector, as the neighbour tilted the rod further upwards, and the key slid down toward the near end of the rod, and the hole in the door where the glass used to be, and Darren's grasping hand, waiting to grab it.

'Bingo!' said Darren, key in hand, and into the keyhole it went, one quick anti-clockwise turn, and the door opened inwards.

Darren and Hector stepped inside.

Lena and the neighbour made to follow.

'No,' said Gibbons. 'Rather you didn't. We'll go and check, and come back and tell you how we get on.'

Lena bit her lip and nodded, half disappointed, half relieved. The neighbour was downright frustrated for he ran the local neighbourhood watch website, and imagined he was onto the scoop of the decade.

Darren hustled into the kitchen. Took a quick look round, including in the pantry and in the big floor to ceiling cupboards, and yelled back, 'Kitchen clear.'

Hector went into the other reception room and took a peek. There was nowhere there anyone could hide, alive or dead. 'Lounge clear!' he yelled, something they all heard, and in the next moment Darren was leading the way up the stairs, all the while calling out, 'Belinda Cooper, it's the police, is everything all right?'

Gibbons pointed Hector into the large rear bedroom. He pushed the door opened and went inside. A nice double bed all made up, no one in the bed, no one in the room. 'Back bedroom clear,' he shouted.

Gibbons went into the front bedroom, the main bedroom, the master bedroom; the one that had to be the favourite, if any room was going to shed light on the mystery.

The front bedroom was not clear.

There was a woman, collapsed in a heap, close to the foot of the bed, and on the bed was a vintage baseball bat. Gibbons rushed to the woman and felt for a pulse. He didn't expect to find one, and he didn't.

'Bugger!' he said. 'She's in here, Heck, we're too late.'

128

Hector came running.

Took one look.

Grimaced and turned away.

Gibbons was already on the phone.

Jenny answered.

'We've found a body, Jen. Foul play looks likely. Can you rustle up the team? Doc Grayling, SOCO, a couple of uniforms to keep the place secure, and you'd better tell Mrs West PDQ, and no doubt she'll want the Guv to know.'

'I'm on it,' and she cut off.

Gibbons and Hector shared a look.

'Murder weapon, you think?' said Gibbons, nodding at the bat.

'Could be,' said Heck. 'Who on earth keeps a baseball bat in the bedroom?'

'A woman living on her own, maybe, unless the killer brought it with him.'

They both heard Lena shouting up the stairs. 'Is everything okay up there?'

'They're in the house,' said an alarmed Gibbons. 'Get them outside. They're contaminating a crime scene.'

'What do I tell her?' asked Hector.

'Nothing, not yet, tell her Guv will be here soon, and he'll decide on that.'

Hector nodded, knowing the woman would give him a hard time, but sometimes that was the job. He went downstairs and ushered the pair of them outside, doing his best to evade their probing questions.

In the offices of ASNB Miroslav Rekatic unlocked the cupboard located along the corridor outside his office.

'That's it?' said Karen, nodding down at a neatly folded up black piece of kit, a piece of machinery in its folded state resembled some kind of fancy picnic chair.

Miro nodded.

Karen slipped on latex gloves and pulled it out.

'Expensive, was it?' asked Walter.

Miro shook his head. 'No, not really.'

Walter nodded knowingly.

They were looking for blood, though none readily showed itself, but it could have been carefully cleaned, though blood spatters are almost impossible to eradicate completely. If there was blood anywhere on the incapacitator, it would be found.

Walter and Karen knew huge advances had been made in forensic science in recent years, and if they didn't fully understand the technology, they knew enough to know that it worked, and incredibly well. Walter thought about it.

It's called luminol chemiluminescence reaction, and is responsible for the glow of lightsticks, the reaction found to detect traces of blood. The luminol solution is sprayed where blood is suspected of being. The iron from the haemoglobin in the blood serves as a catalyst for the chemiluminescence reaction, and that causes luminol to glow blue when the solution is sprayed where there is blood.

It only needs a tiny amount of iron to catalyse the reaction; Walter knew that, he'd read up on the subject, so fascinating was it.

'Evidence,' said Walter.

'Be my guest,' said Miro, apparently happy to see the specialist equipment away and out of the premises.

Karen's phone rang.

She looked at it and nodded and walked away and listened to Jenny, as Jen relayed the news.

'Have you any plans to leave the country?' asked Walter.

'Not in the next three months.'

Walter nodded and said, 'Good. Come to that, I'd rather you didn't leave the city, or if you plan to, you tell us first.'

'I can do that; I'm keen to help in any way I can. I liked Ellie Wright, and I didn't kill her.'

'We'll need to talk again.'

130

'You know where I am.'

'Indeed, we do.'

Karen came back and said, 'We need to go, Guv.'

She picked up Miro's machinery and stared at him hard.

Miroslav licked his lips, but didn't say a word; happy they were on their way. A minute later they were outside, heading back to the car.

'What's happening?'

'Body, Guv, suspicious circumstances, a woman, believed to be thirty-six.'

'Where?'

Karen relayed the address, as they arrived back at the car, and placed the seized equipment in the boot. They didn't have an evidence bag big enough. Every car couldn't carry every piece of necessary equipment, every time. It wasn't possible.

'Who's there now?' asked Walter, settling into the front seat.

'Gibbo and Heck.'

'Just thinking back to Miro for a moment, what did you make of him?'

'A creep!'

'And a murderer?'

'Could be. He certainly had a temper on him. Did you see the way he spoke to the switchboard operator?'

'Couldn't miss it. Can't we go any quicker?'

Karen grinned and opened the window, took out the blue light and stuck it on top of the car, activated it, closed the window, and rattled around the Chester inner ring road as if there was a murderer in town, cars scattering every which way before them.

Chapter Twenty

It was a busy scene outside Belinda Cooper's neat house. Doc Grayling's Jaguar was there; he'd arrived quick, thought Walter. Behind that, a grey unmarked van, the trademark sign of the SOCO people, who'd just arrived by the look of it, busy taking equipment out of the vehicle and lugging it round the side of the house.

In front of the van, half on the pavement and half on the road, was another unmarked car that Karen recognised, almost certainly the transport that brought Gibbons and Browne to the scene, while beyond that was a marked police car. One officer inside, busy on the radio, the other on the pavement talking to a man and a woman, and getting a hard time of it, by the look of things.

Walter opened the car door and heaved himself out. The woman spotted him and rushed over.

'Are you in charge here?'

'I am.'

'Can you please tell me what is going on? I'm Lena Freeman, I'm Belinda's best friend and workmate.'

'I've just arrived, I know as much as you do,' he said, trying to get past her.

'She's all right, isn't she? Please tell me she's alright.'

'We'll let you know as soon as we have something to say,' said Walter, squeezing past her, as the uniformed officer tried to restrain her, as Walter headed toward the side of the house, Karen hustling behind. He heard the neighbour muttering, 'It's always the same; they never say anything at all in cases like this.'

'Cases like what?' said Lena, though any reply was lost in the melee.

Walter and Karen glanced at the busted glass in the French doors, and the shards of glass on the carpet. They stepped gingerly around the debris and headed for the stairs. Hector Browne was at the top.

'Up here, Guv, Doc Grayling's here,' and he pointed toward the front bedroom door.

Inside, Doc Grayling was kneeling down over the body. Gibbons was standing with his back to the window, taking everything in, for no matter how many dead people, and how many cases he had witnessed, there was always something new to be learnt, or some useful tip that the senior bods might impart. Give him his due; he soaked up expertise like blotting paper capturing ink. Never missed an opportunity.

Doc Grayling heard the coming of big black sized 10s and glanced back over his shoulder, expecting to see Walter Darriteau, and he was not disappointed.

'You got here quick,' snorted Walter.

'Pure luck! I had an appointment two streets away.'

'What have we got?'

'Young woman dead, broken neck, and I'd bet my pension on that being the murder weapon,' nodding at the vintage varnished baseball bat that lay on the bed, now ensconced inside a clear evidence bag.

'That's exactly where we found it, Guv,' cheeped Gibbons.

'Who found her?' said Walter.

'I did.'

'TOD?' said Walter, switching back to Grayling.

'Give me a break, Walter, I have been here precisely five minutes.'

'A ballpark figure, man, a rough guess? Your best estimate, give me something.'

Doc Grayling sighed loudly and said, 'She's been dead twenty-four, maybe thirty-six hours, rigor mortis well set in, as you can see, always starts from the head downwards, as you know, stiffening the body to this effect, allowing you guys to refer to dead people as "stiffs".'

'Do we ever refer to dead people as "stiffs", Sergeant Greenwood?'

'No, never, Guv.'

'You know what I mean, plenty of your people do.'

'In films and TV programmes, maybe, but this isn't a film or a TV programme, or a gruesome story, or a blockbusting novel, but someone who has sadly met a premature end. The body will receive every respect.'

'All right, Walter. Keep your hair on.'

'Anything else you can tell me?'

'Not yet. You'll get the full report just as soon as...'

'You can manage,' Walter mumbled, finishing the sentence.

'That's correct, Darriteau.'

Walter nodded and glanced at Gibbons, and then at the mobile phone on the bedside table.

'Bag that up, Hector!'

Hector appeared in the open doorway.

'Go and find any computer equipment, tablets, mobile phones, answering machines, diaries, notebooks, and anything else that could contain emails and messages and letters and other vital information. Bag them all and get them to the station.'

'You got it, Guv.'

'Karen, I want to know everything about the deceased. Marital status, sexual preferences, partners, blood relations, financial status, friends, workplace colleagues, last visitors, et cetera, and especially I want to know if she has any history of prostitution. Get Jenny on that to help you.'

Karen nodded and jumped on her mobile.

'You think she might have been on the game, Guv?' said Gibbons.

'I have no idea, but we are going to find out.'

'Doesn't look like a house of iniquity to me,' suggested Doc Grayling.

'I'll bow to your superior knowledge on that,' said Walter.

'What about the empty wine bottle?' said Gibbons.

'That'll need bagging too, and the glass, you know the drill.'

'Give us a few minutes,' said the young SOCO guy who Walter recognised, and there was a pause, and photographing and filming and recording of everything in that bedroom, and eventually in the entire house, got under way in earnest.

Walter clapped his heavy hands together and yelled to anyone listening, 'And I want more officers here now, pronto pronto, door-to-door, looking for sightings of visitors and callers, pedestrians and cars, and anything at all that could be described as unusual. Get Nicky Barr on that, and don't forget, nothing is to be uttered outside this house about this case without my say so, and if anyone tips off the press they will have me to reckon with.'

'Sure, Guv,' said Gibbons, enjoying every moment of his day. 'Keeping it zipped!'

Strange phrase, thought Walter. Almost American. Keeping it zipped, Gibbons had been watching too much American cop TV.

'And another thing, Hector, check out the immediate neighbours. Are they known to us, are we looking at a neighbour from hell scenario?'

'On it, Guv,' said Hector, and the team went to work, looking for evidence they hoped would lead them to a killer.

That afternoon the main briefing got under way at half-past four. Everyone knew they would be in for a late night, but that came with the job, went without saying; don't sign up if you don't want the hassle. Don't sign up if you can't cope. It would be the first time for Nicky Barr.

It was generally accepted that Karen was the most able presenter, and she kicked things off with a recent colour photo of Belinda Cooper, staring down at them from the Hytec display system, an almost 3D image that looked as though it could speak. If only it would. If only it could. Who was the murderer, Bel?

thought Walter. Did you know him, or her? Anything you can give us could be mighty helpful.

'She was thirty-six, generally well liked, worked in a travel agency in the city centre, she wasn't gay, and so far as we can tell, she did not have a partner at this time.'

'Maybe on the lookout for one,' suggested Nicky.

'Maybe an Internet dater,' suggested Gibbons.

Walter considered that thought. Seemed a fair possibility, and he tried to remember if he had ever accessed her dating info. He couldn't remember doing so, for if he had he might have been interested, though she might not have been interested in him, seeing as he was more than twenty years older than her. A decent line of enquiry though, for everyone knows there are a lot of weirdo's skulking around amongst those characters online.

'Jenny, check the main dating sites,' said Walter. 'See if you can find her details on there, and if she is, find out who's been in touch.'

'Sure, Guv.'

Nicky said, 'Won't all that info be on her phone and computer?'

'It will,' said Walter. 'But we haven't yet cracked her passwords.'

Karen took up the thread.

'Lena Freeman is her best friend at work and a veritable mine of information. She says Bel enjoyed five relationships, talked about it quite a bit, even joked about her five just men. She said Belinda only ever went for tall men, wouldn't entertain what she called "pipsqueaks", a word she used quite often, apparently. One of the five is a guy called Gareth Williams, a solicitor, who works just across the road from the travel agents for a firm called Jones, Rees & Wilbert. Here's his pic from their website,' and they all looked up at the smart looking guy, at his extravagant dark bouffant swept back hairdo, and dark eyes.

'How tall is he?' asked Jenny.

'Not yet known.'

'The second guy she was seeing goes by the name of Iain, note the slightly unusual spelling, with two i's. We want to know who he is and where he is, but the other three are as yet unidentified.'

'Be nice if we could link Belinda with Flanagan,' suggested Hector.

'Or Miro,' said Walter.

'Or Crocker or Nesbitt, come to that,' said Gibbons.

'Yes, all right,' said Walter.

'Do you think this case and the Ellie Wright case are linked?' asked Nicky.

'Nothing as yet to say they are,' said Walter. 'But two suspicious deaths in less than a week sets alarm bells ringing in my head.'

'Let's not complicate matters by splurging all the available intel together at this point,' said Mrs West. 'Treat them as separate inquiries until we know different.'

'What info are we getting from her personal effects?' asked Gibbons.

'It's early days yet,' said Karen, 'but there's sure to be lots of that once we get into her devices.'

'I hear what you are saying about not mixing the two enquiries, ma'am,' said Walter, 'but we could immediately rule out Crocker, Nesbitt, Flanagan and Miroslav, if they have cast iron alibis for the Bel Cooper murder.'

Mrs West scratched her dainty chin and cooed, 'True, but it's a wide time frame. We are not sure yet when she met her end.'

'Should have that back soon, ma'am.'

Walter's mobile rang. Everyone paused and checked him out, as he glanced at the phone screen and took the call. 'Thank you,' he said twice, and then, 'thank you for that.' He looked at everyone, and said, 'There are tiny traces of blood on the incapacitator.'

'On what?' said Gibbons.

'It's a piece of bondage gear we seized from Miroslav,' said Karen.

'Now all we need is some DNA from Ellie to check if it's hers. Get on to the mother. See if she has a hairbrush or something.'

'Be strange if it was Bel's blood,' suggested Jenny.

'Unlikely, but possible,' said Walter. 'We can check for a match on that PDQ.'

'Again,' said Mrs West, 'don't get sidetracked by merging inquiries prematurely. We all know of cases where doing that has brought us nothing but untold grief. There's as yet nothing to say they are linked.'

That's why we are crosschecking, thought Walter, to see if there is a link.

Mrs West again. 'Walter, go and see the solicitor guy. See what he can tell us. He might know who his love rivals were, if nothing else.'

'Will do, ma'am.'

'Did Belinda Cooper have any known enemies?' asked Jenny.

'None as yet identified. She was a popular person, liked by all, so say the early opinions of everyone we have spoken to,' said Karen.

'What about the spouses and former partners of the five just men? There might be a bitter and twisted individual in there somewhere,' suggested Hector.

'Possible,' said Walter. 'Check it out, Heck, as and when we know who they are.'

'Anything on the SOCO report yet?' asked Gibbons.

'Not yet,' said Karen. 'Due anytime.'

'That should be useful,' said Mrs West.

Walter's phone burped again. He glanced at a new message. It was dumping in from Doc Grayling.

Baseball bat definitely the murder weapon.
TOD now thought to be between midnight and 2am yesterday morning. Full report to follow.

Walter relayed the news and said, 'Obviously any and all suspects must account for their whereabouts at that time.'

'We should ask them all,' said Mrs West. 'Rekatic, Flanagan, Nesbitt, Crocker, and this Williams guy.'

'Flanagan's tag curfew has not been breached, ma'am,' said Jenny.

'That's him in the clear.'

'If the tag info is reliable,' muttered Hector.

'Don't start that again!'

'Sorry, ma'am.'

Walter put his phone away and said, 'Karen and I will speak to Williams and Rekatic. I want Gibbons and Hector to speak to Flanagan, Crocker and Nesbitt. All first thing tomorrow.'

'The sooner we get into Belinda's technology the better,' said an increasingly grumpy Mrs West.

'Tech boys say we should be in there before seven tonight,' said Karen.

'If there is nothing more on the Bel Cooper case,' said Walter, 'can we talk about Ellie Wright for a moment?'

Mrs West pulled a face and nodded and muttered, 'Go for it.'

'How did you get on Nick, checking out the pub clientele?'

'I was just going to tell you about that,' he said, grinning and revelling in his moment in the spotlight.

'Well? Spit it out,' said Walter, eager to get his teeth into any morsels of fresh intel.

'As it happens, they did come up with one name.'

'What?' said Karen. 'For one of Ellie's known customers?'

'Yes,' said Nick. 'So they say.'

'And are you going to share that with us?' said Walter.

Nicky Barr glanced down at his notes to make sure he had it right.

'The name they have given me was Ronny, presumably Ronald, Speight.'

'Is he known to us?' asked Mrs West.

'Can't find anything.'

'Did you get a description?' asked Walter.

'I did. Six feet plus, maybe as much as six feet five inches tall, lucky man, slimmish build, dark neatly parted hair.'

'There are a lot of tall people in the world all of a sudden,' said Gibbons, saying what others were thinking.

'Yes,' said Walter, 'and Lena said that Bel only liked tall men. Be nice if this Ronny Speight character was one of the five just men,' and he turned to Karen and told her to ring Lena and ask her if the name Ronny Speight meant anything to her.

They all heard her ask the question and soon gathered there was a positive answer bouncing back.

'I've been racking my brains trying to remember his name,' said Lena. 'How did you know?'

'Just a name that has come up in our enquiries. Do you know where he lives?'

'Not exactly, but I'm pretty sure South Wirral somewhere, Burton, Mollington, Willaston, one of them places.'

'Thanks for that,' said Karen.

'Glad to be of help. Is it true what they are saying?'

'What are they saying?'

'That Bel's dead, that she has been murdered.'

'Just a sec,' and Karen glanced at Mrs West and Walter in turn, and said, 'She's asking if Belinda Cooper is dead?'

'We can't go on saying nothing forever,' said Mrs West. 'It will be all over the media any time soon.'

'Tell her the truth,' said Walter. 'That we have found a body, but it has yet to be formally identified.'

Karen nodded, looked suitably grim, and relayed the info to Lena Freeman. She gasped for breath, started crying, and rang off.

'So,' said Walter, turning over the fresh news in his mind. 'There can't be that many Ronny Speights living in South Wirral. I'll give you fifteen minutes to come up with his address.'

Jennifer Thompson did it in eight, courtesy of the voter's roll, or at least there was definitely a Ronald Colin Speight living in

140

Sandstone Cottages, Burton, South Wirral, and it seemed more than likely he was the first man who positively linked both cases together.

'We'll go and see him in a minute,' said Walter. 'In the meantime, crack on with everything else we have discussed.'

Chapter Twenty-One

Sandstone Cottages lived up to their name, constructed from the local red sandstone. A pair of semi-detached houses with grey stone lined windows, and small neat gardens to the front.

Karen opened the green timber front gate, and Walter ambled through it and up to the matching green timber front door. He reached out, grabbed the brass doorknocker, and banged twice. In the next second, a bolt was drawn across the door from the inside, and the door opened with a slight squeak. He was a big man, was Ronald Colin Speight, and the door wasn't particularly high, so he had to stoop a little to see who was bothering him.

'Ronald Speight?' said Karen.

'Who wants to know?'

'Police,' said Walter, flashing ID. 'Can we come in?'

'Can I stop you?'

'You could do, though we'd think that awfully uncooperative.'

Speight grimaced, clicked his tongue, and nodded them in. They went through to the back of the house where there was a large square kitchen, maybe seventeen or eighteen feet square. In the centre was a rectangular dining table on which sat an opened copy of that night's Liverpool Echo, the crossword half done, an ashtray with a recent cigarette butt, and a half full mug of stewed tea.

Speight sat in front of the tea as Walter sat opposite. Karen remained standing, looking around at pictures and photos on the walls, and at anything else that caught her eye.

'So,' Speight said. 'What can I do for you?'

'You know Belinda Cooper?'

'Maybe.'

'Just answer the question,' said Karen, smiling down encouragingly at the neat cut man.

'Yes, Bel and I had an on-off thing that ran for almost four years. She couldn't get her head round the fact that I was married.'

'Was?' queried Walter.

'Yeah. Was. Though, yes, we are still legally married, and we still share a house, but we have not been married in the true sense of the word for at least five years.'

'What's your wife's name?' asked Karen.

'Debra, though I don't know what that's got to do with anything.'

'Where's Debra now?' asked Walter.

'I'd like to say I haven't a clue, but she did tell me she was going to Spain with a couple of mates. As I say, we share a house these days and bugger all else, so I don't really know where she is, and I don't care either.'

'When did you last see Belinda?' asked Walter.

'About a month ago, maybe more.'

'Not in the last few days?' asked Karen.

'No, just said so, didn't I? Why, what's this all about?'

'Belinda Cooper has been found murdered,' said Walter.

Speight's mouth fell open, though no words popped out.

'Where were you between midnight and 2am the night before last?'

'Here.'

'Alone?' said Walter.

Speight nodded and didn't speak.

'Had you been out at all that night?' asked Karen.

'Yeah, I'd been to the Red Lion.'

'What time did you leave there?' asked Walter.

'About half-past eleven.'

'And it would take you, what, half an hour to get home?'

'About that, certainly no more.'

'And you didn't go out again that night?' asked Karen.

143

'No, I did not.'

'Did you ever stay at Bel's house?' asked Walter.

'Course I did, many times. We were an item for a while, leastways I liked to think so.'

'Did you ever see a baseball bat in the house?'

'That old varnished bat? Yeah, I did. It was her father's. She kept it behind the bedroom door, to deter burglars. That was the theory. Why? Was it used to kill her?'

'No,' said Karen, anxious to bury the thought.

Walter said, 'Did she tell you about her other menfriends?'

'Not directly, no names, oh she mentioned one of them was a solicitor, and I think another one's name was Ian, but she was always reticent to discuss other men. I think she thought it might have upset me, but it didn't. Oh, she liked to say she'd only ever been with five, but I took that with a pinch of salt.'

'You didn't believe her?'

'Course not! What do you think? In my experience you can always add a nought, and then you're not far away.'

'I believe her,' said Karen.

'You would.'

'I believed her too,' said Walter.

'Well, it takes all sorts. I didn't, not that it bugged me.'

'Tell me about your relationship with Ellie Wright?' said Walter.

'Ellie? What's she got to do with anything?'

'Just answer the question,' said Karen.

'Look! Who's been talking?'

'Mr Speight,' said Walter, 'You are going to have to start answering our questions, because if you don't you will leave us no alternative but to take you in for questioning, and if we do that, you could be there for quite some time. Do I make myself clear?'

Speight thought about that for a second, and nodded.

'Ellie Wright?' repeated Walter.

'I am still in shock thinking about Bel. How did she die?'

'I am not at liberty to discuss that. Please answer the question about Ellie?'

'And the question was again?'

Walter sighed loudly.

'You heard!' said Karen. 'What was your relationship with Eleanor Wright?'

'What do you think?'

'We want your version,' said Walter.

Speight grimaced and looked to one side and back and said, 'She was a good-time girl.'

'A good-time girl?' said Walter, getting fed up with hearing that expression.

'Yeah, you know, on the game.'

'You paid her for sex?' asked Karen.

Speight nodded.

'Where?' asked Walter.

'Where what?'

'Where did this take place? Here?'

'No, course not. At her little caravan, it's at the foot of Marigold Lane, as I think you probably know.'

'What kind of sex?' asked Walter.

'Not sure as I follow.'

'I think you do. Answer the question.'

'Normal… Man… Woman… Bonk away, what else is there?'

'There was no torture involved?' asked Karen, studying Speight's face, looking for anything that might be there.

'Course not. What do you take me for?'

'When did you last see her?' asked Walter.

'Last Friday.'

'What time?' asked Karen.

'About two o'clock in the afternoon. I had a free afternoon, thought why not; it's as good a way to spend a blustery day as any. And then…'

'Then what?' said Karen and Walter together.

Speight scowled and shook his head, and said, 'And then the dopey bint set fire to herself.'

Walter repeated the words, 'Set fire to herself.'

145

'Yeah, isn't that what happened? Later that night. Talk of the pubs; it was, in the days that followed. Oh, I don't think she did it on purpose, probably got pissed and knocked a heater over, summat like that.'

'You don't think it's possible that someone set fire to her?' said Karen. 'Was that not the talk of the pubs as well?'

'Course not! Why would anyone do that? She was a good-time girl. She gave the fellas a good time, what's not to like? Who'd want to kill her?'

'You tell us?' said Karen.

'Hey, now look here, it's nothing to do with me.'

'It's everything to do with you!' said Walter. 'You were there on the day she died, and hey ho, you were also regularly present in Belinda Cooper's house, and guess what? Both of those women met violent deaths in the past week, and you are the only person on God's earth we know of who knew both of them, and intimately at that. It doesn't look good for you, does it, Ronny?'

'There must be others.'

Walter again, 'Where were you last Friday night between 11pm and 2am?'

'In the pub, on the way home, in bed, alone.'

'Two deaths and he hasn't an alibi for either, Guv,' said Karen, smirking, piling on the pressure.

'Not looking good for you, is it?' repeated Walter.

'Only one thing wrong with your argument, but it's quite an important thing. I wasn't there when either of them died, and I didn't have anything to do with either death.'

'So you say,' said Karen.

'Yes, I do, and you can't prove any different.'

'And you can't prove you weren't there either,' said Karen.

'And the funny thing is, I don't have to.'

'Are you involved in drugs?' asked Walter.

'Yeah, sure, paracetamol, every time I get a feckin' hangover.'

'So you didn't supply Ellie Wright with cocaine?' asked Karen.

'Course not!'

'But you know who did?' said Walter.

'No! Well, not exactly, but…'

'But what?' said Karen.

'There's a bloke in the pub. Everyone knows if you want anything like that he can supply. I saw him sitting with Ellie once or twice.'

'What's his name?'

'I don't know.'

'What does he look like?' said Karen.

'Ordinary looking, quite tall, modern short haircut, dark hair, I think.'

'A bit like you?'

Speight grinned. 'Yeah. A bit like me, young woman, 'cept it wasn't me. Anything else you want to know? I wanna get changed, I'm going out, socialising.'

'How did you get down to the caravan?' asked Walter.

'Got the old 4X4, and by hell, I needed it, that road is dreadful, feckin' disgrace it is, ruined the suspension, shouldn't wonder.'

'So your tyre tracks will be down there?' said Karen.

'Most likely.'

'What size shoes do you take?'

'Eh? 10s. Why?'

'Just checking,' said Karen.

'You're not planning on leaving town, are you, no nice holidays in Spain, or somewhere like that?' said Walter.

'Not a chance.'

'Good,' said Walter. 'Because if you left the area without advising us first, I'd take a dim view of that.'

'I have no reason to run away.'

'Let's hope so, for your sake,' said Walter. 'We'll be in touch.'

Five minutes later, they were outside in the car. It was already full dark and getting noticeably colder. There was an old 4X4 parked in the lay-by opposite, dark green by the look of it.

'His?' you think, said Karen.

'Probably, check the number.'

Karen switched on ANPR and fed in the number, and back came the answers. Owned by Ronald Speight, taxed by Ronald Speight, insured by Ronald Speight. All legit, and no penalty points on his licence either.

'Quite the model citizen,' said Karen.

'Yeah, looks that way, the thing is, I don't think he's the murderer.'

'Neither do I, Guv, but he is a sleaze-ball of the first order.'

'Can't lock him up for that.'

'More's the pity. Could the drug dealer be the killer?'

'Maybe, but who is he?'

'Good question. Someone in the pubs should finger him. Did Belinda Cooper do drugs?' said Karen.

'Nothing to suspect it, we'll have the toxicology report in the morning, that'll confirm it.'

'Someone here is a murderer, someone we're close to, but which one?'

'Buggered if I know. Come on, Greenwood, I'm getting hungry and I'm getting tired, and you must be too, and no one sees things well through tired eyes, and a tired brain. Let's get back and wind it up for the day, and get home.'

'Sounds like a plan, Guv. Sounds like a plan.'

Chapter Twenty-Two

Karen arrived home at half-past eight. She'd only been in the flat ten minutes when her mobile rang. It was David, and she wondered what he was going to say. Only one way to find out, take the call.

'You're in, are you?' he said.

'I've just come in. What can I do for you?'

'Maybe it's what I can do for you. Fancy going out for something to eat?'

'Oh I can't, Dave, I'm bushed, and very tense too, we're so busy at work.'

'It's David, actually.'

'Sorry! DAVID,' she said, pronouncing the word deliberately, smiling at his mild rebuke.

'You have to eat.'

'I'll grab something from the freezer, maybe a tuna steak.'

'I know a perfect cure for tenseness.'

'I'll bet you do.'

'No, not that… Leastways, not yet. No, I was thinking of my neck massage, it's well renowned, I'm famous for it.'

'Bet you are,' she said, but on thinking about it, it was true she did have an aching neck, and right there a soothing neck massage sounded like pure heaven, and with that thought in the forefront of her mind she found herself saying, 'Okay, but neck massage and nothing more, and you are not staying over, do I make myself clear?'

'Yes, Miss Greenwood. Perfectly!'

'Don't be a prune. Come over in an hour.'

'I'll be there.'

Walter did something he rarely did on the way home. He stopped off at the local fish and chip shop and bought a jumbo sized battered cod, together with a large portion of chips, and a tub of steaming mushy peas. Yes, they were dreadfully bad for you, but by hell they were delicious. The steaming aroma seeping through the damp paper wrapper.

As soon as he was home, he tipped them onto a large dinner plate, added tomato sauce, vinegar and extra salt, that should annoy the salt police, and sat in his favourite chair before the TV and ate the lot, as he followed and giggled his way through the latest cops and robbers caper from the States.

He'd eaten the dinner too quickly, and inevitably that brought on indigestion and heartburn, and that meant a trip to the kitchen, and a dose of pink indigestion medicine. Ghastly. Whilst there, he opened the fridge and grabbed a can of black stout and a glass, and returned towards the lounge. On the way, he spotted the landline phone in the hallway. Should he ring Carlene again? He'd sure liked to have talked with her, but she'd been so offhand with him last time, leastways he thought so, and by his reckoning it was her turn to call him. In any event, he'd not ring.

The TV show was so bad it wasn't true, and he snapped it off and grabbed his new tablet, and found his way back to that Internet dating site, purely as research, he reassured himself, looking to see if he could find any entries for Belinda Cooper. It went without saying that if she had used the site she had probably used a false name, as so many users appeared to do, as he'd discovered through personal experience. Probably disguised her address and locality, too. That went without saying, and a sensible thing for any woman to do. But the number of fresh photos he had seen of her in the office gave him a head start on anyone else looking. Surely she must be there somewhere. What middle-aged woman living alone in the twenty-first century wouldn't be?

But if she was there, she had buried herself well, for he could not find her. There were huge numbers of interesting women on display, and many of them local too, and some of them more than passable, and some of those, voluptuous, just as he liked. There was nothing wrong in looking, was there? And he had to admit; it was more interesting and entertaining than the TV.

Little wonder there were more than half a million people currently online, accessing that site, so the stats boasted at the top of the screen, the figure forever updating, and invariably increasing. The twenty-first century, eh? He said aloud. What would his old aunt Mimosa have made of that?

David Baker arrived at Karen's flat clutching a bottle of Australian chardonnay. He smiled his cute smile, a grin she couldn't ignore, as they kissed in the hallway.

'You're not staying,' she whispered.

'I know... so you said.'

'Just as long as that is understood. Do you want a drink?'

'Maybe a little one, I'm driving, and I don't want to fall foul of the local law.'

'Quite right, too,' she said, taking the bottle to the fridge. She dropped it inside and took out a half drunk cold one, and poured him a drink.

'Ta,' he said, taking it from her, as she sat on the sofa. She smelt nice, but she always did. Expensive perfume, that was clear, and even though she was dressed in ordinary grey slacks and a plain white cotton blouse, she looked fab.

'So,' he said. 'David Baker's famous neck massage.'

'Yes,' she said, and she reached behind her and rubbed her slim neck. 'Where do you want me?'

'On the sofa, on your tum, and undo the top two buttons of your blouse.'

That made sense, as she assumed position; and he took hold of the blouse collar and gently tugged it back a tad, brushing her blonde hair to one side with his hand, exposing her porcelain like neck. He clapped his hands gently, rubbed his fingers together, crouched beside her, and set them to work.

'Ooh, that's lovely,' she cooed. 'Yes, please. More.'

'Good?'

'Fantastic.'

'I can tell you're tense; your neck is not relaxed at all. Just relax, Miss Greenwood, let all your troubles float away. Relax.'

'Yes, Mr Baker. Ooh, that's so good. Who taught you to do that?'

'Can't remember now. One of my many hidden talents.'

'You have other talents, do you?'

'Many.'

'Such as?'

'That would be telling.'

'Do you mean in or out of the bedroom?'

'Both,' he said, grinning.

Karen giggled. He was good fun, that was undeniable, but he still had plenty of making up to do after he had let her down so badly last time.

'Don't stop,' she said. 'I could get used to this.'

They talked about her day, though not in any great detail, though he was interested in everything she said, as he always was.

An hour later, he refused a sandwich and another glass of wine; but insisted on another dinner date that Karen agreed to, before he helped himself to a more passionate and lengthy kiss in the hallway, and after that he was on his way, happier than he'd been when he'd arrived, and she was too, judging by the look on her face.

It was already after eleven and she was bushed. Went to bed, slept well, dreamt better, and got up early, refreshed and relaxed, and ready for another busy and long day. They were going to be much more productive in the day ahead. She was confident of that. Sometimes great results could be achieved through positive thought; she was a great believer in such things. It had served her well in the past, it had served the whole team well on many occasions, and it would do so again. Bring it on.

Chapter Twenty-Three

No one had actually said to be in extra early, but everyone was there, not a soul missing. Mrs West thanked them for their dedication, as the early morning briefing got under way. Walter growled, 'Overnight reports?' and Karen said, 'Quite a few in, Guv.'

'Well, let's hear them.'

Jenny read out the toxicology report on Belinda Cooper. It showed that Bel had not been into illegal drugs, in fact she was totally clean, other than alcohol, and even that figure wasn't over bad, considering she'd apparently dispatched a full bottle of white wine, unless she'd enjoyed company while doing so.

'And one other thing, I could not find her on any dating site.'

'No, neither could I,' said Walter.

'You looked, Guv, did you?' said a grinning Gibbons.

'Yes, I did, Darren, purely as research, you understand.'

Gibbons muttered, 'If you say so, Guv,' and he moved on to read out the report on the scrapings of mud he and Hector had taken from Crocker's mother's old car. It was definitive; there was no match to the soil at the foot of Marigold Lane.

Jenny came back with a more detailed SOCO report on the greater Marigold Lane site.

'There were numerous footprints in the mud down there, though many of them were downgraded by the heavy rain. But a number of recognisable footprints in more shaded positions, were recovered,' and she pointed to the Hytec screen, 'and as you can see, the vast majority of those were size 10.'

'So,' said Mrs West, 'If we have a murder down there, and if the killer's footprints have been recorded, we are saying he probably has size 10 boots.'

'That's about the size of it,' said Jenny.

'Two too many "ifs" for me,' she said coolly.

'It's not conclusive,' agreed Walter. 'But it might help us somewhere further down the track.'

Jenny switched tack and changed reports.

'But there is a positive report. We did get DNA from Dorothy Wright for Ellie, and we did a comparison on the incapacitator, and the traces of blood thereon definitely belonged to Ellie Wright.'

'Why would that be?' asked Nicky Barr, coming to after an unplanned late night.

'Why would what be?' said Walter.

'Why is there blood on it?'

Karen jumped all over that.

'Presumably because Miroslav Rekatic assaulted Ellie Wright with sufficient force to spill Ellie's blood.'

'I can't see it,' said Nicky, not yet willing to back down.

'The luminol chemiluminescence can see it, and that's good enough for me,' said Walter.

'I don't mean that, Guv.'

'So what do you mean?' snapped Mrs West, becoming irritated that precious time was being wasted.

'I don't know,' he said, scratching his head. 'Seems odd, that's all.'

'It's clear enough to me,' said Karen. 'That man is a serial abuser of women, even went to the trouble of going to Germany and buying a specialist piece of equipment, a product that is probably not available here, to assist him in doing precisely that, equipment that now has Ellie Wright's blood all over it. How much more do we need than that?'

'We need to check his alibi for Bel's murder for a start,' said Walter. 'We'll go and see him this morning.'

'Do you want to bring him in?' asked Mrs West.

'No, not yet, ma'am, need a bit more before we do that.'

'How did you get on with Ronald Speight?'

155

Walter deferred to Karen, and she recounted their meeting. Yes, he had known and met both women, and admitted visiting both women in their homes, so it would be no surprise if his DNA turned up there. He also admitted to a sexual relationship with both, and yes, he wore size 10 shoes too, and it was also true he had no alibi for the TODs on either women. On the other hand, he had no known history of violence against women, or anyone else, and they hadn't been able to come up with a motive. He'd also confirmed the baseball bat was Bel's. It had previously been her father's, and that it was kept to ward off possible burglars.

Walter jumped in. 'He also knew that Ellie was a drug user, and after some pressure came up with an image of Ellie sitting in the pub with a known drug dealer, where he, Speight, imagined that Ellie was buying gear.'

'Do we have a description of this guy?' asked Jenny.

'A vague one,' said Walter. 'Tall, dark hair, clean cut.'

'So,' said an exasperated Mrs West. 'Do we now have a prime suspect?'

'Speight is the only one we positively know knew both women,' said Jenny. 'That weighs heavy for me.'

'The Mirror man for me,' said Karen. 'We have proved he is violent towards women. He has demonstrated he does not care one bit about anyone else's opinions, or feelings. Look at the way he has treated his beautiful wife and family. He went to Germany and bought equipment that can be used in torture, gear that has Ellie's blood on it, and it makes me wonder what exactly he did to that girl. And maybe, there were others too.'

'Some people like excitement in the bedroom,' said Gibbons. 'It's not unusual, and it could be nothing more than that.'

'Yeah, but not in his own bedroom!' shot back Karen. 'That's the point! He's playing away from home and spilling blood whilst doing so. How much more excitement do you want?'

Gibbons grimaced and glanced away. Maybe the sarge had a point.

'We seem to be forgetting here the one man who has already been convicted of killing a woman,' said Hector.

'Flanagan?' said Jenny.

'Correct.'

'Tagged,' said Mrs West. 'Both times.'

'You know my views on that,' said Hector.

'Well, you're wrong.'

'We need to see Miro again,' said Walter. 'And we need to speak with the solicitor guy, Williams, too, and I'd also like to talk to Lena Freeman again. She might know more than she's told us.'

'You mean you think she's holding back?' said Mrs West.

'Not necessarily, ma'am, just that she may know a little more about Belinda that she doesn't think, or imagine, is in any way important. There could be something there.'

Mrs West nodded hard and said, 'Get it done!'

Walter glanced at Hector and said, 'You and Darren go and see Flanagan again, seeing as you have such a bee in your bonnet about him. See if you can get him to confess with tag tampering. He'd need advanced computer skills to do that, find out if he has such abilities, and after you have done that, go back to the pubs and flesh out this description on the drug dealer. Track that guy down. We want to talk to him.'

'Sure, Guv,' said Hector, as Gibbons nodded.

Walter again. 'Jenny, you and Nicky, go and see Nesbitt and check his alibi for Bel Cooper, and do the same thing with Crocker, just to be on the safe side, and will everyone please remember that we have not yet identified and ruled out this Iain character, one of Bel's five menfriends, and two others from the five are still totally missing too, so think on about that.'

'Has Bel's technology been broken into yet?' asked Mrs West.

'Not yet, ma'am,' said Jenny, knowing the question was coming.

'Why not?'

'Seems there is some kind of backlog delay. They have assured me it will be done by this afternoon.'

'We have a potential double bloody murder inquiry here,' she snapped. 'That's not good enough! Tell them I said so. And tell them to get a bloody move on. Today... Or else!'

'Yes, ma'am.'

'Any questions?' asked Karen.

No one had.

'Let's get to it,' said Walter. 'Time is slipping by. We don't want the trail going cold.'

Karen grabbed her water and jacket and headed for the lift, and the garage down below, to grab a car before all the good ones had gone. The meeting broke up. It was half-past nine.

'Where to first?' she said, as the Guv got in the car and scratched his cheek.

'City centre, solicitors and travel agents. Two birds with one stone.'

Karen bobbed her head and eased the accelerator down, and the car cruised out into another dismal November day.

Chapter Twenty-Four

The offices of Jones, Rees & Wilbert were located in the ancient Rows, over an upmarket indie dress shop. Two entire floors of small queer shaped rooms, lots of paperwork, new office equipment, a permanent smell of stationery being turned over, and quiet people with earnest faces and new glasses.

Lots of white skin and swept back hair, and a good supply of coffee and apples and bought in sandwiches, just like many other solicitors' offices across the kingdom. A pretty trainee showed Walter and Karen into Gareth Williams' small odd shaped office.

Walter went to the window and stared down and across the road, and directly into the travel agency. He could see Lena Freeman jabbering on the phone, and he wondered who she was talking to, and what she was talking about.

'Take a seat,' said Gareth, pointing at two small red chairs set before his desk, but they couldn't sit down because both chairs were covered in piles of files and papers.

'Chloe!' he yelled. 'Come and shift these files,' and the pretty girl returned and murmured, 'sorry about that,' and grabbed the manila files and took them away.

Gareth pointed at the chairs, and they all sat down.

Walter and Karen stared across the desk. By crikey, the bouffant hairdo had put on even more weight, and height too. It was mesmerising. Neither of them could tear their eyes away. It was like a bushy creature living on top of his head, with a life and mind all of its own. Mind you, thought Karen, the Guv had odd bad hair days when he let it grow too long, when it stood up on end as if it had seen a ghost. But Gareth's dark swept-up-and-back mop was something else.

'What can I do for you?'

Walter kicked off. 'It's about Belinda Cooper.'

'Thought it might be.'

'You know…' said Karen. 'That's she dead?'

'Yes, I bumped into Lena. She told me about it.'

'You had a relationship with Belinda Cooper?' asked Walter.

'I did… For my sins.'

'Sins?' said Karen.

'Just an expression.'

'You're married?' asked Karen.

Gareth nodded and muttered, 'Look, I'm not proud of it.'

'Does your wife know?' asked Walter.

'Yeah, she's forgiven me, at least I hope she has.'

'Where were you on…' and Walter relayed the time of death.

'Home in bed.'

'Can your wife confirm that?'

'Sadly, she can't. She had a bridge night with her friend, and the crazy woman took a few wines too many, and rather than drive home she decided to stay there.'

'You could have gone and fetched her,' suggested Karen.

Gareth shook his head. 'I'd been drinking too.'

'There's such a thing as cabs,' said Walter.

'True,' said Gareth. 'It was just more convenient for her to stay.'

'Do you know a young woman by the name of Ellie Wright?' asked Karen.

Gareth's bottom lip came out, as if he was thinking, and he shook his head and said, 'Not that I know of. Why? Who is she?'

'Just routine enquiries,' said Walter. 'How tall are you?'

'Six, one,' he said, without hesitation, though Karen imagined he was lying, because men often lie about their height and weight, exaggerating their height, and being economic with the truth over weight, but no matter.

'Belinda Cooper mentioned on more than one occasion that she had only been involved with five men…' said Walter, and though he hadn't finished the sentence, Gareth answered anyway.

160

'Yeah, she told me that too.'

'Did you believe her?' asked Karen.

'Had no reason not to.'

'You're one, we have identified one other, can you help us out with the other three?' asked Walter.

Gareth grinned. 'Well there's so sorry sad Iain, for one.'

'Iain who?' asked Karen.

'Iain Donaldson.'

'And why is he so sorry sad?' asked Walter.

'Well, he was pissed off with me for a start. She left him for me, you see, and I'm not surprised. She said he could bore for Cheshire, a geography teacher, the poor lamb, works at the high school.'

'And this was before she discovered you were married, and messing her around?' said Karen.

Gareth bobbed his head and sighed and said, 'I guess. Look, I am not proud of it. It just kind of happened, mid life crisis, if you will, I'd like to turn the clock back and do things differently, but that ain't going to happen, is it?'

'Do you know where this Iain bloke lives?' asked Karen.

'No, she never told me, but you'll find him at the school.'

'And the other two?' asked Walter.

'There was the gay fella.'

'She had a relationship with a gay man?' asked Karen.

'She did, though he liked to say he was bi-sexual. You can imagine how upset and betrayed she felt about that when he told her one night in the pub: "Excuse me darling, but I fancy men at least as much as I fancy you!" Did he really expect to get away with that? He must have been a bit simple.'

'Name?' said Walter, his pencil poised over his notebook.

'Marcus something, she might have mentioned his surname, but I can't remember it. If it comes back, I'll give you a bell.'

'Appreciate that, if you would,' said Walter, glancing at Karen as if to say, anything I've forgotten?

Put on the spot she was momentarily lost for words, which wasn't like her, or for the pair of them, before Karen blurted, 'What size shoes do you take?'

'Nine and a half or ten at a push. Why?'

'Just routine,' said Walter. 'Do you know a man by the name of Miroslav Rekatic?'

Gareth shook his head and said, 'Nope.'

'Thanks, you have been very helpful, we'll be in touch.'

A minute later, and they were walking down the narrow and twisting staircase, and Karen said, 'Amazing, isn't it? Even a solicitor thinks it's okay to deceive his wife and have an affair, and write it off as a midlife crisis, as if it means nothing.'

'The way of the world, Karen, and I don't suppose that will ever change.'

'Doesn't make it right.'

'It doesn't.'

They crossed the road and went into the travel agency. Lena looked up and tried a smile.

'Have you got a minute? A few more quick questions.'

Lena glanced nervously down the office and caught eye contact with the boss. He pulled a face and turned away as if he had more important business to deal with.

'Crack on,' she said.

'It may seem a strange question,' said Walter.

'Now you've intrigued me.'

'Did Belinda ever mention anything about...' Walter paused and scratched his chin, thinking of his words.

'About what?'

Walter tried again.

'To your knowledge did she ever go with men for money?'

'What, Bel? You must be joking! You're way off beam if you think that. She was very particular and most selective about which men she would go with, no pipsqueaks, remember, and as for

162

doing it for money, absolutely no chance! Whatever gave you that idea?'

'Just another inquiry that's overlapped into this one,' said Karen. 'We needed to be sure.'

'You can be.'

'Have you ever heard of a man called Marcus something?' asked Walter.

'Oh yeah, the gay one! I'd forgotten all about him. She was so embarrassed about that, when she found out she'd been sleeping with, well, you know,' and she lowered her voice, and mouthed rather than said the word, 'a homo, God, she was so upset with him about that, went the very next day and had a blood test, just in case, came back negative, thank the Lord, but she felt so… so… betrayed.'

'Do you know where this Marcus character lives?' asked Karen.

Lena shook her head and said, 'I think he moved away, yeah, I think Bel told me he was so upset and annoyed, with himself, as much as anything, that he upped sticks and moved away, she thought Brighton or Blackpool or Bournemouth, one of the B's anyway, I think that's what she said, though I could be wrong on that. It's a while ago now.'

'Do you have a surname for him?'

'Not that I recall.'

'Thanks for your assistance,' said Walter. 'You've been most helpful.'

'Anytime. Has she been officially ID'd yet?'

'Ah yes, that's another thing I meant to mention.'

'Oh?'

Karen took up the thread.

'She has no relatives; none at all, and it would appear you would be her best friend, so we were wondering if you might identify her.'

'What? Look at her dead body, you mean? Oh, I don't know about that, I've never seen a dead body, I'm not sure I could.'

Walter frowned and said, 'I know it's difficult, but someone has to do it, and it has to be a friend, a real good friend. There's nothing to it, and it will only take a minute or two. You'd be really helping us.'

'Oh, go on then, the things I get talked into. Maybe it's not even her, have you even thought about that?'

'That's why it must be someone who knows her well,' said Karen. 'So we can be sure.'

'Where do I go?'

'The morgue, you can go anytime, right up to midnight, but it needs to be done as soon as…'

'Yeah, I get you; I'll go after work.'

Karen grabbed a pen from the desk and wrote the address on a piece of scrap paper.

'Thank you,' said Walter, and they said their goodbyes and the officers left.

In the car on the way to the ASN Bank Karen said, 'Can we rule out this Marcus guy, if he's left the area?'

'We don't know he has, so no is the answer to that, though I agree, he is looking a rank outsider.'

'Unlike the Mirror man who, in my humble opinion, is in it up to his neck.'

'Let's see,' said Walter, as she pulled the car into the car park outside the bank.

Inside, the same bright young thing was on display behind the shiny reception desk. Walter and Karen headed for the door on the left to the corridor, and he grinned across at the girl and said, 'Just another few questions for Mr Rekatic,' and they disappeared through the door, but not before Karen glimpsed the girl jumping on the phone.

Miro's office door was open; Walter and Karen hurried in to find the man on the phone, looking disappointed his day was being ruined again.

'Just a few more questions, Mr Rekatic,' said Walter. 'If you don't mind.'

'What now?' he said, as Walter and Karen sat down.

'Your charming piece of equipment,' said Karen.

'What about it?'

'It has blood all over it, Ellie Wright's blood, to be precise, care to explain how it got there?'

Miro grimaced.

'How would I know?'

'Not a good answer, Mr Rekatic. I think you need to give that a little more thought,' said Walter. 'You are close to being arrested for the murder of Eleanor Wright. I'd come up with a better answer than that, if I were you.'

Miro coughed and said, 'Ah yes, I remember now, she had a nose bleed.'

'A nose bleed?' said Walter. 'How convenient.'

'Wonder how that was brought on,' muttered Karen.

'Yeah, you know, blood coming from the nose.'

'I know what a bloody nose bleed is!' said Walter.

'What brought it on?' said Karen. 'Did you hit her?'

'No! Course not. Well, maybe a few playful taps.'

'A few playful taps,' said Karen, making an issue of writing the comment in her notebook.

'Yes, look, she liked the submissive role, she got off on that.'

'Yeah, sure. Isn't the truth of it that you like to play the dominant one, and you got off on that, as you beat the hell out of the poor girl, as she was trussed up like some Christmas turkey,' said Karen. 'And that maybe you even lost your cool and assaulted her so badly you spilt blood all over the place, and eventually killed her? Isn't that nearer the mark?'

'And seeing what you had done,' continued Walter, 'you cooked up a plan to dispose of the scene by setting fire to that old

165

caravan? Though "cooked up" might not be the best phrase in the circumstances. Perhaps you imagined that no one would miss or care about a lonely little tart of a girl who'd taken some wrong turns in life.'

'No! That's not what happened at all. If you are going to persist with this, I think my solicitor should be present.'

'He wants a solicitor present now, Guv.'

'Yes, interesting that, he needs someone else to speak for him, in case he says the wrong thing, the incriminating thing. But no matter, let's continue, and regardless of that, we'd appreciate your cooperation for a little while longer.'

Miro pulled a face and slowly nodded.

Karen asked, 'Where were you between midnight and 2am on the night of,' and she added the day and night of Belinda Cooper's death.

'At home, in bed,' he said confidently. 'Why?'

'Could anyone confirm that?' asked Walter.

'Yes, of course, my wife, Grizzy.'

'That's good,' said Karen. 'Is she at home now?'

'Yes, she should be, why?'

'What's your address, Mr Rekatic,' said Walter, pen poised.

'I live in Rossett.'

'Address?' said Karen.

'But I don't want Grizzy dragged into this.'

'I'll bet,' whispered Karen.

'Why are you asking me about that time?'

'Because, Mr Rekatic, a woman in Chester was murdered in her own home at that particular time. It's just to eliminate you from our inquiry. It's in your best interests to do that, isn't it?'

'What woman?'

'Her name is, or was, Belinda Cooper. Did you know Belinda?'

'Not that I know of.'

'Are you sure about that?' said Walter. 'Because we have a description of the kind of men Belinda Cooper was attracted to, and guess what, that description fits you to a T.'

Miro shook his head hard.

'This has gone far enough.'

'What's your address, Mr Rekatic?' asked Karen.

'You can bugger off!'

'Charming,' said Karen.

Walter made a note in his notebook; spoke it aloud as he wrote. 'Suspect being most uncooperative.'

'Just a minute,' said Karen, and she jumped up and left the office. She hurried down the corridor and out into the reception area. No new customers at the counter. Went to the shiny desk and smiled at the girl. Flashed her ID again for gravitas and said, 'I need Mr Rekatic's home address, can you supply it please?'

'I'm really not sure…'

'You have two choices, you can either help the police in a murder inquiry, or I will arrest you right now for wasting police time, and obstructing the police in their duty. I really don't mind which.'

The girl gazed into Karen's steady blue eyes and saw she meant every word. She took a small piece of paper from her pad and scribbled an address.

'You'll get me sacked.'

'Doubt that, but if I were you, and just between you and me, I wouldn't work for a piece of dirt like that.'

'Eh?'

Karen leant over the counter and whispered, 'Have you ever been alone with him?'

'What, outside of work?'

Karen remembered the incapacitator that formerly slept in the cupboard along the corridor. 'Inside work or outside work, you know what I mean, have you ever been alone with him?'

'No, course not. I'm engaged to Jason. But…'

'But what?'

'I've heard rumours.'

'What kind of rumours?'

'The girl who worked here before me…'

'What about her?'

'She left, said she'd been approached.'

'By Miro?'

The girl nodded.

'To do what?'

'Don't know, but it wasn't good. Not good at all.'

'What was her name?'

'Marilyn Webb.'

'Thank you. You've been very helpful.'

'I'll get into big trouble now.'

'No you won't. I'll see to that,' and Karen turned tail and returned to the office.

Not much seemed to have changed in there, almost as if they had been waiting for her return.

'12 Sunflowers Close, Rossett,' she said, grinning. 'That wasn't so difficult, was it?'

'Look, I really don't want you bothering Grizzy.'

'That's as maybe,' said Walter. 'But we need to check on your alibi. If we can do that, you are in the clear, at least so far as Belinda Cooper is concerned. You must see that.'

'I'd rather you didn't mention anything about Ellie.'

'Can't make any promises,' said Walter. 'But if you could help us some more...'

'How can I help you? I've done nothing wrong.'

'Tell me about Marilyn Webb?' said Karen.

Walter sat up and paid attention.

'Who's been talking?'

'Never mind that. Marilyn Webb left here under a cloud in a bit of a hurry. Why was that?'

'She said she'd been suffering from sexual harassment.'

'By you?' asked Walter.

'No, course not!'

'Did you ever use the incapacitator on her?' asked Karen.

'No! Definitely not.'

'Would we find her blood on it too?'

168

'No, I told you.'

'We could ask her,' said Walter.

'Please do!'

'I think that's all for today,' said Walter. 'Thank you for your assistance.'

Miro didn't reply, as Karen said, 'And don't you dare put any pressure on the young woman on reception, or I will have your guts for garters.'

Miro pulled a face and said, 'Are you going to see Grizzy?'

'Yes,' said Walter, 'and no doubt you will ring her first to prime her with answers.'

'I won't.'

'That's the most sensible thing you have said all day,' said Walter. 'Good morning.'

Chapter Twenty-Five

During the short journey south to Rossett Karen said, 'It's amazing, isn't it?'

'What is?'

'We are investigating murder, and looking into another suspicious death, and we end up uncovering all kinds of creepy nonsense.'

'Like sexual harassment at work, you mean?'

'Yeah, among other things. Adultery, deceit, lies, you name it. It all comes tumbling out.'

'The human condition, Karen.'

'Yeah, but it doesn't always look great does it, Guv?'

'Too true.'

Three and a half thousand souls lived in Rossett, a small border town, or large village if you prefer, just over the Welsh border, 7.5 miles south of Chester, 6.5 miles north of Wrexham. It's a smart little place standing on the banks of the River Alyn, a tributary of the big River Dee a couple of miles away. It's a pretty place too with a cute watermill, and a couple of quaint country pubs that are always packed out at the weekends, with city people paying a visit to the country, and country people eager and willing to meet the city folks. Pretty girls in short skirts, and handsome hunky farm guys looking for company, and maybe more.

Karen knew the pubs well; she'd frequented them many times herself, but so had Walter, though not for a while. It was a pleasant place to be, and a pleasant place to live.

Sunflowers Close consisted of not more than twenty executive style detached houses, precisely the kind of place one would expect a locally based banker to live. Number 12 looked like most of the others, large gable to the right side, red brick, white windows, red tiles, white people, three large windows to the left, and a double garage with white up-and-over doors to the left of that. Reasonable sized gardens that still housed a few flowering roses, chrysanths, and dahlias, despite it being November, the very last ones hanging on for dear life, courtesy of global warming.

'Nice place,' said Walter.

'Very nice,' said Karen, as they ambled up the path and Walter rang the doorbell.

A young blonde woman, presumably Grizelda Rekatic, came to the door straight away. Opened up, looked out, saw a big bear-like black man, and a slim blonde. Grizzy hadn't applied any makeup, though she didn't need it. She must have looked dreadful, she imagined, though Walter thought she looked incredibly beautiful, in tight jeans and white blouse, not unlike Karen herself.

'Grizelda Rekatic?' said Walter.

'Yes. And you are?'

Karen flashed ID and did the intros.

'Police?' she said, alarmed, as people always are. 'There's nothing wrong is there? With Miro? Or the children, there's nothing wrong with the children is there? God forbid!'

'Nothing like that,' reassured Karen.

'We just need to ask you a few questions, routine enquiries, nothing for you to worry about.'

'You'd better come in.'

Walter smiled and entered the smart house. Grizzy showed them into a luxurious front sitting room, where everything was new and neat and just so.

'Take a seat,' she said. 'Would you like a cup of tea? The kettle's just boiled.'

Normally they'd always say no, but Walter's throat was dry, and the chair was particularly comfy, and he found himself saying, 'That would be nice, thanks, milk no sugar.'

Karen said, 'No thanks,' and Grizzy left the room.

There was the same silver-framed photo on the glass coffee table featuring the two beautiful girls, and smart pictures on the walls, but nothing else of interest.

Grizzy came back and set a mug of tea before Walter, and clutching her own cup, sat down and said, 'So what can I do for you? It isn't every day the police come calling.'

Walter sipped the tea. It was good.

Karen said, 'Can you tell us where Miro was between midnight and 2am on the night of…' and she repeated the date of Bel's murder.

'Miro?' said Grizzy. 'Why do you ask?'

'Was he here?' asked Walter.

'Of course he was here, we were in bed, sleeping, he is very busy at present, with all the expansion. He's often very tired when he gets home, he needs his rest.'

I'll bet he does, thought Karen.

'Are you certain he was here?' said Walter. 'You wouldn't lie to us, would you?'

'Of course I would not lie. My mutter always taught me not to lie. I never lie. Not ever. What is this all about?'

Walter took a deep breath.

'There was a woman murdered in Chester that night.'

'Murdered? What has this got to do with my Miro? I not understand.'

'We are just eliminating people from our enquiries, that's all.'

'You don't think Miro had anything to do with it, do you?'

'As I said, we are just ruling people out,' said Walter.

'I think you not tell me everything.'

You're right there, thought Karen, biting her lip. Did the woman have a right to know that Miro visited prostitutes, that he restrained them and beat them till they bled, and harassed the beautiful young women at work, and heaven knows what else.

Walter drank tea and took a card from his top jacket pocket and set it on the glass table.

'If you think of anything else, you can ring me anytime.'

'Is that it?' she said, glancing at the card.

'Yes,' said Walter. 'That's it.'

The phone in the hallway rang.

'Excuse me,' she said, getting up and going through and answering it.

They heard her say, 'Yes, they're here now. What's this all about, Miro?' and they guessed he said something like, 'I'll tell you later.' She put the phone down and came back into the room.

'It was Miro. He was as evasive as you.'

'You've answered our questions, Mrs Rekatic, thank you,' said Karen, and they got up and headed for the door.

'I'm not sure I understand what's happened here,' she said, opening the front door.

'Thanks, again,' said Walter, 'nothing to it,' and in the next second they walked away from the house and got in the car.

A couple of minutes later Karen said, 'That was tricky.'

'It always is.'

'Do you think she had a right to know?'

'Probably, but it's not down to us to bugger up other people's marriages.'

'I think he's doing a good enough job of that himself.'

'Yeah, the fool. But I imagine he'll be in for some tough questioning later.'

'The least he deserves. Did you believe her?'

Walter pondered on that. 'What, about him being at home at the TOD? Yes, I did. You?'

'Yes, I did too, unfortunately.'

'You know what that means don't you?'

'It means he's innocent of the Belinda Cooper murder, if nothing else, if she's telling the truth.'

'The more of them we can rule out, the quicker we can rule someone in.'

'Yeah, but he's still in the frame for whatever happened to Ellie Wright,' said Karen.

'Maybe we have two separate cases after all.'

'Could be, so where to now, Guv?'

'The high school, and Iain Donaldson.'

Walter glanced at the car clock. It was just on noon.

'Put on the radio,' he said. 'See if there is anything on the news.'

She flicked the controls on the steering wheel and the midday news, courtesy of the local radio station, came on.

A woman has been found murdered in Chester in her own home. Police say she has not yet been identified. Our sources tell us that she was bludgeoned to death with a baseball bat, and some people are referring to the death as the Baseball Bat Murder. In other news the local MP has called for greater action to help youth unemployment...

'Turn it off,' said Walter.

'Didn't take long for that to get out.'

'Indeed,' said Walter. 'Inevitable, I suppose, and she wasn't bludgeoned to death.'

'No, someone's got that bit wrong. Who do you think leaked the story?'

'Could be Ronald Speight, he seemed to relish and deal in lurid gossip.'

'Possibly, just so long as it isn't one of the home team. Here we are, the high school,' and Karen turned right off the main road, and down the long straight approach to the redbrick school. The car park was half empty, and they slid into a space close to the main entrance, jumped out, and headed for the door.

The doors were locked. Maybe not such a surprise in the twenty-first century. So many schools and churches were no longer operating an open door policy, with constant worries over theft and security. On the wire reinforced glass window within the double doors was a handwritten note.

Will all visitors please ring the bell and wait.

Walter rang the bell, and waited.

174

A couple of minutes later a frumpy middle-aged woman came to the door. She half smiled, opened up and said, 'Can I help you?'

Karen flashed ID and did the intros.

'We need a quick word with Iain Donaldson, nothing important, just routine.'

'You've picked a good time, he's on his lunch, I'll show you through.'

They went along a long corridor, turned right, another twenty yards or so, or was it metres these days, thought Walter, and knocked on a door on the left, and opened up without waiting to be invited.

There was just the one person in the office, studying a quality newspaper, whilst munching on a decent looking beef sandwich. He glanced up at the unusual visitors.

'Iain,' said Miss Frumpiness. 'These two people would like a quick word, they are police officers, I have seen their ID.'

'Police?' said Iain. Standing up. Slim guy, short dark hair, noted Karen, six feet'ish. 'Nothing wrong is there?'

'Well, yes and no,' said Walter, pulling out a canvas and tubular steel chair, and sitting down, as Karen studied the information on the notice board. 'It's about Belinda Cooper.'

'Bel? What about her?'

'She's been murdered.'

'What!'

'It's true, I am afraid. And you knew her well, I believe?'

'Yes, I did, we were... for a short while...'

'Lovers?' suggested Karen.

Iain nodded and said, 'Yes, I had hoped it might have gone on from there.'

'But she met Gareth Williams and promptly finished with you,' said Walter. 'That must have been hard.'

'Now hold on a minute...'

Karen jumped in. 'Where were you between midnight and 2am on....' reciting the date of death.

'At home in bed.'

'And where is home?'

'I have a new flat in the city,' and he gave an address.

It wasn't a million miles from Karen's pad.

'Can anyone confirm that?' asked Walter.

'Thankfully, yes. My new fiancé, I only proposed to her two weeks ago. She was with me.'

'And your fiancé's name is…' said Walter, pen at the ready.

'Andrea Dennehey.'

'Thanks for that,' said Walter. 'We have it on good authority that Belinda Cooper only ever had five boyfriends.'

'She was indeed very selective,' said Donaldson, happy to give himself a backhanded compliment. 'I can't believe she's dead. It's a big shock.'

Walter gave the guy a moment. 'You were one, Gareth another, a guy called Ronny Speight, a bloke named Marcus, who turned out to be bi-sexual.'

'Was he! I didn't know that.'

'Nothing to worry about,' said Karen. 'So I'm told. Blood tests aplenty. All in the clear.'

'So who was the missing mister number five?' asked Walter.

Iain shook his head and said, 'Search me. I've no idea.'

'Do you know anyone who might have wanted to harm Miss Cooper?'

'Certainly not. She was a very likeable person; and a popular woman too. I'd still be with her now, but for…'

'Quite,' said Walter. 'Do you know a girl called Ellie Wright?'

'No. Should I?'

'No matter. What size shoes do you take?'

'Ten, why?'

'Do you drive a car?' asked Karen.

'Course I do, who doesn't?'

'Model?'

'New Cayton Cerisa, landed a better job here, thought I'd get a better car. Andrea loves it.'

'Did you kill Belinda Cooper?' asked Karen.

'Course not! What do you take me for?'

'I'd rather you didn't leave town,' said Walter.

'I have no intention of leaving town.'

'That's good. Thank you for your help.'

They retreated to the door and down the corridors and through the main doors and out into the dank November air, and back to the car.

Sitting quiet for a moment, Karen said, 'That's interesting.'

'What is?'

'I know Andrea Dennehey.'

'Do you? How?'

'I charged her when you were away on that canal boat holiday.'

'I didn't think I'd heard the name before. Charged her with what?'

'That's the interesting thing, Guv.'

'Go on.'

'Affray, and GBH.'

Chapter Twenty-Six

Earlier that morning DCs Darren Gibbons and Hector Browne paid another visit to Michael Flanagan's modern townhouse in Christleton. They half expected to find him out and away at work, but he was there, and not in the best of moods.

'Don't you people ever leave hardworking folk alone?'

'Just a few more questions, nothing too demanding,' said Gibbons smiling, hoping to win the guy over.

'Can we come in?' added Hector. 'You don't want the whole world to know your business.'

Flanagan scowled and stood to one side and the detectives went inside.

'No work today?' said Gibbons.

'Everyone is entitled to a day off.'

Gibbons sat down and glanced around.

Hector stood in the lounge doorway, observing.

'Nice place you have.'

'Do we have to go into all that again? What exactly do you want?'

'You're tagged?' said Gibbons.

'I am,' and he lifted his trouser bottoms to reveal the grey technology.

'We don't think it's working,' said Hector.

'What gave you that idea?'

'Just a theory that Hector has,' said Gibbons.

'Well, it's news to me, no one has said anything.'

Hector wandered into the small kitchen, took a look around.

'Do you have a computer?' asked Gibbons.

'Yeah, course I do, who doesn't?'

'And I'll bet you're something of a whiz on it?'

Flanagan grinned, happy to accept a compliment.

'I guess. I know a bit, that's for sure,' and he glanced over his shoulder and saw that Hector was missing. 'What's he doing in there?'

'Just getting a glass of water, I should think. He suffers from dry throat syndrome. Have you cracked the coding on the tag?'

'What?'

Hector returned and said, 'You heard him, Michael. We think you are one clever bastard when it comes to computers, and you've cracked the coding on the tag, enabling you to take it off without central control realising it.'

'I wish.'

'Did you go out last night?' asked Gibbons.

'Course not, you can check.'

'Ah, but can we though?' said Hector. 'That's the whole point.'

'Not sure I understand what you are getting at.'

'Did you go out on the night of...' said Gibbons, adding the date of the Belinda Cooper murder.

'Ah! I see. I get you. You're trying to fit me up for that baseball bat murder because you can't find the real culprit.'

'No,' said Hector. 'We are trying to ascertain if you are slipping out undetected, because I think that is what you are doing.'

'You're heading up a blind alley.'

'No, we're not,' said Hector. 'You are.'

'How do you do it?' asked Gibbons. 'You can tell me, I'm impressed.'

'Do what?'

'Fool the system.'

'I'm not fooling the system.'

'If we were to examine your computer,' said Hector. 'And took a look at the browsing history, I reckon that would tell us a lot.'

'Can we see your computer?' asked Gibbons.

'Not without a warrant.'

'You're out on licence, aren't you?' said Hector.

179

'You know I am.'

'It only takes a word,' said Gibbons, 'from the boss, and you'd be back inside before your feet could touch.'

Flanagan stared at the police officers and insisted, 'You are not looking at my computer.'

Hector and Gibbons shared a look.

Hector pulled a face. Gibbons shrugged his shoulders.

'Your choice, Mr Flanagan,' said Hector, and the detectives made their way to the front door, Flanagan following.

Hector leant over and whispered, 'Crash coding, is it?'

'What?'

'We're on to you.'

'I have no idea what you are talking about.'

Hector nodded and the officers ambled outside and jumped in the car.

'What the hell's crash coding?'

'I have no idea,' said Hector laughing. 'But it sure sounded good.'

Gibbons laughed too.

'You're mad. Still think he'd fiddling with the tag?'

'Course he is.'

'Why are you so sure?'

'One thing I have learnt to do in this job is to spot liars, and he's lying about something.'

'Well if he is, he could be our man.'

'That's what I reckon. Where to now?' said Hector, firing up the engine.

'The pubs. Guv wants us to ID the drug dealer.'

'Oh yeah, forgot all about that.'

Walter sat back hard in the car seat and said, 'Tell me all about Andrea Dennehey.'

'Hard woman, in more ways than one,' said Karen.

'Tell me more.'

'Mutton dressed as pilchard.'

Walter guffawed.

'She goes to the same gym as I do. She's there every day. Does the running machine, and weights. She's slim, toned, and strong.'

'Go on.'

'She's been on the lookout for a husband for ages. Everyone knows that. She'll eat Iain Donaldson alive; he won't know what hits him. Don't get me wrong, Guv, she's attractive enough, pretty face, shoulder length auburn hair, but her soul is as cold as ice.'

'I gather from that, you don't like her.'

'I can see right through her. Her whole life is an act. She's a fraud.'

'What was she done for?'

'Affray and GBH.'

'I know that! So you said. Details of the case?'

'Oh right, I'm with you. She beat up two women in a nightclub lav. Broke one girl's nose, cut the other one's eye.'

'What did she get?'

'Big fine, and fifty hours community service.'

'She was lucky to get that.'

'She damn well was. The magistrate said she was lucky the case didn't go up to the Crown Court, which on another day it would have done. He gave her some benefit of the doubt, said something about it being two onto one, and that Andrea pleaded self defence, saying the other two kicked it off, and there was some doubt as to who was telling the truth.'

'Do we know what the row was about?'

'The usual, Guv, over a man she'd taken a fancy to, and they were making eyes at, another potential husband, I reckon.'

'Do you think she's capable of murdering Belinda Cooper?'

'Certain of it, Guv. She's tall and very strong, you should see her on the weights, obsessed by it, she is. She could snap a neck like a chocolate bar, I kid you not.'

'And she'll give Iain an alibi, and he will do the same for her.'

'For sure.'

'So we have another one to add to the list.'

'The list?'

'Of suspects.'

'Yep, we do.'

'I think we need to find out a lot more about Andrea Dennehey.'

'That we do, Guv.'

'Come on, let's get back to the station, I want to get something to eat.'

'Good idea, and I want to find out how we are progressing with analysing the Mirror man's phone.'

'And Belinda's technology too, we should be inside that by now.'

'Yeah, that too, there could be all sorts of intel in there.'

Karen booted up the car and pointed it at the city centre, back to base, and a busy afternoon in the land of secrets and lies that sleeps and hides in all modern tech.

Jenny and Nicky were busy at their desks, frustrated at making little progress, unable to break Jimmy Crocker's alibi, unable to contact Derek Nesbitt, who'd gone away for a few day's fishing.

Chapter Twenty-Seven

Walter popped out for ten minutes to visit his favourite purveyor of sandwiches where he picked up two hot beef rolls and a chocolate muffin. Sometimes comfort food had its place, he reassured himself, though could he restrict his visits in future?

Karen remained at her desk and gnawed on a hard green apple and a packet of almost as hard low fat crisps.

She was scrolling through Miro's many phone calls. Like so many others he sure as hell used his tech to the max. Hundreds of logged calls, text messages, and voicemails, but nothing that looked out of place, nothing that caught her eye, nothing that incriminated the man, no matter how hard she looked.

The cute young guy from the Tech department came in and hustled up to her desk and grinned and said, 'Belinda Cooper's computer and phone?'

'Yeah?' said Karen. 'What about it?'

'All open and readable.'

'About time too.'

'Don't you start.'

'What took you so long?'

'Got hung up on a big regional job from Manchester. Three local Uni's in big trouble.'

'Oh?'

'Yeah… you know, that ransomware scam.'

'Meaning?'

'Big time cyber crime. They hack into the Uni's mainframes and lock everyone else out, then demand a big ransom to free up and allow access to the data again. It's becoming quite common, and damn difficult to break. Looks like it's based in Romania, or

Bulgaria, one of those places, but it's cloaked so many times it's almost impossible to track down, and to make it worse they constantly shift things around.'

'Was the ransom paid?'

'Oh no, we got lucky. Cracked it wide open. No sweat. Do you want Belinda Cooper's gear?'

'Yeah, set it down there,' and he plonked it on the side of Karen's desk.

'What's the password?'

'Highfive555.'

'That didn't sound so difficult to work out.'

'They never do when you know the answers. Bloody difficult when you don't.'

'Thanks,' she said, thinking about Highfive555.

Belinda Cooper sure seemed hung up on that number.

'No probs, glad to be of service,' and he smirked and scuttled off back to the tech lair, wherever that was currently located.

Bulgaria or Romania? She thought. Where was the Mirror man from again? Serbia, didn't he say? How far was that from Bulgaria and Romania? Just a coincidence maybe, thought Karen, but like most of the members of the team, she didn't believe in coincidences, for they often pointed the way forward. Maybe worth remembering. Sometimes whole cases fell open like a ripe sweet chestnut on such morsels. She glanced across the office at Jenny and Nick.

'Are you busy, Jen?'

'Not particularly.'

'Fancy a trawl through the Mirror man's phone.'

'Sure, glad to,' and Jenny came over to Karen's desk and collected the latest model mobile. 'What am I looking for?'

'Anything that links him with Ellie Wright, or better still, Belinda Cooper, or anything that looks weird, calls and messages to women, and dating sites, and anything that suggests financing or organising cyber crime.'

'Cyber crime?'

'Yeah, the local Uni's have all been hit, coming from Eastern Europe, played havoc with their systems, apparently, costs them a load of dosh in downtime and stuff.'

'Okey-doke,' and she took the phone away.

Karen plugged in the laptop and booted it up. The tech guys had set it up so that it overrode any existing passwords. Well done them. All the stuff about the number 5 was now redundant.

Walter came back in the office and walked past her and grunted.

'Bel's laptop?'

'Sure is.'

'Anything interesting?'

'Just opened it now.'

'Crack on, I'm going to have a word with the boss,' and he ambled across the office and tapped on Mrs West's open door.

Karen went straight to the emails. Sure, people texted a lot, but for the real meaty stuff, that was still to be found in the emails. Love letters, juicy gossip, hopes and aspirations, secrets and lies, diaries, stuff like that, that's where she'd find it.

And they were all there too, going back over the previous three years. First, the semi-gay Marcus Royce, for that was his name, and his wacky sense of humour and bawdy jokes, some of which Karen understood, and some she didn't. Moving on as their relationship developed, until the final phase when Bel finished with him after his gay revelations, and his subsequent pleadings to be given another chance, all to no avail. Begging rarely worked, didn't everyone know that?

Ronny Speight, writing masculine filth, something he thought exciting, and imagined that she would too, though it was obvious to Karen's eye that it made Belinda uncomfortable, as she tried to steer him away from such things, though he apparently didn't see the advice tactfully written between Bel's lines, and in the end he paid for it. And there was something else there too that caught her eye, within Ronny's increasingly furious writings, as their relationship crashed and burned. How could it not? One Saturday

185

night/Sunday morning at 1.28am he'd written: "I could strangle you!" Maybe something there. She printed it off and circled it in red and set it on Walter's desk.

Iain Donaldson followed, and his gentler more cerebral caring line, and maybe that came as something of a relief after Ronny's queer pitch and violent tongue, though by the cringe, he came across as an awful bore, writing overlong emails on how he'd like to travel to Chile and explore the Atacama Desert, to further his knowledge of South American geography, so he said, and would she like to go along with him on the trip of a lifetime? Something she evidently did not wish to do.

Somewhere around that time she began seeing Gareth Williams, and somehow Iain found out. Or maybe she told him, or left hints he was meant to find. Iain mounted his high horse and issued her with an ultimatum. It's him or me, never a good move, as Karen's former boyfriend Rodney once discovered. Belinda chose Gareth, much to Iain's chagrin.

Onto and into Gareth's feisty stuff, kind of somewhere between Iain and Ronny, definitely more exciting than Iain's dull style, but not as bad as Ronny's over the top rantings that some men imagine attract women. There were some photo attachments there, on Ronny's emails, photo attachments for God's sake of close-ups of excited male body parts, presumably big Ron's, as he liked to refer to himself. Though he wasn't identifiable, or that big. Karen laughed aloud. No one noticed. Did men really think such things turned women on enough to win them over? It didn't attract Karen, not one jot, and by the look of Bel's replies it hadn't worked on her either.

But back to Gareth, and his gentler more supporting style, but all the while including little digs along the lines of how she was better off with him than with that loser, Iain, or as he described him, the Jogman, geography teacher and daily jogger to boot. The Jogman could jog off into the sunset, and eventually he was forced to do precisely that. And still it came.

186

Details of frequent secret weekends away they'd enjoyed together, Gareth and Bel, in five-star hotels in Hereford, Lytham, Buxton, Ludlow, and others too, quite a list, and exciting as well, judging by the detailed descriptions written after the events, equally enjoyed by Bel and Gareth, if the emails were to be believed, before the electronic letters took a serious downward turn, when he admitted he had been married all along, though in his words: It shouldn't make any difference, we're strong, for what we have is so special.

Yeah, right. Yuck! Karen tut-tutted aloud, and thought about bouffant man. He's a solicitor for God's sake, and yet clearly he didn't understand a thing about Belinda Cooper, and how she ticked, and how she felt, and what she really wanted and needed and desired.

Karen felt sorry for Belinda. Who wouldn't? It wasn't just Iain Donaldson who was a loser, or Ronny Speight, they all were. The whole damned lot of them. But someone had murdered poor Bel, but who had committed the filthy crime? Was the evidence, the pointer to the culprit, hidden amongst those hundreds of pages, and thousands of words that displayed themselves before Karen's sharp blue eyes?

There was something vaguely wicked about reading other people's emails, even if that person was dead, even if you enjoyed the full authority of the British government, and hence the British people, to do so. It was a little like taking a quick sneak at someone else's diary. Karen did that once, way back when, back at school, when she and her best friend, Kayleigh Mortimer, as thirteen-year-olds, had first discovered boys.

Karen knew that Kayleigh and herself had both taken a liking to the clean cut and white shirted Colin Hart, and she knew that Kayleigh kept a vivid diary, recounting all her hopes and dreams and fears, and no doubt juicy titbits about Colin too. Karen so wanted to see it and read it, and when Kayleigh was away for a matter of minutes, she had weakened and taken a quick peek.

Kayleigh came back and saw Karen's eye's rushing over the pages in that old red diary, and she ran up and snatched it back, yelling and calling her an "Utter Shit!" That was undeniably fair comment in the circumstances. Karen apologised countless times afterwards, but the damage had been done, and Kayleigh never spoke a civil word to Karen again. Karen never told a soul about that sorry episode and banished the event from her mind.

She turned her thoughts back to Belinda and whispered an apology for going through Bel's most private communications, emails and texts and messages that were never meant for anyone else but Bel and the receiver, or Bel and the sender, including a huge amount of detail of Belinda Cooper's intimate life. Karen hoped and prayed that Belinda wouldn't appear at that moment and snatch back her laptop and scream: "You Utter Shit!" That wasn't going to happen of course, or at least if it ever did, it could only be in Karen's darkest dreams.

There were hundreds of pages in the directory of emails, as she yawned and turned over the page on the screen. Another huge list of messages and letters, another full day's work, but a fresh email address smacked her in the eye. It was not one she had seen there before. She shivered, and a cold tingle crept up her spine and across her shoulders. Her heart raced, and she felt sudden sweat in her armpits. She blinked and looked at it hard, her racing brain ordering her eyes to zoom in on the handle. No, she wasn't mistaken; she'd read it correctly.

There it was, black letters on a beige background.

Dozens and dozens, nay hundreds of times.

Shushshish@Comptech.co.uk.

Shushshish@Comptech.co.uk happened to be David Baker's unforgettable, if faintly ridiculous email handle.

'Hell,' she said, breathing out hard, while rushing to open the first communiqué.

'Did you say something, sarge?' asked Nicky, glancing across the office, never one to waste an opportunity to check out his sexy sergeant.

'Nothing, Nicky, get on with your work.'

After knocking, Walter was invited into Mrs West's office. She was correcting some kind of long report, pen poised, plenty of crossings out and suggestions in red ink, testament to her zealousness in all things administrative.

'Sit down, my man. What is it?'

Walter collapsed in the visitor's chair and blew out hard.

She took off her pink specs and adopted a sympathetic face and said, 'If I didn't know better, I'd say you were getting stuck.'

'Not stuck exactly, ma'am.'

'What then?'

Walter sighed. 'We have yet another suspect ma'am, and to complicate matters, this time it's a woman.'

'That's different. Is she capable of breaking Belinda Cooper's neck?'

'She is, ma'am. Karen knows her. She shares the same gym. She goes every day. Weights apparently, is her forte. Very strong, so Karen says.'

'And she's known to us?'

Walter nodded.

'When I was on holiday she was done for GBH and affray. Got off lightly too.'

'I remember. Andrea somebody, Donohue, or something.'

'Dennehey.'

'That's the one. Where does she fit into this?'

'She's Iain Donaldson's fiancé, can you believe?'

'So she'd have some kind of twisted motive, coming to the moral aid and defence of her spurned partner, et cetera.'

'Something like that, though I am not sure it stacks up.'

'Have you spoken to her?'

'Not yet, but she's got an alibi.'

'Don't tell me, she was with Iain, and he was with her, so they think they are both off the hook.'

'That's about the size of it, ma'am, in fact, that's what bugs me most about this whole case. If you take out mother's and lover's alibis I don't think any of them are in the clear.'

'So what's the roll call now?'

'Nine, maybe ten.'

'Namely?'

'Speight, Gareth Williams, the gay Marcus, the Mirror man Rekatic, Iain, and now Andrea, Flanagan, Nesbitt, and Crocker. And the tenth possible is a sighting of a drug dealing guy who also fits the profile of the kind of man Belinda was attracted to.'

'You can forget Flanagan, I trust in tags.'

'Hector and Darren think…'

'I don't care what they think. Tags work.'

Walter nodded and said, 'We know that Speight, Williams and Iain Donaldson have all been in Bel's house, and in Bel's bedroom, so any DNA we find there can immediately be explained away. What bugs me is that all these guys, even the unidentified drug dealer, vaguely look alike, six foot or above, slim and fit, dark hair and eyes, and smart, I've never known anything quite like it.'

'What about the missing fifth lover? Any progress there?'

'Not yet, ma'am. It could of course be that drug dealer. We are into Bel's tech now, Karen's going through her laptop as we speak.'

'That's good. That's where the answers usually lie.'

Walter nodded and sniffed and wished he hadn't, and said, 'I hope so. We need a break.'

'So the prime suspect is?'

Walter gave her a quizzical look and his forehead creased.

'At this moment it's throw a bunch of balls in the air and catch one.'

'Wish I hadn't asked. Go and see this Andrea woman. Find out if she ever met Bel. You might get lucky.'

'Pencilled in for the morning.'

Mrs West nodded and said, 'Good. I am getting a bit of flak on this case.'

'Oh?'

'You know how it is, Walter, if the case isn't solved within three days flak begins to fall, and the longer it goes, the heavier the flak.'

Walter bobbed his head and said, 'And the trail can go cold.'

'Too true. Are you confident the killer is one of the nine?'

'As confident as I can be.'

'You know the drill, Mr D, keep asking them questions, until one of them trips themselves up. We all know they will, sooner or later.'

'That's the plan.'

'Was Eleanor Wright murdered?'

'I think so ma'am. Just can't prove it.'

'If she was, I'd bet my new caravan on there being one killer involved and not two.'

'I'm with you on that, ma'am.'

'Anything else?'

'Not right now, and thanks.'

'No problem, Walter, you know my door is always open.'

Karen discovered David Baker was Belinda Cooper's fifth lover, and she also knew it put her in a difficult position. If she revealed that fact to Walter and the team, she would be removed from the enquiry for being personally involved, and that was the last thing she wanted. She also knew he was taking her out to dinner that night to some swanky place.

She hated not being straight with Walter about anything, but surely it was better to have her there at the centre of things, pushing the inquiry forward, rather than have her excluded, especially as she was as close to David Baker as anyone alive, to the best of her knowledge.

There was another small matter too. If it came out later she deliberately withheld information she could be for the high jump, and that spelt big danger. Yet sooner or later that info would come to the fore, nothing was more certain. The best thing she could do was delay it for a day or two, and see what David had to say for himself.

And there was another factor.

To her knowledge, David Baker didn't have an alibi for Belinda Cooper's TOD. Could he possibly be Belinda's killer and maybe Ellie's killer too? She couldn't prove he wasn't, and that was a thought to make her think long and hard about being alone with the guy. But right there, that was the thing she wanted most, to be alone with him, in order to find out.

She was reading more of his old lovey-dovey emails to Bel, and that was a strange experience. Seeing the evidence before her eyes of how her potential partner-to-be had wooed and won a slightly older woman, a pretty lady with a succession of tall and dark lovers, just like David. It was unsettling, to say the least.

The one thing that Karen took comfort from was that Bel and David had stopped going out together a while before she met him online. That was something. Maybe Karen got him on the rebound, and that was another thing that was odd. They just seemed to stop, the emails between the pair of them. Their meetings came to an abrupt end, with no hint of a fall out or the strife to come. It was like an airliner blown out of the sky, with no time for a mayday call, no time for anything, just total silence, a complete break, and not even a black box to search for in the wreckage to garner clues.

She'd have to ask him about that, but she couldn't outright. She'd have to be clever and canny, more clever and cannier than she had ever been before, and that was going to be challenging and tricky. Her train of thought was interrupted by Walter's voice booming across the room. She hadn't noticed he'd come back.

'Well that's a bloody thing, isn't it!'

'What?' said Karen, turning to look at him.

'This!' he said, waving Karen's printout, and the red-circled words. 'I could strangle you! I could strangle you! If that's not a threat to murder someone, I don't know what is.'

Karen brought him back to earth.

'People always say things like that, Guv, as you well know. I could kill you. All the time, and she wasn't strangled either. She had her neck broken.'

'Yes, they might say that in the heat of the moment, but they don't write it down in bloody black and white, not like he has.'

Maybe Walter had a point.

Darren and Hector returned, grinning and playing about, as they often did.

'Well?' said Walter. 'How did you get on?'

'The drug dealer's name is Marty,' said Gibbons.

'Is that all you've got? Marty what?'

'No one seems to know any more.'

'He must have used a surname to someone sometime, maybe used a credit card to pay for a meal, or something.'

'That's one thing drug dealers never do,' said Gibbons. 'It's cash only with that crew, always cash.'

He had a point there, and Walter knew it. The money laundering laws and rules and regs and systems had been tightened hard and were working pretty well. Drug dealers always had too much cash and nowhere to spend it, and would constantly face the major problem of working it back legally into the system. Of course he would have bought all meals with cash. Went without saying, drip, drip, drip it away. There was no doubt about that.

'You're right, Darren, thank you for reminding me. How did you get on with Flanagan?'

'The guy's taken the day off. He was at home, and get this, he is something of a computer whiz, even liked to brag about it, until he saw it was something we were taking an interest in.'

'A computer expert, eh? That's convenient.'

'He sure is. But he would not let us see his computer.'

'What do you think? Can he somehow bypass the tag?'

'I can't see it myself, but Hector is convinced that's what he is doing.'

Walter stood still and breathed out heavy and took a moment to think, and said, 'Can we link him to Belinda Cooper? No. Can we explain how he bypasses the tag? No. Can we prove he killed Ellie Wright? No. That looks dead in the water to me.'

'He killed his wife,' said Hector. 'Known indisputable fact, that says a lot.'

'Mmm,' said Walter. 'Nick, do you know what is happening with the complete SOCO report on Belinda Cooper's house?'

'They are still there, Guv. Working hard. They'll be a while longer yet.'

'I wish they'd get a bloody move on,' and raising his voice he said, 'For those of you that don't know, we have yet another suspect, and this time it's a woman.'

'That make's a change,' said Gibbons.

'Who?' said Jenny.

'Andrea Dennehey. Already known to us, convicted within the last twelve months of GBH and affray.'

Hector sniggered and said, 'Belinda Cooper's neck was broken. I think we can discount her.'

Karen glanced up from the laptop.

'Andrea Dennehey could snap you in half like a twig,' and in the way she said it no one had any doubt that Andrea could.

Walter looked down at Karen.

'Anything more in those emails?'

'Not yet, Guv. Just lots and lots of graphic lovey-dovey messages.'

'I could do with some graphic lovey-dovey messages,' said Gibbons, grinning.

Most of them laughed at the thought.

'I could fix you up with Tracey Day for fifty quid,' said Hector, laughing at his little joke.

'Oh, funny, yeah!'

'Maybe we should seize Flanagan's computer,' said Walter, thinking out loud. 'He's out on licence. We could do that.'

'I'm up for it,' said Hector.

'I'll think about it,' said Walter, sitting down and closing his eyes for a big think.

Chapter Twenty-Eight

Corla Revelation resembled Oliver Cromwell, high forehead, large flat nose, and hefty warts, aplenty. Yet for all that, she was a vivacious woman, and rarely short of admirers.

She made a decent living through her full-time counselling work, and part-time fortune telling business, though where one finished and the other began was becoming increasingly blurred. She liked to say she was a spiritualist, and a medium, and had gone to the trouble of inventing highfaluting sounding associations that she christened, "The British Spiritualist Congress" and the "European Mediums Association" and proceeded to have printed expensive and impressive looking Articles and Certificates, that she framed and set on her walls. They sure as hell impressed Corla, and in due course wowed her clients too. That was the plan, and most times, it worked.

In a good light and on a bright day she could pass for thirty-nine, as her friends would eagerly confirm, especially after Corla had bought the drinks. But on a bad day after a heavy night out, and maybe not standing her corner, those same friends would swear she was fifty-nine, looking sixty-nine. Fact was, no one really knew how old Corla Revelation and her close-knit family of warts were, and that was exactly as she liked it.

She'd always had an eye for the main chance, and that had served her well in the past, and would continue to do in the future. She always paid close attention to the criminal cases covered in the press, and especially ones from Chester and surrounding areas, and most particularly the ones where financial rewards were offered. Of special interest to her were the worst crimes imaginable, and that invariably meant rape, murder, and death.

The Chester baseball bat murder had piqued her interest, as she devoured all the media coverage she could find. It was causing quite a stir, for it wasn't every day a well-liked and well-known local woman was murdered in her own home in the genteel city of Chester.

In her quiet moments Corla believed she possessed ESP powers, and she would test that ability to the max by sitting back in her favourite wing-backed armchair, a bottle of whisky on the small table close by, with her favourite crystal cut glass, as she attempted to reconstruct the face of the killer in her mind. If you don't believe in yourself, she mused, how could you expect others to believe in you? He will come to me, she would say aloud. He will come.

He's a tall man, and dark too, that was eminently clear, though whether that intelligence had been garnered through her imaginary powers, or subconsciously, via the increasing media coverage, it was difficult to tell.

Corla sipped twenty-year-old malt whisky, closed her eyes, blanked her mind, and let the force swirl over and through her. She spoke aloud in a strange, deep voice: *It will appear, as it always does, everything about him will materialise, and sooner than we think, and then I shall be famous.*

She reached out and topped up the glass. Always nice to whet the whistle before she went out on the town. She glanced at her expensive wristwatch, a present from a long ago wealthy lover. She'd quite forgotten his name. The watch ticked on as it always did, never missed a beat. 8.22pm. Give it another ten minutes and she would slip on her favourite faux leather coat, and head down to the city centre, meet friends, and drink the night away.

Across town, Karen was getting ready too. She'd slipped into a tight-fitting red dress. Okay, maybe it was a tad too short, but that was the idea. She wanted to excite him, engage him, and relax

197

him, for she figured that was her best chance of teasing vital information from the man.

She'd put on her most expensive red stilettos too, the ones she'd bought the previous Christmas, and had only worn once. It made her instantly taller, though she would still have to look up to David when he kissed her, and that was how she liked it. The doorbell rang from down below. Karen went to the security phone.

'It's me,' he said.

'Glad to hear it,' she replied, smirking, an intonation that transmitted itself down the line. 'You'd better come in,' and she pressed the button and the door below sprang open.

A minute later he was in her apartment. His eyes widened when he saw her, in that dress, in those shoes.

'Lady in red,' he said. 'Ooh la la!'

'You like?'

'I love,' and he grabbed her and pulled her to him and kissed her hard. He smelt good, as if he had just showered. Karen kissed him back, and it was good too, better than good, and she hadn't kissed a man like that since she and Gregory Orlando had gone their separate ways. But she couldn't keep a negative thought inveigling itself deep into her brain like a burrowing worm. Was she kissing a killer? Could that be the case?

Two minutes later, and they were motoring away from her apartment block.

'Are you sure you won't be cold,' he said.

'I rarely get cold.'

'Hot blooded, eh?'

'Very. Where are we going?'

Maybe he was taking her into North Wales. There were lots of quiet and remote forests in North Wales, ideal places for a killer to go about his dirty business, she knew that well enough, for she had often driven rally cars through those pinewoods at breakneck speed. She comforted herself in knowing that she was as fit as she had ever been, and possessed the latest most powerful pepper

198

spray in her black leather bag, a spray so potent it was on trial with the police, and had not yet been released to Joe Public and his sweaty chums, for it would find its way into the wrong hands, such as bank robbers and muggers, and rapists, and worse.

But he, David, was fit too. She could never imagine herself being attracted to any man who wasn't, and he was tall and powerful as well, and that should not be underestimated. But first, she needed to extract information from him, and that was the objective of the evening, for now.

'It's a secret,' he said, and that wasn't the answer she wanted to hear, for they were heading out of the city, southbound, on a quiet and poorly lit country road. She glanced across at him. He looked fab, perfect husband material, as no doubt Andrea Dennehey would have said if she had ever spied him in the gym. He appeared relaxed and contented as he drove, and that was as he should look, for the lucky man was dating a beautiful blonde in her prime. It didn't get much better than that.

'You're full of secrets, Mr Baker.'

'You can talk! You didn't tell me you were a police officer until we'd met for the third time.'

'That's normal,' she said. 'One can't be too careful in my line of work.'

'You're right there,' and still they were driving south into a black and breezy night, and try as she might she found it hard to relax.

Walter sat alone in his favourite armchair. The curtains were drawn, and the TV on low, though he wasn't watching. He squished open a can of stout and poured and sipped and pondered on the case.

If he could eliminate enough suspects, then the one remaining must be the killer. Either that, or it was someone else entirely, and that was still possible. Eliminating people was the first step. He began with Flanagan. Mrs West was adamant that tags worked. In

Walter's world, that was compelling enough. He dismissed Flanagan. Next!

The solicitor, Williams. What possible motive could Gareth Williams have for murdering his former lover? The fact that she had eventually spurned him? Possible, though he didn't seem unduly upset about it, and more than that, happy to be back with his wife, and add to that, he was, after all, a solicitor. Could solicitors commit murder? Of course they could, anyone can, but were they less likely to do so than others? Maybe. In the court of Walter's mind he would give Gareth the benefit of the doubt, for now. He would be excused.

On to Iain Donaldson. Another professional man, a teacher this time. Did teachers commit murder? Of course they did, but statistically they were far less likely to do so than others. When did you last hear of a teacher committing murder? It doesn't happen often. And he had an alibi, something that Walter would test in the morning when he interviewed Andrea Dennehey. He also seemed something of a wet week of a man. Was he capable of it? Walter couldn't envisage Iain holding a baseball bat to Belinda's throat, and coldly snapping her neck. That didn't seem likely at all. He just couldn't see it. For now, Walter would give him the benefit of the doubt. He didn't believe it was Iain.

Maybe he was eliminating the easy ones first, but the field was whittled down to Miro, Nesbitt, Crocker, Andrea, Speight, Marty the drug dealer, and Marcus. Who next to look at again? Miro the Mirror man. Walter took another drink and brought Miro into his mind.

David Baker finally pulled off the road and into a small car park. Ahead of them was a long single-story stone building. It looked a little like a traditional Welsh cottage, and that wasn't surprising for they were only a couple of miles from the Welsh border. There were five or six other cars in the car park, and a warm glow coming from the small square windows.

'What's this place?' asked Karen.

'It's the best kept secret in Cheshire.'

'You've been here before?'

'Yes, two or three times.'

'How did you find it?'

'A former girlfriend brought me.'

That was a little nugget. Could that former girlfriend be Belinda Cooper? In any event, it gave Karen an easy way in to starting a casual conversation about previous partners without it appearing too obvious, at least that was her hope.

'What's it called?'

'Ali's place.'

'Ali?'

'Yep,' David said, getting out of the car into the freshening wind. 'Come on, let's get inside.'

Walter breathed out heavy and thought of Grizelda Rekatic. She had quite specifically said that she never lied. Her mother had drummed that into her, and Walter believed her. She said that Miro was in bed with her, sleeping at the time of Belinda's death, and if that was the case, Miro was not the killer. He could only have done it if he had woken up, dressed and left the house without his wife noticing. Murdered Belinda, raced home again, and slipped back into bed without waking his wife. Was that possible? Yes it was. Was it likely? Not in Walter's world.

Plus, he had left Ellie's caravan at around 8pm, that fact was supported by the cab company, and the fire hadn't gone up till around midnight. It had been witnessed by Mr Duffield who lived up the lane. That all pointed to someone else, at least one other person going down Marigold Lane after Miro had left. If that were the case, that let Miro off the hook. Walter was reluctant to set him free, for in his mind he was a man full of dreadful faults and weaknesses, an incredibly unlikeable person, but facts were facts, and honest people were honest people, and he believed

Grizelda Rekatic was honest. He'd bet his pension on that. For now, Miro appeared innocent, and the Mirror man was excused.

Next up, Ronald Speight, another most unlikeable person, in Walter's eyes. Perhaps deep down Belinda Cooper was attracted to unlikeable men, maybe without realising it. Some women are. Though Iain and Gareth didn't fit into that box. Walter squished open a second can and poured and sipped, and poured and sipped, and thought and thought.

Ali Camperdown was a Scot who'd come to Chester twenty-five years before, to take up a position as a Sous Chef in a top Chester hotel, which sounded grand, but sous chef simply means under chef in French, or deputy chef, or assistant chef, if you prefer.

But like many others before him he worked hard, moved up the table, salted away a little capital, and helped by his Scottish acquisitiveness and careful nature, he set about opening his own small restaurant. He'd launched Ali's place five years before, and though it was still something of a hidden gem, he was building a decent business based on quality and selectivity.

Unsurprisingly, he specialised in Scottish produce, maintaining his sources of supply from way back when, importing from north of the border the majority of his ingredients. River caught Scottish Salmon, none of your fish farm frauds for him, and Aberdeen Angus beef were staples, as were hand collected shellfish and seaweed, and the sweetest raspberries you could ever find, grown on the slopes of the pretty Ochil hills where as a boy, he had spent many happy hours, picking and eating the juiciest fruit, and getting paid a few pennies for doing so.

The only way to obtain a table in Ali's place was by booking, and David Baker had done that; determined, as he was, to impress Karen Greenwood. Inside the restaurant to the right, was a blazing log fire, and opposite that a tiny stone bar, where Ali held court, greeting his diners personally, warm handshakes and mwah-mwah's all around.

He remembered David Baker. He'd been in a few times before, and Ali Camperdown made a point of remembering his clientele, and their names, and why not, for his prices were sky high, and anyone willing and able to splash the cash into Ali's till at least deserved to be remembered. This time Baker had brought with him an incredibly attractive blonde in a yes-yes-yes dress that no man would ever miss. She was younger than the women he usually accompanied too.

Intros and aperitifs duly over, they were shown through to a small and intimate table in the far corner. The little place was almost full with a gentle of hum of satisfied conversation reverberating back from the ancient grey stone walls.

'It's fab in here,' she said, allowing David to tuck the chair in beneath her.

'Wait till you've eaten before you decide that,' he grinned, taking his seat and smiling across the table.

He handed her the small menu, only four choices, but wasn't that better than fifty-four? Four choices alone meant more attention to each, and the greater probability of fresh and carefully chosen ingredients.

'Don't look at the price,' he said. 'My treat.'

Too late, for she had already glanced at the tariffs.

Goodness me. What was he after?

Predictably, she chose the salmon, and he the steak, and both were perfect.

'So,' she said, 'tell me about the lady who first brought you here.'

'Just a woman I once knew.'

'No, Mr Baker, you are not getting away with that, I want all the goss,' she said, linking her hands and smiling and gazing into his dark chocolate eyes, while leaning slightly across the white cotton cloth.

Ronald Colin Speight, Walter muttered his name aloud, and pictured him in his mind. What the heck did a lovely lady like Bel Cooper see in the man? He came across as something of a bully, occasionally uncouth, intolerant, impatient, and unbearable, though it wasn't unusual for Walter to be found wanting when trying to figure out a man's attraction to women.

Before he'd left the office Karen had showed him the stark photos that Speight had emailed to Bel. What was the point? What was the thinking behind such a move? Did he imagine that such pictures would turn her on? Excite her, make him more desirable, and cement their relationship? It seemed unlikely to Walter, and that judgement stood up, for not long after, Bel brought the final curtain down on not so big Ron.

I could strangle you. Walter wondered what brought on the thought in the first place. I could strangle you. That infamous phrase that was not only inside Speight's head and brain, but he had seen fit to write it down and email it to his partner, his lover, his lady, knowing that it would be there in her computer forever. I could strangle you. Okay, it was issued in the wee small hours when alcohol was almost certainly in play too, but that was no excuse. The thought was there, even if it were meant in a jokey fashion.

The fact that Belinda was not strangled but murdered with a baseball bat meant nothing. Who would ever say, "I'm going to break your neck with a baseball bat?" It didn't slip off the tongue in the same manner as: "I could strangle you," or, "I could kill you." And he had a motive, and some might say the most powerful motive of all. Jealousy, and Walter had seen first hand that Ronny Speight could be a jealous man.

The man was in a jam. One week he had a beautiful woman on tap, presumably providing him with all his bedroom needs, and in the next, he was reduced to visiting a downmarket call girl in a scruffy and smelly caravan to get his fix at the sexual well. What a comedown that must have been.

That was the picture in a nutshell; throw in threats of attack, even to the extent of murder, a serious motive present in jealousy and revenge, and lo-and-behold the man had no alibi, and through his arrogance he even thought that was something of a joke.

Walter snorted. It was time to bring Ronald Speight in for a serious quest-session, in fact it was overdue, and that would be done sooner rather than later, and yet… and yet, the bottom line was that Walter did not believe Ronald Speight to be the murderer. True, he was the only name in the frame so far to have had a relationship with both dead women, if visiting a call girl could ever be described as a relationship.

The more one juggled the facts, the more likely it looked that Ronald Colin Speight was the killer, yet Walter didn't concur. He'd been wrong before, and he was well aware of that, and many times too over his long career, and no doubt he would be wrong again before the final curtain came down on his working life. But he did not think he was wrong this time.

What was it that ma'am had said? Keep asking them questions until they trip themselves up. The stock tactic of detectives going back millennia, and Walter would do just that. But the annoying thing was he thought they could go on asking Speight questions until the sun went out, with no discernable results. In other words, it was a waste of precious time, his, and the team's.

No matter, he made a mental note to send the boys, and maybe boys and girls, round in the morning, to bring Speight in to discover if an intensive questioning session might reveal something. Anything would be nice. Unlike the others, Speight was not excused. Not yet.

David Baker sipped his drink and tried to avoid Karen's question.

'Come on,' she said, smirking. 'Where did you meet her? Is she another online dater?'

'No,' he said. 'Not a computer babe, in fact you are the first woman I have ever met online.'

'Yeah, right,' said Karen. 'And see that flying pig?'

'That isn't a flying pig, it's best Scottish pork loin, Ali's well known for it.'

They laughed together.

'So where did you meet her?'

'Is it important?'

'I don't know. Is it?'

'I met her at her place of work, if you must know.'

'Whereabouts?'

'Forgive me for saying, but this conversation seems to have morphed from friendly banter, to a police interview. Would that be fair to say?'

Karen giggled and said, 'Course not, sorry if I sound a little officious, it's just with asking people questions all day in a certain manner, inevitably, I guess sometimes I relapse into enquiro-speak out of hours. I've been told off about that before.'

'I'll bet you have.'

'Why did you stop seeing her, or is that a secret too?'

'She stopped seeing me, she said I was too young.'

'She was older than you?' asked Karen, though she thought she knew the answer.

'A little, but not by much.'

'Do you miss her?'

'No, not now, not when I am with you,' he said, his dark eyes piercing into her blue, holding her gaze, hoping she believed him.

She thought that was so much flannel. She'd always seen through disingenuous male compliments, always been wary of them, but she wanted him to keep talking, and maybe even wanted to believe him. Truth was, she wanted to believe everything about the guy. But he still fitted the profile of the man wanted for murdering Belinda Cooper, and she knew he had a possible motive. Rejection. Simple as that. Plenty of people have been murdered for less.

Walter finished the can of stout and pondered on whether to go to the kitchen and fetch another. Maybe in a second. There were still a few names in the frame to review. Derek Nesbitt? No, there was nothing to suggest he was involved with Bel, unless Karen could come up with something via Bel's broken passworded tech.

What about Marcus Royce, as Karen had discovered his name to be? What was it Lena Freeman had said? He'd run off to one of the three B's: Bournemouth, Blackpool or Brighton, seaside resorts all. If Walter had to bet, he'd choose Brighton, though a case could be made for all three. For now, the guy was beyond the reach of questioning, and there wasn't sufficient intelligence warranting a nationwide search to bring him back to Chester for interrogation. That could change, but for now he was, in Walter's mind, ruled out.

It didn't leave much.

Speight of course, a nagging picture that would not go away. Andrea Dennehey, a tough young woman not averse to using violence. A so far unidentified drug dealer called Marty, and that left just two other possibilities. The fifth man, Belinda Cooper's mysterious fifth lover, also yet to be identified. Surely to God there must be something within Bel's tech to ID him, and Walter made another mental note to ask Karen about that in the morning. While the final possibility was someone yet to enter the picture. Someone new. Someone unknown. Someone mysterious. Seemed unlikely, but not impossible. But who could that be? He glanced at his overlarge watch. 11.32pm. That wasn't too late to ring someone, was it? Not when a murderer was at large. He wandered through to the hall and picked up the phone.

David Baker paid for the excellent meal and drove Karen straight back to her apartment. It was something of a relief, though if he had suggested a late night drive out into the wilds of North Wales it might have brought things on a little. Earlier, he had parried her questions, and she realised she was going to give her true intentions away if she persisted.

They'd only been in the flat for a couple of minutes when the phone rang.

'Sorry to trouble you so late,' mumbled Walter.

'No problem, Guv. What's up?'

'I was wondering how you were getting on with Bel's laptop.'

'Good. There's a lot of stuff in there. It'll take a bit of time to get through it all.'

'I was wondering about the fifth man. It would be weird if there was nothing in there about him.'

'If he exists.'

'You think he doesn't?'

'We only have Bel's word for it,' said Karen, glancing across at David, who was busy standing and admiring some Greenwood family photographs on the far wall. He had a cute bum.

'I don't see why she'd lie.'

'I am not saying she did, but we don't have a fifth man until we have proof that such a person exists,' said Karen, knowing she was misleading her boss.

'I think there is a fifth man, and I want you to step up your search in Bel's tech. He must be in there somewhere.'

'I'm on it, first thing in the morning.'

Walter sniffed and said, 'I think the fifth man is the killer.'

'Really?' said Karen, still looking at the handsome Mr B who had turned round, and was smiling at her through his fab eyes. 'What makes you say that?'

'Because I don't think it's any of the others. Our man is smarter than the ordinary Joes we have in the frame, much smarter, and more dangerous with it. He's a cunning foe to be reckoned with.'

'You think?'

'For sure. I wonder where he is now, and what he's doing.'

Karen's mouth fell open, and she shivered.

David smiled. Walter sighed.

'God knows,' she said, pondering, maybe he's right in front of me, about to go to work again, God forbid.

'Sorry to bother you so late.'

'No problem, Guv. You've discounted Andrea?'

'Not entirely.'

'Neither have I.'

'Ah, well,' said Walter. 'Early start tomorrow, yeah?'

'Yeah sure, Guv, I'll be there. Sleep well.'

'You too.'

Karen put down the phone as David said, 'Who was that?'

'My boss.'

'Does he always ring so late at night?'

'Sometimes.'

'Does he fancy you?'

'Good God, no.'

'I should hope not.'

That was an interesting thing for him to say, I should hope not, but maybe not surprising. Men are fiercely territorial creatures, they never like other males on what they see as their territory. But it was interesting that David Baker appeared to imagine that she might be part of his domain. Taking a bit for granted, a little arrogant too, but hey, it was a lot better than showing no interest at all, far better, for she liked him, and a bit more with each passing day.

She shook her head and closed on him and said, 'Now listen, Mr B, I have to be up real early in the morning, and you are going to have to go.'

'So soon?'

'Yes, soon, like now.'

'But not until I have done this,' and he reached out and tugged her close and kissed her like he meant it. He was strong, really strong. It was good too, though she never let herself go, not completely, for that weird thought was there again, nagging away. Was she kissing a killer? Had this man murdered Belinda Cooper, snapping her neck with a baseball bat as if it were a twig? Walter seemed to think so, and that was worrying.

They agreed to meet again in three days. That would be enough time, she hoped, to prove his innocence, or guilt. Later, in bed alone before she fell asleep, she pondered on her predicament. One lie led to another, or one half-truth to another, or one misleading comment to another, and it had. She had already denied in the office she knew of a fifth man, and his ID, and she had done so again, while looking into the fifth man's smiling face.

She would have to come clean about it, and soon, and that was going to be mighty tricky. The worst thing was she realised what delicate ground she was crossing. Her entire career was at stake. Nothing less. She tried to switch her mind back to what could have happened if DB had stayed over, stayed the night, stayed with her, in her bed.

It would have been good, beyond good, she was certain of that, and on another day, and another night, she might have forced the issue, though she didn't imagine she would have to do much forcing. She wondered what it would be like, sleeping with David Baker, or sleeping with a killer, or were they one and the same? In any event, he excited her. That was beyond doubt. Killers often excite.

Chapter Twenty-Nine

It was a new dawn and a new day and I'm feeling good, thought Walter, as he knotted his favourite red and blue striped tie. But it was a dark one, one of those horrid November days that never gets light, dank and cold and miserable and negative. Was there anything good about November in England?

But Walter wasn't negative at all, as he went outside and ambled down the road to catch the single-decker bus on the ten-minute trip into town. The usual four early birds were at the bus stop. They were all on nodding terms, like some kind of special club of hard-done-by-ers, out alone, working early, when the lucky world slept soundly on.

'Be along in a minute,' said the plump woman, forcing a smile, as she glanced away from her mobile.

'Hope so,' said Walter, ramming his hands deeper into his coat pockets. It wasn't raining, but there was a creeping cold chill and dankness in the air, capable of attacking anyone who was going to stand about in it for too long.

The little bus appeared like some kind of happy dog, its headlights grinning a good morning, bringing relief. Walter imagined a frantic tail wagging at the backend, and all those waiting at the bus stop smirked at one another, and muttered positive vibes, as they changed weight from one foot to another, formed an orderly queue, the woman first, and then the men, strictly in order of time of arrival, Walter bringing up the rear. Then they were aboard, half full, plenty of seats at that hour, lots of room to spread out, and the beautiful heater blowing out comfort and joy, as the bus glided almost silently into town, so much so the November blues were obliterated, almost.

In the office everyone was in early, even Mrs West. They were a good crew; Walter couldn't help thinking that, though they were in because of him, though he would never have realised that in a month of Sundays. A month of Sundays would be like any other month, seeing as Sunday was no longer different to other days. Empty churches, full bookies, frantic shopping, horseracing on the telly, pubs open all day, X-rated pics on the flicks. Things had changed, and Sundays were not like they were.

Hector brought him a coffee and set it down on Walter's desk.

'Thank you, man.'

'Welcome, Guv.'

Walter wasn't in any mood for gentle introductions, or a gradual build up. He was straight on it.

'Karen, I want you to stay in all day and get on with disseminating any intel in Bel's tech.'

'Sure, Guv.'

'Nicky, I want you to stay with Karen and give her any help necessary.'

'Sure,' he said, grinning at his sarge.

'You know what we are looking for. Any clues the killer may have left in there, any hints that he was about to do what he did.'

'You said "he", Guv, but it could still be a "she",' said Jenny.

'Yes, that too. Jenny. I want you to find out where Andrea Dennehey is right now, I want you to get us a good unmarked car, and I want you to take me to see her as soon as we have finished here.'

'Sure, Guv, leave it with me.'

'Hector and Gibbons, I want you to find out where Ronald Speight is this morning, I want you to go and see him later, and bring him back here to answer my questions around lunchtime.'

Mrs West nodded and looked happy.

212

'What happens if he refuses to come?' asked Hector.

'Tell him I'd appreciate his cooperation. If he still won't come, arrest him on suspicion of the murder of Belinda Cooper, that should concentrate his mind.'

'Sure, Guv,' said Hector.

'Looking forward to it,' said Gibbons.

'There's a £20,000 reward been put up for information leading to the conviction of…. et cetera,' said Mrs West.

'Who by?' asked Karen.

'Not sure, some local businessman.'

Walter nodded and said, 'Thank you, ma'am, anything that helps is good. It's come to my attention that some of you are not reading all the reports relevant to this case, or these cases, the deaths of Wright and Cooper. Put that right today. Toxicology reports, SOCO reports, fire reports, autopsies, the whole bloody lot. You can't afford to miss things, so make sure you all read the reports, and I don't care how long it takes, or how boring some of them may be. That clear?'

'Sure, Guv,' mumbled a few.

'Any questions?'

No one had.

'Get to it… Today's the day…'

And people started to move, as Gibbons added, 'The teddy bears have their picnic!'

'Shut up, Gibbons,' said Karen, as Walter nodded to her and said, 'Use Nicky wherever you can. I know there's loads of stuff to get through, but use him, he's supposed to be bright. We need to get finished.'

Karen nodded. 'Sure, Guv. I'll see you later.'

Jenny came over to Walter and said, 'Andrea Dennehey works in Austerity Hayes old department store in the city, on the perfume counter, and she's there this morning.'

'That figures,' said Karen. 'She uses enough of the stuff, and wears false lashes like big black hairy caterpillars. You won't miss her, or them.'

'Car, Jen?' said Walter.

'On my way, Guv, see you downstairs in ten.'

Walter glanced back at Karen.

'Have a good morning, I'll want you in on the Speight interview later.'

'Sure, Guv,' and Walter turned about and limped towards the lift. After he'd gone Karen pondered on her continuing predicament. It was even worse, for she had the little runt Nicky there snooping around; and how bad would it be if he found evidence of the fifth man before she did? That didn't bear thinking about. She'd have to give him something to keep him busy that didn't jeopardise her own position, and that wouldn't be easy. One thing was clear, she needed to reveal the ID of the fifth man soon.

Nicky ambled over, smirked down and said, 'I'm all yours.'

The idiotic little guy seemed to think he had a chance with her. The fool. She gave him Bel's bank statements, going back five years.

'What am I looking for?'

'Clues, DC Barr, clues.'

'Meaning?'

'Anything that looks out of order, any payments to and from anyone involved in the case. You have read all the reports involved in these cases, I take it?'

He looked guilty. 'Maybe not all of them.'

'Well do that now!'

'Sure, sarge,' and he ambled away, as Karen grinned.

Austerity Hayes old department store hadn't changed that much in forty years, and it was still busy, even first thing. It didn't matter that it was a dank November day; there were still plenty of tourists about. Chester is a touristy town, and they kept the tills ringing with their euros and dollars and yen and yuan, and a goodly proportion of visitors had chosen to pack out the perfumes and cosmetics department on the ground floor.

Walter and Jenny stepped through the recently modernised double glass doors to be hit with an aroma that reminded them of first dates, and Christmas gifts, and romance, and, dare one mention the word sex, too? though Walter would keep that colourful observation to himself.

They sought out the floor manageress, explained to her that they needed somewhere quiet to talk to Andrea Dennehey. She wasn't in any trouble, simply helping with their routine enquiries, and the manageress was most accommodating, providing them with a quiet furnished room.

'Do you want me to fetch her for you?' she asked.

'That would be great,' said Walter, sitting at the modern desk. Jenny to one side of him, as she took out her notebook.

A couple of minutes later the manageress showed a pair of hairy black caterpillars into the room, Andrea Dennehey following immediately behind. The manageress made her excuses and left, as Jenny did the introductions.

'What's all this about?' asked Andrea, still wary of the police after her last brush with the law.

'Take a seat,' said Walter, pointing to the chair before the desk. 'Just a few questions, nothing to worry about.'

It was hard to take the eyes away from the lashes. Maybe it was because Karen had mentioned them, but by hell they caught the eye, and not all of it was good.

Andrea grinned and sat down and crossed her legs with a flourish, and smoothed down her short black skirt. Walter looked up and across the desk and tried not to see the 'pillars.

'You're Iain Donaldson's fiancé, I understand?'

'Yeah, that's right. He said you might want a word with me.'

'Did he? and what would that be about?'

'Presumably the baseball bat murder, everyone's talking about it.'

'Are they?'

Andrea nodded and said, 'What do you want to know?'

'You were with Iain on the night of the murder?' said Walter, as Jenny chipped in with the date.

'Yes, I was. All night... you know, together, just the two of us.'

'Quite,' said Walter, 'and you wouldn't lie about that, would you?'

'Course not. What do you take me for?'

'You're a member of the gym, I believe?'

'Yep, gotta keep in shape, you know how it is. Mind you,' she said, looking at Walter's ample figure, and she glanced at Jen and pulled a face and said, 'I thought you lot had to keep in shape too.'

Walter ignored the barb.

'They tell me you are very strong?'

'What? For a woman you mean?'

'No, I mean as a human being.'

'I am strong, I can whack Iain at arm wrestling, lots of fellas come to that, you want to try me?'

'That won't be necessary. What would you say if we found your fingerprints on the baseball bat?'

'I'd say you were lying twats! Because that ain't possible,' and she thought about that for a second and said, 'Hold on a minute, is this what you are about? Trying to fit me up with that murder, 'cos you can't find the real killer? What's your game?'

'We are not trying to fit anyone up. We just want to get at the truth. Iain, your Iain, was once the partner of the deceased. It's standard procedure to look at all ex-partners, and their new partners.'

'You mean me?'

'Yes, in this instance, that's you.'

'Do you like my lashes or something?'

'Pardon.'

'It's just you keep staring at them.'

'Do I? My apologies if you think that.'

'They're not expensive,' and she glanced across at Jenny and back at Walter and said, 'your young friend here could do with some, if you don't mind me saying. Improve her no end.'

'Tell me about when you attacked two young women in the lavatory?'

'Oh, here we go! They attacked me, is the truth of it. You know all about that. It went to court and I was punished, wrongly in my opinion, but there we are, end of.'

'Have you ever attacked anyone else?'

'I have not!'

'Have you ever been in Belinda Cooper's house?'

'Certainly not!'

'Iain has.'

'Of course he bloody well has, and it ain't the only thing he's been in, in that house, if you get my meaning,' and she smirked at the two coppers in turn.

'Were you upset with Belinda Cooper?'

'No, not really. Why should I be? He dumped her, and then found me, lucky him, and quite right too, for she was messing around with other men, lots of them, if truth be told. You should be looking at that greasy bouffant-haired solicitor of a dick for one. Belinda was a bit of a stuck up cow, that's all, so I gathered, from what Iain told me, but I never met her.'

'What else did Iain tell you?'

'Nothing special, just odd things here and there that painted a picture of a frustrated woman, who'd never found happiness.'

'And you've found happiness?'

'I have. Iain and I are good. We're going to make a real go of it.'

'Do you know anything about Belinda Cooper's other menfriends?'

'No, not by name, though Iain said that one of them turned out to be gay, and that really freaked her out, but it would, wouldn't it?' And she turned and pulled a face and addressed that question to Jenny.

Jenny glanced at Walter, remained silent, and noted the conversation.

'On the night of the murder did Iain leave the house at any point? Think very carefully before you answer, for an untruthful reply could bring you serious trouble.'

'He never left the apartment. Not once. We were too busy creating the eight-limbed beast.'

Walter grimaced and continued.

'Could he have nipped out when you fell asleep?'

'Nope, not possible.'

'And why would that be?'

'Because I'd tied him to the bed, I think he quite likes it. Anything else you want to know?'

'No,' said Walter. 'Thanks for your help. You can go now.'

'Thanks,' she said. 'And another thing, if it had been just you and me when I had that other nonsense, it would never have gone to court.'

'Why's that?'

'Because I am sure we could have sorted things out between us. Know what I mean… Walter, love. Ta-rah,' and she stood up and grinned, and flashed her lashes, and left the room in a swirl of expensive gratis perfume.

'Geez, give me strength,' said Walter. 'What did you make of that?'

'She's a tramp,' said Jenny. 'Imagines all men are overwhelmingly attracted to her. Can't see what a hard-faced bitch she really is. Thick as a plank, if you ask me.'

Walter pulled a face, never one to be surprised by the outspokenness of the women on the team, and that was cool.

'But a murdering bitch, you think?'

'I think she's capable of it, but I don't think she did it.'

'My sentiments, exactly. Come on, back to the office. Ronald Speight awaits.'

'Lovely,' she said, grinning.

Chapter Thirty

The interview with Ronald Speight got underway at 12.25pm. He was furious at being dragged out of work. He was a draughtsman, though not qualified, though he didn't advertise that fact, got by as an assistant, but harboured a grudge against the fully qualified university educated wallahs, who he hated with a passion, many of whom were younger, and paid far more.

He moaned he could lose his job because of Darriteau and the bird, as he called them, and if he did, he was threatening to sue Cheshire Police and Darriteau, personally.

Walter shrugged. Bluster and braggadocio deserved nothing more. Karen turned on the recorder and said, 'Interview with Ronald Colin Speight, I am Detective Sergeant Karen Greenwood, also present is Inspector Walter Darriteau.'

Walter set the ball rolling.

'We've invited you here to assist in our enquiries into the deaths of Eleanor Wright and Belinda Cooper.'

'You didn't invite me, you dragged me out of work against my wishes.'

'Whatever the circumstances, we appreciate your cooperation.'

'Get on with it, I haven't got all day.'

'In one of your emails to Belinda Cooper you said, and I quote, "I could strangle you". What did you mean by that?'

'Yeah, and I could kill you for dragging me here, but it doesn't mean I'm going to do it. Get my point?'

'It was meant in jest?' asked Karen.

'Not exactly. It was meant as a rebuke. She was pissing me around, and I felt I needed to make a point.'

'Despite extensive enquiries you are the only person we can trace who knew both dead women, and you had a motive for Belinda's murder.'

'Then you're not looking hard enough.'

'Your DNA is all over Bel's house.'

'No shit, Sherlock. I was there enough times.'

'Yes, but not for a while, and DNA degrades over time.'

'You're clutching at straws and not particularly strong ones at that. I know it because I wasn't there when Bel was murdered, and I suspect you know it too, because you haven't anything better. My guess is you're under pressure to get a result, but you're looking in the wrong place.'

'Where should we be looking?' asked Karen.

'How the hell would I know? Do you want me to do your job for you? I would if you paid me enough, and by hell I couldn't do it any worse.'

'Let's talk about Ellie Wright,' said Walter.

'Talk about what you like.'

'We believe you went there again, late that Friday night.'

'I did not.'

'We think she didn't appreciate your return visit. Maybe she was busy, maybe she was tired, perhaps she was cheesed off after a long and hard week.'

'Didn't happen.'

'We think you argued, maybe you hit her, had a fight, you're a big and powerful man, a man known for his temper, a man who routinely threatens women, and maybe you hit her and she fell over and banged her head. So you thought, the best thing you could do to cover your tracks was burn the place down. You're a regular smoker, you had matches or a lighter to hand, and before you knew it there was a big fire, and you were running for your life.'

Speight pulled a face and shook his head. 'Fairy tales.'

'You have no alibi for that night, because you couldn't possibly have an alibi because you were there.'

'Nope, you're wrong.'

'And would you know it, but you haven't got an alibi for the night Belinda Cooper was murdered either.'

'That's what happens when you live alone, no one can say whether you were in or out.'

'You were angry at Ellie because she didn't want to know, and you were even angrier at Belinda Cooper because you could see your idyllic way of life going down the tubes. One day you have a hot girlfriend on tap, the next, you were reduced to visiting prostitutes.'

'I can get sex any time I want.'

'Doesn't look that way to us. You were reduced to pay and display, or starve.'

'I do all right.'

'You are an angry man with a quick temper, a man who writes threatening messages late at night to vulnerable women living alone, and I quote again, "I could strangle you", and lo-and-behold what happens? That same threatened lady is murdered in her own home.'

'You're firing blanks, Darriteau. Is that the best you've got, because you've got bugger all! Charge me or let me go.'

'Is your wife back?'

'Eh?'

'You heard the Inspector.'

'What's that got to do with anything?'

'Just answer the question.'

'No, not yet, and don't ask me where she is, for I have no idea.'

'When she returns could you ask her to ring me?' and Walter slipped his card across the desk.

'No chance!'

'Thanks for your help Mr Speight, that's all for today.'

Speight sighed and looked surprised and said, 'You mean I can go?'

Walter nodded. 'For now. Unless there's anything you'd like to tell us.'

'I've got bugger all to say to you two,' and he kicked the chair back, muttering something about seeing his solicitor, and then he was gone.

'That was a complete waste of time,' said Karen.

'You think?'

'Don't you?'

'No, not entirely. Mrs West said we keep asking them questions until they trip themselves up.'

'So?'

'We have, and he didn't, and that's probably because he's telling the truth. I don't believe Speight's the killer.'

'So who do you think is?'

'More and more likely it looks like the fifth man.'

They exchanged glances, and Karen knew the question coming next and pre-empted it.

'I'm on the tech now.'

Walter nodded. 'How's Nicky getting on?'

'He's going through Bel's finances. Nothing so far.'

'Crack on with it, KG.'

'Will do, Guv.'

Corla Revelation sat alone in her house. The radio was on, but it always was because Corla liked to keep fresh with the up-to-date tracks. The set was permanently tuned to the pirate station, Dee Bee Cee, and there was a solid reason for that. The station was owned and run by young blokes who happened to be good friends of her two nieces. Many of the local families rarely listened to anything else.

DBC pumped out mainly non-stop music, and not just current stuff, but classics going back to the sixties. But in between the sounds there was a decent news round-up, and just as pirate stations have always done, those news stories were cribbed from the BBC, ITN, SKY, and the local radio stations.

The catchy on-the-hour station signature tune came on, and Corla hummed along. The news would follow in a second, and the lead story could only be the Chester baseball bat murder, for nothing like it had happened in the city for quite some time.

There had been slight developments too. A little more information had been released. The deceased woman; named as thirty-six-year-old Belinda Cooper, resided not far from Corla, in a wide and pleasant street called Berryland Avenue. And there was more too. A twenty thousand pound reward had been put up by a local solicitor, one Gareth Williams, available to anyone who could provide information to bring the perpetrator to justice.

A radio station run by her nieces' friends, a news item pinched from legit broadcasters, a murder in a house not so far away, and a decent reward on offer, four facts that didn't have a great deal to do with one another, but combined and sent through the airwaves, out of Corla's modern radio, swishing through her dyed blonde hair, down her ears, into her brain, and suddenly everything became crystal clear.

She remembered it all. She remembered everything. She had seen the killer on the night of the murder, and could identify him too if required. She'd always known she'd become involved in the case, and she had. She opened her diary and spotted the direct number for Chester central police station, she'd used it several times before, and carefully dabbed in the number. A minute later, and the call found its way to DC Darren Gibbons.

Chapter Thirty-One

Walter and Karen came back from the interview room. Gibbons was talking on the phone. He stood up and waved and caught their attention. They heard him say, 'Yes, someone will be with you in about twenty minutes. Yes. Don't go out, we're on our way.'

'What?' said Walter.

'Witness, Guv, says she saw the murderer coming out of Belinda's house on the night of the murder.'

'Fan-bloody-tastic! What's her name?'

'Bit of an unusual one. Corla Revelation, so she says.'

'Where does she live?'

'Warren Drive, number 20, not far from Bel's house.'

'Car, Guv?' said Karen, not wanting to miss out on a thing.

Walter nodded. 'I'll be down in a sec,' and he hurried across to Mrs West's room, tapped on the open door, held it open and peeped around the side to bring Mrs West up to speed.

'Let's hope she's not a time-waster,' said Mrs West, staring at her crammed screen of multi-coloured spreadsheets.

'We're overdue a break, ma'am, this could be it.'

'Hope so, my man, keep me posted.'

Karen grabbed a newish navy blue BMW, no police markings, as he liked them, though for once they weren't interested in the car.

Karen said, 'We have to drive down Berryland to get to Warren Drive,' and ten minutes later they were doing precisely that. Outside Belinda's house a solitary Community Support Officer stood guard, while on the verge were two large grey vans, lots of personnel in the house, working hard, beavering away, seeking vital intel. A couple of minutes later, and they pulled into Warren

Drive, a very similar suburban road packed with well-heeled old houses, some detached, some semis, and all built between Victoria abandoning the throne in 1901, and Edward VIII desperately trying to clamber aboard in 1937.

Karen pulled the big car to a gentle halt outside number 20, a small 1920s detached house, not unlike Walter's.

'Here we go,' she said, turning off the engine and getting out.

'Please God, don't let this woman be a dreamer motivated by gold,' muttered Walter, heaving himself out of the car and into the cold November afternoon.

Karen opened the squeaking wrought iron front gate, went to the door, and rang the bell.

Corla opened up fast, nodded at them, and said, 'Come on in.'

They stood in the hallway and Walter said, 'You live on your own?'

'I do, and I suspect you do too.'

Karen suppressed a smile.

Walter said, 'You have an unusual name. Corla Revelation.'

Corla smiled, not unattractively, and nodded and said, 'I do, but it's all my own. I had an old aunt named Corla, but no one knows where the Revelation part came from. My mother used to say one Revelation in the bible, and one Revelation in the town. We'd always laugh about that. Come on through, would you like some tea?'

Walter thought about that for a second. Was this a lonely lady desperate for company and attention, a woman with an eye on the reward, who would say anything to get it, or was she a potential reliable witness with something serious to contribute? He gave her the benefit of the doubt.

'If it's not too much trouble.'

'No, of course not,' and she showed them into a neat square rear sitting room overlooking a neat square rear garden. 'Take a seat, I won't be a minute.'

Walter and Karen shared a look and glanced around. Pictures on the wall, but no photos, no dead husbands on display like

226

trophies, forever staring down at a former wife who didn't love them that much. Corla came back almost straight away; the kettle must have been on the go all along, anticipating thirsty police officers. She carried an old wooden tray and on the tray were primrose patterned china cups and saucers, something rarely seen. She set them out on the coffee table and poured from a matching yellow teapot. Karen rarely touched tea, but it was too late to refuse. Steam wafted away, and the tea looked good and strong, as Walter liked it.

Walter checked Corla out. She was a neat woman, tall and slender with a pinched waist, long dark skirt way below the knee, plain white blouse finished off with a flourish by a red silk scarf knotted around her neck. Pity about the warts, but none of us are perfect. The heavily dyed and shiny blonde hair bouncing on her shoulders didn't do anything for her, making her a hard woman to age. There was something vaguely hippy-ish about her, and the house too, though whether she had any direct connection to the sixties, it was hard to tell.

'So,' said Walter, cradling hot tea. 'My colleague at the station tells me you might have seen something in Berryland Avenue.'

Corla sat in the matching armchair opposite and smiled and said, 'That's right. I did.'

'Would you like to tell us what you saw?'

Corla nodded and began. 'Before I tell you about that, just to be clear, I understand there is a reward on offer in this case.'

Oh, here we go, thought Walter, his worst fears re-emerging.

'There is, if your information results in the killer being apprehended, and successfully prosecuted.'

'Good,' she said, happy to see Karen taking notes. 'So long as that is understood.'

Walter prompted again. 'What did you see?'

'I saw a tall young man coming out of Belinda's house.'

'You knew Belinda?'

'No, not to speak to, but it was her house all right.'

'How old was the young man?'

227

'Thirty, maybe thirty-five.'

'Can you describe him?'

'Tall, fit, dark-haired, a good head of hair.'

Just like David Baker, thought Karen, but also like Ronald Speight, Miro, Gareth Williams, Michael Flanagan, Iain Donaldson, and Derek Nesbitt, to name but seven.'

'What time was this?'

'Around a quarter to one in the morning.'

'Where were you?'

'I was sitting on a garden wall on the other side of the road, four or five houses down.'

'What were you doing there?'

'I'd been out. I always go out that night, there's a group of us go together, socialising, it's a regular thing, you know, have a nice time, a few drinks, maybe something to eat. I was walking home when I felt like a sit down, you know how it is, and naughty I know, but I needed a ciggie. I was going to wait till I got home, but I thought, to hell with it, I'll sit and have a quiet fag. The rain had just stopped. Of course everything was sopping wet, and I ruined my coat when I sat down, but you don't think, do you?'

'You were by yourself?'

'Oh, yes.'

'Tell me exactly what happened.'

'He came out of Belinda's house. I noticed him particularly because he stood there for a second on the pavement and glanced around. I thought he'd see me, but he didn't. He hunched into his jacket and walked smartly away from the house, and away from me. The streetlights were popping out, one by one, almost as he went past. I thought that weird.'

'What was he wearing?'

'Dark trousers, they could have been black jeans, though I couldn't be sure, and a casual jacket, and gloves. I noticed that too, dark gloves.'

'No hat?'

'No hat.'

'He was a white man?'

'Oh yes, as white as me.'

'And he didn't have a car?'

'Nope, not that I saw.'

'Was he carrying anything?'

She shook her head and again said, 'Nope.'

'How tall was he?'

'Six feet, maybe more. He looked like a man who could look after himself, and a man who could look after other people too, if necessary, a man's man, as they used to say.'

'What about his feet?'

'His feet?'

'Yes, trainers, boots, shoes, what?'

She shook her head and thought hard. 'Dark shoes, I'd say. I think I would have noticed if he had worn boots, or flashy trainers.'

'What happened next?'

'I finished my ciggie.'

'And you didn't see anyone else?'

'Nope, not a soul. It was very quiet.'

'What did you do then?'

'I got up and noticed my dirty coat, brushed it down, and ambled home.'

'So you walked right past Belinda's house?'

'I did. There were no lights on in the house, and I…'

'You, what?'

She shook her head and grimaced and continued. 'I know I shouldn't have, but right there, I thought naughty thoughts.'

'What kind of naughty thoughts?'

Corla nodded and continued. 'You'll think me crazy, but I imagined he was a lady's younger lover, and he'd been paying her a night-time visit, passionate like, and they'd enjoyed a lovely time, and she was peacefully sleeping. I was just a little jealous, I guess, and she was perfectly content, and he had a spring in his step, but in truth she wasn't content at all, was she?'

'No, she wasn't. She was dead.'

'Dreadful business. It beggars belief. Why are so many men so bloody awful?'

'I can't explain that,' said Walter, glancing at Karen.

She said, 'Women kill too. I don't suppose you would recognise him if you saw him again.'

Corla smiled.

'Of course I could, that's why I rang. I may be getting on a little, but my vision is perfect. 20/20, I have never worn glasses in my life. I saw him as clear as day, he paused under the light, just for a second, and he looked my way down the road. I saw his face. I'd recognise him again for sure, especially now we know what he's done. The filthy git. He needs to be put behind bars. I'd string him up if I had my way... But you don't want to know that.'

'Just to be clear,' said Walter. 'We don't yet know the man you saw was the killer.'

'Well, who else would he be?'

'Do you think you might be able to pick him out of an ID parade?'

'What? Men lined up in front of me, you mean?'

'Yes, but you could be hidden behind a glass screen, if you prefer. They couldn't see you. You'd be quite safe with us.'

'I think that would be better.'

'Could you do that tomorrow, say late afternoon, if we arranged it? We'd send a car for you.'

'Yes, I'd do that, be happy to, so long as I received my just rewards.'

'You would, on completion of a successful prosecution.'

Corla nodded and said, 'Okay, I'll do it.'

'One thing I don't understand?' said Walter.

'What's that?'

'Why has it taken you until now to tell us what you saw?'

'That's the funny thing. I didn't put two and two together until I heard it on the news today, about the murder being in Berryland

230

Avenue. To tell you the truth, I'd forgotten all about it. You know what it's like when one goes out and has a few drinks. I'd forgotten even seeing him. But then I have special powers, and it all came tumbling back. I can see his face in my mind now. If only you could see that too.'

'Special powers?'

'Yes, didn't I say? I'm a medium, a spiritualist, I do fortune telling as well, and sometimes I receive ESP moments.'

'ESP?'

'Yes, extra sensory percept…'

'I know what it is, I'm just not sure I believe in it, and I know a court would never do so.'

'What I have told you is not an ESP moment, Inspector. It's the truth, fact, and when you put me in front of a line-up, I will point the killer out to you, so long as he is there, of course. I am not in this for the money, I can assure you of that, though I'll admit anything would be gratefully received.'

'We'll organise something.'

Corla nodded and said, 'I know you think I am a stupid woman, but I am not. I have gifts. I could tell you a lot about yourself, you'd be surprised. After this is over, you should consider booking an appointment and come for a consultation. Would you like my card?'

Walter grinned and glanced at Karen. She was grinning, too.

'I'll tell you what I'll do,' he said. 'I'll take your card if you take mine,' and he pulled one from his top pocket.

'Deal,' she said, swapping cards.

'So what could you tell me about myself?' he said, reaching out and setting the empty cup on the tray.

'Loads, Walter. Your current girlfriend,' and she stroked her lightly pinkened lips and shook her head. 'That won't last five minutes.'

'Nothing new there,' grinned Karen.

Walter looked glum and regretted asking.

'Anything else you can tell us?'

231

'Not yet, but there could be.'

'How do you mean?'

'Information is re-materialising all the time.'

Walter pulled a doubting face.

'But everything you have told us are true facts, not conjecture, or imaginings, or dreams of any kind?'

'I don't do dreams!' she said coldly. 'Dreams are for ordinary people. Dreams are the devil's work.'

Walter glanced at Karen as if to say, anything else, have I forgotten anything? She nodded and stood up and said, 'We'll be in touch, Mrs Revelation.'

'Please do, and it's "Miss" actually.'

Five minutes later and they were outside in the BMW.

'Well?' she said.

'I thought it was going great until all that nonsense popped out about ESP and spiritualism, and mediumship, and fortune telling, for God's sake, and all that ragbag rubbish. It all kind of went downhill after that.'

'You don't believe in it?'

Walter breathed out heavy and hard and said, 'All I believe in are checkable facts. I thought before she might have been in it just for the money, and I still think that could be the case. Let's hope she's not a total fruitcake.'

'I know it's borderline weird Guv, but I thought she sounded quite convincing.'

'You would.'

'Was she right about your current girlfriend?'

'Maybe, but you don't need to be an expert to see that.'

'And how did she know you lived alone?'

'Lucky guess maybe, or perhaps she could tell from my clothing and body language or haircut, how would I know?'

'That's the thing, Guv; she's a clever woman. Insightful.'

232

'Yes, up to a point. It wouldn't surprise me if she had claimed rewards before, fiddling the facts to fit the case. If she's doing that, in the end it won't stand up. When we get back to the station, see what we have on her; see if she's claimed rewards before. If she's taking us for silly Charlies, she's in for a big surprise. We'll charge her with wasting police time.'

'I think she's kosher.'

'I don't know what to think, but hopefully we're a little further forward than we were this morning.'

'Back to the station, Guv?'

Walter nodded, still thinking about something.

'I'll take a bet now that she's made any number of claims against insurance companies. I'll bet she knows every trick going, anything to make a quick buck, and if we think that and can see that, imagine what a smart-arsed defending barrister would do. They'd rip her a new one. Geez, that doesn't bear thinking about. Makes me shiver, just the thought of it.'

'A tenner,' she said, starting the car.

'A tenner what?'

'A tenner says she hasn't claimed a reward before.'

'You're on, and don't forget.'

Chapter Thirty-Two

Back in the office, Mrs West was missing. She had some kind of quarterly update meeting with the local city councillors, something that Walter would do anything to avoid. Walter glanced at Karen and said, 'Let's have a chat in private; there's an interview room free, there's something I want to talk to you about.'

Karen stiffened and glanced at him. He didn't notice, for he was looking away toward the interview room door. They went across the office and into the room and closed the door and sat down.

Karen jumped in first, fearing the worst.

'What do you want to talk about?'

'The ID parade.'

'What about it?'

'I'm thinking of doing something a bit off the wall.'

You and me both, thought Karen, though she didn't say. Instead she found herself saying, 'I presume it's Ronald Speight you want to put up?'

'That's the thing,' he said. 'I don't want to have to do eight or nine bloody ID parades.'

'So?'

'I thought I'd just do the one, have them all in the same line-up.'

'But you can't do that!'

'Why not?'

'Oh, come on, Guv. You know why. For a start, if you tried to use the result in a court of law any judge would almost certainly throw it out, and for two, surely it's against the rules.'

'At this stage, I don't want to use the result as evidence. I want to get a positive ID on the killer. And as for rules, if by bending one a little it saves another woman from being murdered, I'd say it was worth bending, wouldn't you?'

'Of course,' she said, thinking of her own rule bending.

'If we know who it is, we can concentrate all our resources on nailing the bastard.'

'I'm all for that, but it's a risky strategy.'

'Okay, your objection is noted, DS Greenwood, that will be in my report, you'll be in the clear.'

'That wasn't what worried me, Guv. You know I always support you where I can. So who do you want in the line?'

'Speight, Miro, Donaldson, Nesbitt, Flanagan, and Williams. Crocker's out of the frame, good head of hair, not. We'll tell them all they're not the prime suspect; they are there to make up the numbers, due to their similarity to the description we now have of a man leaving Belinda's place at the dead of night. All we are trying to do is eliminate them from our inquiry. Tell them it's in their best interests, blah-blah.'

'I don't think they'll buy that, especially that solicitor bloke, Mr Bouffant. He'll see through it straight away.'

'Maybe, but we'll appeal to his community spirit, helping the police in such a tragic case, et cetera, and we'll throw in two ringers as well, just as token bodies, nothing to do with the case.'

Karen shook her head and grinned and said, 'This is one crazy idea.'

'Yes, it is, but it might just work.'

'Mrs West won't like it.'

'Mrs West won't know about it until it's all set up. Look, I know it's a bit unusual, but sometimes unusual tactics pay big dividends.'

'It's not like you, Guv, but okay, if that's what you want. I'm with you all the way, but I did think you might have used VIPER.'

Walter thought about that for a second and scratched his head. VIPER, the new digital recognition system: Video Identification Parade Electronic Recording, to give it its overlong and pompous title. VIPER had its place, showing witnesses in the comfort of their own home video line-ups of suspects, but it was better done in the flesh where you could smell the fear on the guilty, see the twitchiness in their eyes, and monitor their body language. You couldn't beat up close and personal.

'VIPER has a place, but not here, not now, especially with a woman who supposedly possesses superhuman powers.'

'I thought you didn't believe in all that tosh.'

'I don't, but if there's anything in it at all, I want to have her up close to the killer, to be able to look into his eyes.'

'If he's among them.'

'Yes, Karen, there is that, but at least we'll know if we are looking in the right place, or the wrong one.'

'Actually, Guv, talking about doing things a little off the wall…'

A heavy knock came to the door and Gibbons barged in. He didn't wait to be invited, or to speak; he was straight in there.

'Did you know, Guv, who's put up the reward in the Belinda Cooper case?'

'No. Who?'

'Only Gareth Bloody Williams!'

'He can't do that!'

'Why not?' asked Karen.

'Because he's a suspect, without an alibi,' said Walter, 'when I last looked, and no matter how unlikely a suspect he might be, he's still in the frame, and he can't be putting up financial inducements to put someone else in the frame.'

'Thought you'd better know, Guv.'

'Yeah, thanks Gibbons, we'll be with you in a minute,' and Walter turned back to Karen. 'What were you going to say?'

Karen scratched her head.

'Oh, nothing important, Guv, another time maybe, let's get on with setting up the ID parade to end all ID parades.'

Walter grinned.

'I couldn't have put it better myself. We'll set it up for half-past four tomorrow afternoon. Someone will have to go and fetch Corla Rev at say half three, so she's here in plenty of time.'

236

'Gibbons and Hector?'

'No, send Jenny and Nicky. Corla might be happier to see another woman on the team.'

'Okey-doke. I'll fix it.'

Outside, in the general office, Walter filled the team in on developments. Hector was assigned the job of finding two ringers, Jenny and Gibbons the duty of making sure everyone else attended.

'Don't forget,' said Walter. 'They must all wear dark trousers, short casual jacket, gloves, and no hat.'

As it turned out, Derek Nesbitt had come back bored and early from his fishing trip, and actually said he was looking forward to it. Miro, Speight, Flanagan and Donaldson all moaned like hell, but agreed that if it put them in the clear they would attend, albeit under protest.

Walter phoned Gareth Williams and mentioned he was out of order in putting up a reward. Gareth advised Walter that he had indeed put up a reward, and would continue to do so, and as he believed he knew and understood the law at least as well as Inspector Darriteau, that was how it would remain. The reward stood, and at least that might encourage Corla Rev. Walter was too busy and too tired to argue. At least Williams had agreed to attend, though he too protested long and hard about it.

Everyone went home a little earlier than usual, all hoping and praying the next day the quaintly named Corla Revelation would steer them towards a positive result.

An hour later Walter threw a beef curry ready meal into the oven and slammed the door. He squished a can open and sipped direct. He thought about Corla Revelation and her offer of a consultation. She hadn't mentioned anything about a discount, but surely that would be forthcoming if she collected cash on the

237

case. He'd be flavour of the month. It might be worth thinking about. What had he to lose?

He thought about Carlene Henderson and how nice it would be if she came round, though right there a phone call would have done, but nothing like that happened, and he wasn't going to weaken and ring her, not yet a while. And he thought again about the neat woman in yellow, Nesbitt's neighbour, what was her name again? Mary Warner, that was it. He wasn't losing his memory yet. What was it she had said? *Every woman knows you, Walter; you're quite famous around Chester these days,* something like that.

She had a way of speaking to men that pleased them, that was obvious, and when the case was over, he might go round there, by way of thanking her for her assistance, and see what developed. Seemed like a plan. He turned on the TV and watched an old black and white war movie starring Kirk Douglas, or was it an anti-war movie; he was never quite sure with some of those too clever by half pictures, and after that he went to bed earlier than usual, and slept surprisingly well.

Karen lounged on her sofa, eating a lightly done tuna steak with an avocado on the side, and thought about David Baker. He would fit right in amongst the planned line-up, but how could she suddenly blurt out that she knew who the fifth man was, that he matched Corla Rev's description spot on, but don't mention the tiny fact she was dating him. It wasn't going to happen. She hoped to god Corla would pick someone out, finger the killer, and anyone would do.

Her mobile on the coffee table rang. Her heart skipped a beat. She reached across and grabbed it. It was him. She smirked and smiled and felt good about life, and took the call.

It was a long call, and a warm call, but in truth one that consisted of trivia and gossip, a typical conversation between two people who maybe cared about one another, and perhaps thought they could care about each other a lot more. He had a beautiful telephone voice, manly yet soothing, clear diction without any discernable accent, as similar thoughts swirled through his head about her.

It was only afterwards she realised she knew so little about him. Where he came from, what his parents were like, what they did, how he'd fallen into the job he said he adored, and so much more. How had all that been overlooked and neglected?

Had he been cunning in steering away from discussing such things? They always seemed to talk about her, but rarely about him. Fact was, she still knew little about him, and that would have to change. Had he shielded his background for fear of incriminating himself in ways that made her shudder. That didn't bear thinking about either, yet she did, for several hours, her mind racing to improbable places she would rather not have visited.

What was it that Walter had said about the fifth man? Karen thought hard. It was something like: *Our man is smarter than the ordinary Joes we have in the frame, much smarter, and more dangerous with it. He's a cunning foe to be reckoned with.*

A cunning foe to be reckoned with, a phrase to stick in the mind. But was David Baker a cunning foe, or *the* cunning foe? The following day might shed light on that crazy idea. But if it didn't, what then? The only thing for it would be to set a trap. She could be cunning too, she had always known that. Maybe it came with the job. She would have to set a trap that only the killer would know how to trigger, but how, and where, and when?

It wasn't an easy problem to solve. She would much prefer to have bounced ideas off Walter about that, but that wasn't possible. Later, much later, she came to a decision. If the ID parade produced no definite result, and no clear trap plan presented itself by close of play, she would miraculously uncover the identity of the fifth man in Bel's technology, as if for the first time, and tell Walter everything. It wasn't perfect, but it was

239

progress, and she would stick with it, and that brought her a better night's sleep than had seemed possible earlier.

Chapter Thirty-Three

He sat alone, late at night, in his modern apartment. The TV was off, he didn't often watch television, but the music was on, loud. Occasionally it brought strife with the neighbours; the late night music listening, but he was in the clear. The sound was muted, headphones only.

He reached forward and increased the volume. Holst's planet suite, Mars to be exact. The bringer of war thundered into his ears. It relaxed him, cleared his mind to the point of making thinking easier.

He had always thought two would be enough, that he would have been sated. But recently he'd come to question that judgement. Truth was, he did not feel as fulfilled as he'd imagined he would, as he wished to be. There was still something missing. A measure of dissatisfaction was growing within him. He was now sure a third incident would finish it off. A third one would signal the final end of things, closure, as the people who knew about these things liked to say.

Yes, that seemed to fit together so well. A third one it would have to be, but who? And where, and when, that was the greater question. Who, where, and when? He reached out again and turned the volume up high as to be unbearable, thinking that it might drown out such complicated and difficult thoughts. Yet it did not, not completely, for they refused to go away. They were growing still, those dark ideas, like dry rot, as if they were some kind of alien creature that could never be slain.

In his mind he began sorting through potential suitable candidates, and that brought a smile to his handsome face and satisfaction to his soul. If only they knew what he was thinking, wouldn't they be surprised and terrified? They damned well should be.

There were several women in the frame, and the thing was, this time the lucky one, or unfortunate one, depending on your line of thinking, would also want to kiss him, or so he imagined, or be kissed by him, which was almost the same thing.

The faces slid through his head, one to six, like slides slipping through an old-fashioned projector, click, bang, show, click, bang, show, and there were pros and cons for each of them, so much so that it made it hard to choose. But a decision would have to be made, and soon. He knew that now. It had to be done.

Click, bang, show, was a maybe, click, bang, show, perhaps not, this time, click, bang, show, another maybe, click, bang, show, a definite possible, click, bang, show, a maybe/maybe not, click, bang, show, oh, right up there, for sure, in fact the favourite to date, definitely, and back to the beginning without any resolution in sight. Perhaps a second screening might clarify things. Click, bang, show, and off we go. Perhaps a good night's sleep would bring clarity to the mind. That seemed an appropriate thought.

Mars came to an end. His favourite part. He reached forward and switched off the sound technology. In his brain he switched off the slide projector too. He wouldn't think about number three again until the morning. He could do that, switch things on and off at the touch of a button. It was a rare talent he didn't know he possessed until recently. Not many people could do that, turn things on and off in the mind at will.

He stood up and turned everything off, switched the light out, and headed for the bathroom. Undressed and jumped under the shower, admired his fit and taut body, flexed his muscles, washed and gently dried himself, and went to bed, and dreamt the dreams of a God.

The whole team was in early again for they understood the importance of the day, the entire team that is with the notable exception of Mrs West, who had succumbed to one of her occasional and very frightening migraines.

242

On hearing that news, Walter and Karen shared a look as if to say, someone must be looking down kindly on us today. There would be no need to explain to Mrs W the reasoning behind an ID parade containing not one but six suspects. By the time she returned, the whole pantomime would have been played out.

Perhaps inevitably, the morning and early afternoon dragged by, as they often did when something significant, something important, something exciting, was planned for late afternoon. But it gave Karen the time to check on Corla's history. She had attempted to claim rewards before, so that looked like her bet had lost. But she had been unsuccessful, so that muddied the waters sufficiently to perhaps get her off the hook. They'd have to look carefully at the terms and wording of the bet, and that brought some temporary merriment into the office when she informed Walter of the news.

At two o'clock Karen said, 'Shall I ring Mrs Rev to tell her everything's on track?'

'No, I'll do it, and it's "Miss",' and he pulled her card from his desk drawer, picked up the phone, and dabbed in the numbers.

The phone rang four times and was picked up.

'Amazing Revelations,' said the voice in a singsong fashion.

'Corla Revelation?'

'That's me, Inspector. Have you rung to book an early appointment?'

He laughed and said, 'No, not today, just a quick call to advise you that we're all arranged at this end. Everything's on track. Jenny and Nick will call for you at 3pm, for you to be here in plenty of time, so we can prepare you, and explain the procedure.'

'It all sounds most daunting.'

'It's not. It'll be a cakewalk, and I'll be by your side every step of the way. You'll be fine.'

'I hope so.'

'We'll see you soon.'

'Yes, Inspector, you will.'

Everything started at half-past two. Hector was sent to the local Job Centre to pick out two smart looking guys who vaguely fitted the bill, guys who'd imagined they were there for a job interview. They were in the police station by ten-past three, being briefed about the ID parade to come, as fillers, you understand, and reasonably happy about collecting thirty quid expenses for their trouble. Hector had a dental appointment after that and went off to visit the killer driller fiend for urgent attention.

Jenny and Nick departed on the short ride to Warren Drive to collect Corla Rev, and they returned with the star guest by half-past three. She looked smart too in a long fitted beige raincoat and good white shoes. Walter greeted her and asked if she'd like a tea or coffee. Corla declined and muttered something about getting it over as soon as possible.

They took her downstairs to view the set-up. First, Walter took her into the interview room. All the furniture had been removed, and along one wall was a large mirror.

Walter beckoned to the floor.

'See the line,' he said, 'the men will stand on the line. They'll be holding number cards.' He turned back to the mirror. 'You'll be on the other side of the glass, safe with me. No one in here will be able to see you or hear anything you say, but you'll be able to see them and hear everything.'

Corla nodded and went to the glass. Put her hands around her eyes and peered through from up close. She couldn't see a thing.

'I'm impressed,' she said.

'Good,' said Walter. 'It's a tried and tested system. None of the men will ever know your identity. There's nothing to it. You walk up and down the line, take as much time as you want, go back and forth as often as you like, and only when you are ready, and only if you are certain, you indicate to me who you think the man is who you saw coming out of Belinda's house on the night of her murder. You do that by saying his number. Is that clear?'

'Perfectly. I'm not stupid.'

'I know that, Miss Revelation, there are just certain procedures I have to follow by the book.'

'I see. Sorry, if I was a little brusque, and please call me Corla.'

'Not a problem, Corla. Do you have any questions?'

'I feel as if I should have, but I don't.'

'That's okay.'

'How many men will there be?'

'Eight.'

'And are they all criminals?'

'I'm not allowed to discuss the men involved.'

'I see, makes sense, I guess.'

'Let's go into the other room,' and they went outside and into the viewing room.

Walter pointed at the glass and said, 'You've a great view from here.'

'It's amazingly clear.'

'It is, perfect vision, and the glass has been freshly cleaned today.'

'And they can't hear a word we say?'

'Not a whisper.'

'I'm impressed,' she said again.

'Good. That's the way we like it.'

'Thank you for putting my mind at rest.'

'You're welcome. Anything else?'

Corla shook her head.

'Okay. We're done here for now. Karen will take you back upstairs and we'll wait there until everything is ready.'

'Do you know what this reminds me of?'

'What?'

'An American prison movie.'

Walter grinned knowingly and said, 'I can see what you mean, we're both law enforcement agencies, after all, but the similarities stop there. We're not American, and we're not in a movie.'

'No, pity,' she said, grinning.

The guys in the line-up had started booking in. Michael Flanagan was first, grizzling that he was losing vital fare money, and who was going to compensate him for that? Derek Nesbitt, chipper and happy and confident, for he had never done anything remotely like it before. He'd once considered becoming a policeman, though the thought of wrestling with vicious armed thugs had persuaded him into another career path, though for a moment he was having second thoughts about that.

Next in was Iain Donaldson. He'd taken the afternoon off, and Andrea Dennehey had come with him for moral support, to act as a witness, she said, in an overloud voice. Though she was miffed when informed she would not be allowed to witness events. She would be held in a holding room for friends and family upstairs until it was done.

A subdued Miroslav Rekatic was next up. He listened hard and said little, and both Walter and Karen were surprised at his subdued demeanour, and wondered if he'd been interrogated and rebuked by his fine wife, and if that was the case, it was the least he deserved.

Gareth Williams turned up next, looking confident, freshly preened bouffant prominently on display. He moaned a minute or two about the ludicrousness of the whole exercise, but settled down, realising the quicker the charade was completed, the sooner he could get out of there, and back to his hectic office.

Ronald Speight was late, and no one in the station was surprised at that. The first thing he said was, 'I didn't think I was going to come. I shouldn't be here at all because I'm completely innocent of any crime. But if this is the only way to prove it, then so be it.'

Bob Barnes, an avuncular old bloke of fifty-three, though he seemed much older than that, was the on-duty station sergeant, and it was his responsibility to get the scene set up and ready to go. All eight men were present in the cleared interview room, and all stared at each other and gazed down at the line on the floor that Bob pointed out. He grabbed the two bemused ringers and set one at either end.

The other six were invited to stand in any order, and as usual, much to-ing and fro-ing took place before they settled into final positions.

'Now, gents,' he said. 'Are you comfortable where you are before I give you your number placings?'

'I'm not comfortable being here at all,' moaned Speight.

'I second that,' said Flanagan.

'Let's just get on with it,' said Gareth, 'and we can get out of here,' and that advice had merit, and the grumbling stopped, and the line-up was ready to go.

Bob took the large square white number cards from the top of the radiator and passed them out, left to right, numbers one to eight. He took a step back and made a mental note. From the left, a Job Centre ringer, Nesbitt, Speight, Rekatic, Williams, Iain Donaldson, Flanagan, and the second Job Centre fella.

'Right,' he said. 'No more changes, let's get the show on the road,' and he picked up the internal phone and dialled upstairs.

Karen picked up.

'Bob here, we're ready for you now.'

'Be down in five,' and she set the phone down.

Walter glanced from Corla and back to Karen.

'Are they ready?'

'They are, ready and waiting.'

Corla stood up and pulled a face.

'I feel like I am about to witness an execution.'

'Nothing like that,' said Walter. 'All we are trying to do is serve justice.'

'Yes,' she said. 'You're right, of course,' and in the next moment they were out of the room, and heading for the stairs to take them down one flight, to inspect a line-up of faces that Corla Revelation would never forget.

Downstairs, Karen opened the door to the room with the false mirror, and Walter stood back and beckoned Corla inside. She smiled and stepped through, and caught her first glimpse of men, all in a line, all waiting on her inspection and decision.

'Stand still please,' they all heard Bob Barnes say. 'Please raise your number board and hold steady in front of your chest.'

The boards went up. Faces went dull and disinterested as they always did, as if inspected men always imagined an ordinary face might help. Walter placed his palm on the small of Corla's back and eased her to the end of the room. 'Let's start with number one,' he said. 'Take your time, there's no hurry, you have all the time in the world.'

'And they can't see me?'

Walter shook his head. 'Not one jot.'

Corla nodded and stood closer to the glass. She studied the face of number one, the Job Centre ringer. He was a good-looking fellow, a little younger than her, but the kind of man who always gravitated towards Corla on a night out, and she might let him buy her a whisky if she was in the right mood. But she wasn't there to inspect potential dates, though weirdly it had that feel to it. Speed dating, with potential criminals. Yes, she liked him, but he wasn't the man who'd come out of Belinda Cooper's house at one o'clock in the morning, or whatever time it was.

On to number two. Derek Nesbitt. Right on cue he grinned at her through the glass, as if sensing his moment in the limelight had come. Corla took a step back and glanced at Walter for reassurance.

'It's all right,' he said. 'He can't see you. Keep going.'

It wasn't number two. He was too young, and not strong boned enough, and she didn't fancy him one bit.

Number three was Ronald Speight, the tallest of them all. There was something mean looking about this guy, and maybe he even resembled the archetypal picture that some people have of a murderer. She didn't like the look of him at all. He appeared to her as something of a bully, though whether one can tell such things on looks alone was debatable. He looked pushy and cocksure and was all the things she hated about men. There was

248

no doubt he would be able to look after himself in certain situations, and look after other people too, if the feeling took him. But Corla did not fancy him at all, but neither did she think he was the man she had seen coming out of Belinda's house.

Number four was the Mirror man, Rekatic. Even though he had a decent alibi for Belinda's death, Karen harboured hopes that he had somehow managed to slip away from Grizelda in the dead of night to commit the crime. She held her right hand behind her back and crossed her fingers. It would be brilliant if Corla Revelation could ID Miroslav Rekatic, not simply because they would proceed to charge him with murder, but also because it would let David Baker off the hook.

The thought occurred to Karen that he, David, would have looked right at home amongst the other suspects, and that didn't bear thinking about. She and Walter observed Corla taking a definite pace toward the glass, as she stared through at the Mirror man. Was there something there? Had she seen something in him that struck a chord? She was certainly taking a lot longer over Miro than any of the others.

Corla sighed and shook her head, and took a sideways step to the right, to be confronted by the bouffant hairdo of a smirking Gareth Williams. She pulled a startled face and took a second look. It detracted or distracted from his slightly fattening face. Had it been him, retreating from the house in Berryland Avenue? He was dressed right, but he didn't look right, and he looked better off financially than any of the others, not that that meant anything.

He also looked married, and Corla Revelation had experienced umpteen men who had said they were single when they were not. So much so, she could spot them a mile off. It wasn't him. She would have liked it to have been, and fleetingly that potential reward money came back into her mind, but to no avail. There would be no bounty paid out on bouffant man.

Another pace to the right. Another bland man's face, Iain Donaldson, the geography teacher, though Corla was not to know that. He was the right height and almost the right build, but the wrong body shape and the wrong body language, as if he didn't believe in himself. He wasn't broad enough or strong enough, but he was somehow involved in the case, her gifts told her that. But he was not the man strolling away down Berryland Avenue in the wee small hours.

Another step to the right, and there was Flanagan, and there was danger. He was a man who could kill women, she instinctively knew that, but had he killed Belinda Cooper? Maybe. It was possible. The height was right. The build was right. The body language was spot on; this was a man confident in his own skin, a man who knew what he wanted and how to get it. The best looking man there by a distance, in Corla's eyes, the kind of man she could have fallen in love with, even if he was a little younger than her.

A dangerous man too, that was self evident, but also an exciting man, the kind of guy women gravitate towards in pubs and clubs, maybe without even realising it. She stood stock-still and stared into his face. His neat hair looked recently cut, his dark eyes staring directly ahead, rarely blinking. Number seven was a man she would have liked to have known, but was he a killer?

Had he murdered Belinda Cooper with a baseball bat, as the press said? Was he the man who had looked straight at her in Berryland Avenue before turning and walking away? She so wanted it to be number seven, but she couldn't be sure. She wasn't positive, as Walter had reminded her that she must be. She couldn't possibly ID him, she couldn't pick him out, much as she would like to.

Pity, for she knew through her peripheral vision, it was not number eight, an irrelevance of a man, too nondescript and weak, too much of a loser, too obviously not right, and probably a police plant, on reflection a little like number one. He did not belong there. She glanced at Walter and pursed her lips.

'Well?' he said, hopefully.

'I need to get closer to them,' she said.

'You mean you want to go inside?'

Corla bobbed her head and said, 'I need to smell them.'

'But you weren't close enough to the man that early morning to smell him, were you?'

'Of course not. I want to smell the guilt on them, I need to smell the fear.'

'Okay, if that's what you want.'

'Will you come with me?'

'Yes, of course, all the way.'

Walter nodded at Karen and she jumped on the intercom and said, 'They are coming inside, Bob.'

They watched Bob nod, and stare at his charges and say, 'Best behaviour now, lads, ladies present,' and unbelievably all the men stood up straighter, shoulders back, chests out, a man thing, as if they were about to experience an inspection by the Queen. They probably didn't know they were doing it.

Corla paused at the door and said, 'May I take your arm?'

'Of course,' and she linked Walter's chunky forearm.

They entered the room, stood still for a moment, without glancing into faces, and turned to face the parade. Corla pursed her lips and looked upward. A dainty sniff at number one. She meant it literally, observed Walter, she was going to smell them all. Mothballs and over-strong soap. It wasn't him. A stooge. Number two, Nesbitt, grinning and enjoying himself, expensive aftershave, probably imagined it would bring him all he desired; yet she knew it did not. It wasn't him.

Another pace along and number three, the tall one, Speight. He smelt of musty and dusty offices, and musty and dusty houses, where an absent wife hadn't kept up with the cleaning. But there was more to it than that. Arrogance and ignorance, for starters. Corla shivered, and it wasn't cold in there, the heating was full on. She didn't like the man, in fact she couldn't stand being near him, and that was often an indicator of a violent and out-of-control guy. But no matter how much she might have liked to, she

251

couldn't ID him, for he was not the man. Far too tall. Best to not waste a second on the cretin.

Man number four, Rekatic, was totally different. He smelt of women. Maybe he had sneaked some of his wife's perfume, or perhaps there was more to it than that. This was a different kind of man altogether, and possibly dangerous too. Beads of sweat formed on his forehead. Fear and loathing oozed from his pores. He looked guilty, and he smelt guilty, and he knew it too, a man with many sins to conquer, but was he the man she had seen in the street?

Deep down she knew he did not like women, enjoyed hurting them, even. Corla had met more than her fair share of such brutes. But that worked both ways. She didn't like him either, and she imagined many women would feel the same. It would have been easy to finger him too, and maybe he deserved it, but sadly, he was not the man she saw.

Number five, the man with the flourishing hair. He smelt of gel, and cosmetics, probably spent a goodly portion of his lunch hour inspecting the latest products in the high street chemist, something of a supercilious guy who imagined he knew everything, and thought that money could and would solve all the world's problems. Up close and personal, she thought she might have met him or seen him before, though she could not place where. She peered up into his dark eyes. He grinned back. He imagined she fancied him. What a prick!

On to number six, Iain Donaldson. He smelt of books, and domineering women, probably an insurance clerk or something similar, mused Corla. He couldn't murder a woman if he tried. Corla doubted he could fight his way out of a paper bag. A time-waster, and a waste of time.

But number seven was not a waste of time. Michael Flanagan, he of the recent haircut. She wondered why he had done that, and how long his hair had been before he'd had it trimmed. He could kill; she knew that from the first moment, though whether he had killed Belinda, she still harboured doubts. She tried to sniff him without appearing to do so. There was nothing there, so she was reduced to a more pronounced sniff that none of those present could have missed. Still very little, just a tiny trace of man.

He wasn't sweating, and he wasn't nervous. Here was a man like Geronimo who could go places and leave little or no trace of his presence. Here was a man totally in control of his own body, and what a fine and strong body it was too, powerful and threatening. Corla lingered. She imagined him wielding a baseball bat. What a sight that would have been. Terrifying, but exciting too. She didn't want to move along the line. Yet still her overlong inspection and presence did not unnerve him. He wasn't only strong in body, but rock solid mentally, and that was a rare combination. God had been unusually generous when bestowing gifts on the gentleman.

She wanted to ask him if he had murdered Belinda Cooper, but guessed that would have been beyond her brief, and though his answer would undoubtedly have been a curt denial, she could have deduced things from the intonation in his words and voice. Maybe she was in the wrong job. Maybe the man Darriteau should make an appointment and employ her for her expertise. For a brief second she let her mind run riot.

'Corla,' whispered Walter, easing her on to the final fellow.

He smelt of cheap burgers and overdone onions, probably unemployed, possibly unemployable, maybe hauled in from the local Job Centre, imagined Corla, a place filler, a deliberate attempt to mislead her by people who didn't believe in her gifts, a red herring who stunk out the place. She shook her head, and Walter said, 'Thank you, Bob, just give us a few more minutes.'

Back in the soundproof room next door Walter and Karen glanced at Corla.

Walter said, 'Well, what did you make of that?'

She scratched her chin and rubbed her warts and said nothing.

'Was he there?' asked Karen. 'The man you saw coming out of Belinda's place?'

'It's none of them,' she said. 'But it's all of them.'

Walter jerked his head back and took a second take of her face, and said, 'I don't follow. How do you mean?'

'They're all involved in the case, aren't they? Except the two ringers you threw in at each end, they were just so obvious. But all the others are in there somewhere, and at least two of them are capable of killing women.'

'Unfortunately we are not here to discuss conjecture or theory,' said Walter. 'Illuminating though that might be.'

'Pity,' she said. 'I could tell you things.'

'Which two?' asked Karen.

'Karen!' said Walter, and he shook his head.

'Four and seven, and maybe number three as well.'

'The only thing that matters is whether the man you saw leaving Belinda's house was in that line-up,' said Walter, and he pointed at the glass.

'No!' she said 'He wasn't there, you are looking in the wrong place.'

Walter sighed and shook his head.

Karen's backbone tingled. The worst result she'd feared had come to pass. Walter turned the intercom back on. 'Thank you, Bob,' he said. 'That is all for today, thank you all for your attendance and patience, everyone is excused. Good afternoon.'

'Thank God for that!' snarled Speight, 'and where's my apology?'

'You'll wait till hell freezes over before you get that,' said Flanagan.

Speight nodded and said, 'Anyone fancy a quick pint?'

Gareth Williams, Iain Donaldson, and Miroslav Rekatic made their excuses and left, but the other four were up for it, and they made a beeline for the nearest boozer, amongst much loud and cocky conversation.

254

Walter and Karen took Corla back upstairs and Jenny produced tea without waiting to be asked.

'So sorry,' said Corla.

'You've nothing to be sorry for,' said Walter.

'I feel as if I have let you down.'

'Not at all, if the man wasn't there, he wasn't there.'

'Some of the others were involved though, weren't they?'

'I can't discuss that.'

'No, of course you can't.'

'Finish your tea and I'll get one of the young men to run you home.'

Corla nodded and drank the tea.

'Nicky! Can you run Miss Revelation home?'

'Course, Guv. My pleasure.'

Corla and Karen and Walter shared a look of gentle disappointment, as Walter said. 'We'll be in touch.'

'I'd like that,' she said. 'I could help you, you know.'

Walter bobbed his head and escorted Corla to the door. Karen left them to it, for they seemed awfully pally all of a sudden.

Twenty minutes later Hector came back in. His face was swollen, his top lip crooked like some kind of fifties rock star.

Gibbons looked across at his face and said, 'That's a big improvement.'

'Funny, funny!'

'What did you have done?'

'Two fillings. All done with now, thank God. How did it go here?'

'Drew a blank, though Karen seemed to think it was worthwhile.'

'I did, as it happens,' she said, 'I think she's a talented lady, that Corla,' and she turned to Walter and said, 'Guv, there's something I've been meaning to talk to you about.'

'Guv, Guv!' yelled Jenny, and everyone turned to her.

She set the phone down and came running.

'You'll never guess what!'

'What?'

'That was forensics, an update report on Belinda's house.'

'And?'

'They have a fingerprint match from Bel's bedroom!'

'Yeah, I'll bet they have, and it will be Williams, Speight, or Donaldson.'

'No Guv, that's the crazy thing, it's Michael Flanagan's.'

There was a moment's stunned silence as communal brains took onboard fresh information.

Karen breathed out heavy.

Gibbons said, 'Oh no, I couldn't bear it, surely Hector hasn't been right all along.'

Walter pursed his lips as if about to whistle, though no sound came. Then he said, 'That is interesting, Jenny, mind you, he could have left the print there anytime. Get on to the tag people again; double double double check to see if his tag could have been faulty. If he was there in Berryland Avenue at the time of the murder the tag must have been interfered with.'

'Triple check even,' muttered Gibbons.

'On it, Guv,' said Jenny.

'I wonder why Corla didn't pick him out,' said Walter, thinking aloud.

'You saw her, Guv, you saw how close she was to doing so.'

'Mmm, yes, but she didn't, did she?'

'What now?' asked Karen.

Walter glanced at the clock. Nearly half-past six. Michael Flanagan would have to be home within the next half hour.

'You and I are going to pay a visit to Mr Flanagan's neat little house in Christleton, where we are going to arrest him in connection with the murder of Belinda Cooper, and maybe Eleanor Wright as well.'

'Get in, Guv!' said Gibbons. 'A result!'

'Not yet, Gibbons, not yet.'

Hector looked real smug.

256

'Do you want us to wait on?' asked Gibbons.

Walter bobbed his head and said, 'Please, just until we get back, you can stay on as long as you like after that.'

'Sure thing.'

'Karen!'

'I know, Guv, a car and an unmarked one.'

'You got it, and Jenny, make sure we have the full forensic report as soon as poss, so we can take a quick scan through it.'

'On it, Guv.'

Chapter Thirty-Four

Outside, it was already full dark and getting noticeably colder. The streets were still busy. On the short trip to Christleton, Walter said, 'What were you going to say earlier?'

'Oh, it's not important, Guv, another time, maybe,' and that fitted in well, for they were already pulling in close to Flanagan's house.

Karen doused the lights and said, 'He's in.'

'So I see.'

The lights were on downstairs, though the curtains were drawn. 'Make sure we seize his computer.'

'For sure,' she said, looking forward to getting inside it and checking it out.

Walter felt deep into his raincoat pocket. The cold steel cuffs were there, ready and waiting for business, and Walter intended on using them. They went to the door and Karen rang the bell. A moment later a large shadowy figure appeared behind the glass. Flanagan opened the door, hiccupped, and stared out.

'Not you again, what do you want now?'

He stank of beer.

'Michael Flanagan, I am arresting you in connection with the murders of Belinda Cooper and Eleanor Wright,' and before the guy could say a word, Walter reached forward and slipped the cuffs round Flanagan's left wrist, grabbed his right, and clipped it shut, as Karen cautioned him.

'You've just had me on an ID parade, for god's sake! She didn't pick me out. I'm innocent! What more do you want?'

'New information has come to light.'

'What new information? You're trying to fit me up.'

'All will be revealed at the station. Karen, collect the computer. We are seizing that as evidence.'

'You can't do that!'

'We can.'

Karen collected the computer from the lounge, as Flanagan slipped into some shoes. She glanced at him and said, 'There are no pay and display girls skulking about upstairs, are there?'

'Don't be absurd!'

'Anything else you need, medication or anything at all?' asked Walter.

'I'm not on bloody medication! It's you lot who should be on the meds.'

'Where are your keys?' asked Walter.

'On the ring, there,' said Flanagan, nodding to some hooks beside the door. 'It's the fat bronze one.'

Karen took it down and turned everything off, TV, lights, and the cooker, where some kind of heavy and meaty dinner was on the go.

'If you take me out of the house now, I'm going to break my bloody tag-time.'

'You don't need to worry about that. We'll let them know you are with us.'

'You'd better! I don't want to do extra time because of you, and I want to see a solicitor.'

'All that can be arranged at the station. Do you want a jacket?'

'Do I hell!'

'Language, Michael,' said Walter. 'No need for it.'

Walter dragged Flanagan outside and put him in the back of the car. Karen closed the door and locked the house and joined them.

'What about my key?'

'All in good time. Let's get back to the nick.'

In the police station Karen turned on the recorder and said, 'Interview with Michael Flanagan starting at 7.26pm,' and she

259

added the date. 'I am Sergeant Karen Greenwood, also present is Inspector Walter Darriteau.'

'I'm starving, I want something to eat, I missed my dinner.'

'We'll get something organised for you,' said Walter.

'And I want to see a solicitor.'

'Do you have a solicitor?'

'No, I shouldn't need one; it's only because of you…'

'Do you want me to get the Duty Solicitor?' said Walter.

Flanagan nodded and said, 'I do, and I am not saying anything until he or she, is right here beside me.'

'Could be a long night,' said Karen.

'Suits me, sister, I couldn't go out anyway. It's your social life that's suffering, not mine.'

He had a point there, and he knew it, as Karen thought of David Baker, and wondered where he was, and what he was doing, and what he was thinking.

'How well did you know Belinda Cooper?' asked Walter.

'Oh, no, you are not getting me on that, sliding questions in when you think I haven't noticed.'

'How well?' asked Karen.

'Solicitor? Chop, chop!'

Walter went to the door and peered out. Gibbons was at his desk, staring at his phone.

'See if you can find the Duty Sol, will ya?'

'Sure, Guv, I'm on it.'

Walter sat back down again and scratched his chin and said, 'When did you last visit Berryland Avenue?'

'Look! I don't want to start no commenting, but I will if you persist.'

'You were having an affair with Belinda Cooper, weren't you?' asked Karen.

'No… sodding… comment.'

'When did you first meet her?'

'How could I have been having an affair with this woman if up until recently I was in prison? Answer me that!'

260

He had another point there, and a good one too. Maybe it was a fresh thing, recent, it had to be, otherwise it didn't fit.

'Did you meet her speed dating?' asked Karen.

'See this solicitor here,' said Michael, pointing to an empty chair, 'I'll ask him or her for some advice, and then I'll get back to you.'

'What's your email address?' asked Karen.

'You've got my computer, look it up!'

'We will, Michael, just thought you might like to speed things up a tad. The sooner we get to the bottom of this, the sooner we get finished and get out of here.'

She thought back to Bel's computer and tried to recall if she'd seen any recent messages between Bel and another man, a man like Michael, but nothing registered. They only had Bel's word to say she'd only had five boyfriends. Maybe that figure needed updating.

'Where's my food? And where's the solicitor?'

'Maybe you could eat the solicitor,' suggested Karen.

'This isn't the time or place for idiotic jokes!'

He had a point there too. Walter hid his smirk well.

'Sorry,' she said, glancing at Walter.

Gibbons came knocking at the door and said, 'The Duty Sol is on the way.'

Walter thanked him and Gibbons retreated.

'And the food?' said Flanagan.

'All in good time.'

'Where did you meet Belinda Cooper?' asked Karen.

'I have never met Belinda Cooper.'

Walter opened the manila file before him. Took out a solitary sheet bearing a large photograph of a single fingerprint. He turned it around and slid it across the table.

'Do you know what this is?'

'Could it possibly be a fingerprint?'

'It is, Michael.'

'So?'

'It's your fingerprint.'

'Yeah, so what's your point?'

'That print was lifted this morning from Belinda Cooper's bedroom.'

'You're having a laugh! That ain't possible.'

Walter shook his head.

'It's no joke, Michael, that print was found in Belinda's bedroom, the same room in which she was murdered.'

'You're full of shit!'

'Do you know whereabouts in the bedroom it was found?'

'How could I know that, when I have never been in Belinda Cooper's house, never mind her bedroom?'

'I'll tell you where it was. Inside the drawer on her bedside table. That's a pretty intimate place, the drawer of a bedside table, by a lady's bed, not the kind of place where just anyone would touch.'

'But a lover might,' said Karen.

'Yes,' said Walter, 'and it's the kind of place where one wouldn't think to go when wiping prints. It would be so easy to miss one there, wouldn't it, Michael?'

'You're talking bollocks; you're trying to fit me up. I was at home, in bed. My tag proves it. It's a rock solid alibi. I don't know what your game is, but it stinks. When I first met you I thought you were a decent guy. I shouldn't have been so naïve. I shouldn't have been so stupid. I should have known better. You're just like all the rest, crooked and bent to hell. I ain't saying another word until I see a solicitor.'

Right on cue, Gibbons knocked on the door and came in.

'Duty Solicitor, Guv,' said Gibbons, and he did the introductions and left the room.

She was a smart young woman, was Gayle Drake, neat and tidy too, as any man would testify. No one ever looked quite so good in a plain fitted grey suit. She nodded across the table at Walter and said, 'May I have ten minutes with my client?'

'Later,' said Walter, 'we are in the middle of something.'

'For the benefit of the tape,' said Karen, 'the Duty Solicitor, Gayle Drake, has entered the room.'

Gayle sat beside Flanagan and studied the photograph on the table, and said, 'And this is?'

'That print was lifted this morning from inside the deceased's bedroom. It matches your client.'

'I have never been inside that woman's house, ever,' said Flanagan.

'This says you have,' said Walter, tapping the photo. 'How do you explain your print being inside Belinda Cooper's bedside table?'

'I can't, maybe you can. And I would remind you my tag proves I was at home.'

Gayle Drake butted in.

'Am I to understand my client is tagged, and your own records show he was at home?'

'At present, yes,' said Walter. 'But your client is also a computer expert, and we suspect he has been tampering with the tag.'

'Have you any proof of that?'

'Not yet,' said Karen. 'We're checking through his computer as we speak.'

'Well, until you have proof, I would like my client released, pending further enquiries.'

'That's not going to happen,' said Walter.

'Where's my food?' moaned Flanagan. 'I haven't eaten in nine hours.'

'Is that true?' asked Gayle.

'We don't know when Mr Flanagan last ate,' said Karen, 'but we have ordered something for him. It should be here soon.'

'It's getting late,' said Gayle. 'Why not chase up the food, chase up the research into my client's computer, and reconvene in the morning?'

Karen imagined Walter would reject that suggestion out of hand, and was surprised to hear him say, 'That's not a bad idea.

Mr Flanagan will be detained overnight, and we'll come back to this at 9am tomorrow.'

Gayle looked pleased with herself and nodded.

Job done, so far as she was concerned.

Flanagan said, 'Food?' and back came Gibbons, knocking and entering, bearing a blue and white cardboard box full to overflowing with fried fish and chips. They did look and smell good, and that reminded Walter he hadn't eaten in hours either.

It was almost 10pm by the time Walter and Karen arrived in their respective homes. Walter bunged a ready meal in the microwave and slammed the door. Karen settled down on the sofa and ate two bananas and a beautiful ripe pear, and afterwards gave herself a rare treat, a portion of mint chocolate ice cream, though she felt guilty about it afterwards.

She thought back on the day, and the last conversation she'd had with Walter. He'd said that everyone was getting tired, and that's when mistakes were made, and a break would do them good, and things would look different in the morning after a good night's sleep. She hoped to hell he was right.

It had been a packed day, with the ID parade, and Corla Rev's revelations, and the forensic info on that print putting Flanagan in the frame, and David Baker out of it. And thinking of Mr Baker, she had thought he might have rung, but he did not. Maybe he was playing tough again, silly mind games, making her sweat, and the annoying thing was; it was working. She thought of ringing him, but that wasn't going to happen. In Karen's world the man did the chasing, and if he didn't, it was clear proof there wasn't much to him, and didn't think anywhere near enough of her.

The good news was, as Walter had pointed out, that Mrs West was back in the morning, and with the latest development of Flanagan being in custody, and likely to be charged, she should be more than happy with that. The weird and wacky ID parade featuring not one but six men, all of whom played some part in

264

the case, or cases, might be glossed over and forgotten, if everything went well. That was the hope.

Karen sank a single glass of cold, sharp white wine, albeit a large one, and headed for the shower, ultra hot and ultra cold in quick succession, and then to bed, where she thought awhile, replaying the day's events in her mind, fantasised for a while longer after that, of a tall dark man who would remain nameless, before she fell into a satisfactory sleep.

Walter was asleep too, dreaming of racing greyhounds made from roast beef he couldn't catch and eat, and hot sunny beaches in the Caribbean; and playing the perfect forward defensive stroke at Lords cricket ground, only to be given out by an incompetent umpire. Plus some snatches of Carlene Henderson in there too.

The man was not asleep, but fully awake, thinking and planning. The next day promised to be a big day in more ways than one. He planned to prune another, the third and final one, the last act that would bring everything to a satisfactory conclusion. Closure; and he said the word aloud. 'Closure.' It would not be easy, it never was. But it was satisfying, and in a weird way, uplifting too.

Anyone who had not travelled the same road would never understand or comprehend the intensity of feeling and exhilaration it brought. Only members of their select club could know.

He smiled a warm smile, and prepared for bed. Sleep would come eventually, and of a satisfying kind. There would be no twisting and turning, no restlessness, and no pangs of conscience. It was too late for that.

Chapter Thirty-Five

8.30am, and Walter brought Mrs West fully up to speed. The unorthodox ID parade barely rated a mention, for all eyes were firmly on the prize. Flanagan's print was inside Bel's bedside table, proof positive that he had been there, in her house, in her bedroom.

Mrs West imagined him resting in Bel's bed, maybe after a steamy lovemaking session, reaching over and slipping open the bedside table drawer, touching the inside, leaving evidence that would convict him.

But what was he looking for? A tissue, a condom, surely too late for that, a pill, maybe he had a headache, the poor love, or perhaps he was getting something for her, a sleeping pill, maybe? Though none had been found. It would be interesting to know why he'd gone in that drawer.

'Ask him, Walter,' she said. 'I'm intrigued.'

Her previous certainty that tags couldn't be broken and interfered with had been washed away, overwhelmed by positive evidence that would stand up in court. She'd speak to the tag people. There had to be an obvious explanation.

9.00am, and the interview began, as Karen read the intros for the recorder. Flanagan looked unshaven and rough, as if he'd experienced a hard night's sleep, which wouldn't have been surprising. Cell beds were not supposed to be five-star comfortable. Some deodorant wouldn't have gone amiss either. Gayle Drake looked good again, businesslike and smart. Walter didn't miss that.

He kicked things off by asking Flanagan when he first met Belinda Cooper. The question brought the first of many curt denials, frequently interrupted by Ms Drake, who consistently pointed out the lack of any other evidence. One hour later, and Walter brought an early end to proceedings by ordering a timeout coffee break.

Karen and Walter sat before Mrs West and sipped coffee, or lemon flavoured water, in Karen's case.

'Just a pity Corla Rev didn't ID Flanagan,' muttered Walter.

'You saw how close she was to doing so,' said Karen. 'She couldn't keep her eyes off the guy.'

'Maybe you should go and see this Mrs Revelation woman again,' said Mrs West. 'See what else she can tell you.'

'I agree,' said Karen. 'She's a gifted woman, she can see things that others can't, and by the way, she likes to be called "Miss".'

'Oh, please,' said Walter. 'Let's not go down that line again, same old hippy nonsense.'

'We need more than we've got,' said Mrs West. 'Or he'll wriggle free.'

Walter bobbed his head and reluctantly said, 'We'll see Corla again.'

Mrs West grinned. 'Keep at it team! The same questions half a dozen times, compare the answers, and there you will find incriminating discrepancies.'

It was the same old mantra, give them enough rope, and all that, and that was what they would do.

'Crack on!' she said, and they got up and returned to work.

Before they returned to the interview room, Walter said, 'Strange we never found anything about the fifth man.'

'Ah,' said Karen.

'What do you mean "ah"?'

Karen bit her lip and said, 'I have ID'd the fifth man.'

'Have you now? And when did you do that?'

'Yesterday, I think it was, but with everything else going on, and then the discovery of Flanagan's fingerprint, it didn't seem so important or relevant,' which was not quite the truth, and they both knew it.

'Would you like to acquaint me with this new intel?'

But before she could answer, he called Gibbons over.

'Go and tell the Duty Sol there will be no more questioning of Michael Flanagan until later this afternoon. Say it's due to fresh information that has just come to hand. She can stand down; we'll keep her informed, and get Flanagan back to the cells.'

Gibbons pulled an impressed face and said, 'Sure, Guv,' and beetled off to give the impressive Ms Drake the news.

Walter turned back to Karen. His face said everything, demanding she told him what she knew, and she didn't need prompting.

'His name's David Baker, he's thirty-six, and works for a grain merchant. Never been in any kind of trouble.'

'Does he fit the description of the man Corla described?'

'He does.'

'What vaguely, exactly, what?'

'Pretty much on the nail.'

'And you didn't think to tell me?'

'It's more complicated than that, Guv.'

'Oh, in what way?'

'He's err, kind of, my bloke.'

'What! Your boyfriend?'

Karen nodded.

'Geez! And does "your bloke", as you describe him, have a rock solid alibi for both killings?'

Karen shook her head, and said, 'Not that he's telling me.'

'Have you discussed the case with him?'

'No, not at all.'

'Forgive me, Karen, but I find that hard to believe.'

'I know it looks odd, Guv, but it's the truth.'

'Mrs West will have to be told. It doesn't look good, does it?'

'I know that, Guv, but once the fingerprint thing came up, it really didn't seem important.'

268

'You know the score KG, ALL intel is important, because it builds up the bigger picture.'

Gibbons came back and shared a look with Walter who said, 'How was she?'

'Miffed! She said both she and her client were being unnecessarily messed around.'

Walter pulled a face.

'That's the least of my worries.'

He turned back to Karen and said, 'I'll need to interview this Mr Baker. Where can I find him?'

Karen gave him the phone numbers and an address.

'You'll not be able to attend, you know that?'

'Sure, Guv.'

'In fact you may need to be taken off the case. I'll check that with Mrs West.'

'I thought that might happen.'

'You thought that would be the case, didn't you?'

'It occurred to me, Guv, of course it did, I just wanted to get to the bottom of it first. I was bending the rules a little, I'll admit, just as you did with the...'

'Oh no! Don't you dare compare my off the wall ID parade with you withholding information, it won't wash!'

'Sorry, Guv, but surely it's all irrelevant now we have concrete proof on Flanagan?'

'There are numerous holes in that argument, don't you think? Why didn't Corla ID him, for one? How did he break his tag time, for two? We still haven't found any evidence he is tag tampering, and how and where did he meet Belinda Cooper, for three? And that's for starters. Hardly watertight, is it?'

'He was in her bedroom.'

'Maybe, but nothing else fits.'

Gibbons phone rang.

They heard him say, 'Just a second, Mrs Revelation.'

How that must have been annoyed her.

'Yes, he's here, just a sec, I'll put him on.'

269

Gibbons grimaced and gawped at Walter.

'It's Corla, and she sounds…'

'Sounds what?'

'She sounds kind of frightened, Guv.'

Walter grabbed the phone and said, 'Corla, what's up?'

'I've seen him!'

'You've seen who?'

'The murderer, of course! Or at least the man who came out of Belinda's house. I've seen him twice.'

'Where? When?'

'First thing this morning when I went for the papers. I always go out early if I can, stretch the legs, that kind of thing. He was across the road, I thought it was him, but he ducked out of sight when I looked his way.'

'And the second time?'

'A few seconds ago, crossing the square.'

'Which square?'

'The one outside Portobello Towers.'

'What are you doing there?'

'I was so unsettled when I saw him earlier, I had to get away from the house, so I decided to come and stay here with my nieces. They live in number 35. Safety in numbers, and all that.'

'You mean Janice and Chantelle are your nieces?'

'Yes, how do you know them? They haven't been naughty, have they?'

'No, nothing like that. They were helping me with something else.'

'That's a relief. Please come over, Walter. I'm frightened. I'm certain he's coming to kill me. I'm the only witness, you see, without me he'll get away scot-free. It's me he wants.'

'Sure. We'll come straight away.'

'Please hurry, and bring plenty of puff.'

'Puff?'

'Yes, the damned lifts are off again.'

270

'Bugger! Stay in the flat, lock the doors, and don't go out. We're on our way.'

'Thanks, Walter. You're a love.'

He set the phone down.

Karen, Jenny, Gibbons and Nick had all gravitated to his desk.

'Where's Hector?'

'He's gone to see Pat the snout. Had some intel for us, apparently,' said Gibbons.

'Okay, Nick you stay here and man the phones. When Hector checks in, tell him to get down to Portobello Towers, PDQ, number 35. Jenny and Gibbons, get yourself a car and get over there and wait for us outside.'

Gibbons nodded. Jenny said, 'Got it.'

Karen slipped on her jacket and headed for the lift to grab a car.

'Nick?' said Walter. 'Bring Mrs West up to speed. Tell her Corla Revelation says she has just seen the prime suspect outside her niece's flat. She says he's there to kill her.'

'Sure, Guv. But if the suspect is there, what's Flanagan doing in the cells?'

'Good question! Let him stew for a few hours. We'll keep you posted.'

'And what about the Duty Sol?'

'Humour her, I'm sure you're capable of that.'

Nicky grinned, 'Happy to, Guv.'

Two minutes later and they were in cars pulling out of the underground car park.

'It's him, Guv, I know it's him?' said Karen.

'Who are you talking about now?'

'David Baker, of course.'

'What makes you so sure?'

'No alibi for either murder. Fits the description to a T. Never talks about his family and background, typical behaviour of the career criminal, and he's the only one who wasn't on the bloody ID parade. And just my luck…'

'I don't follow. Just your luck, what?'

271

'It's always the same, Guv. As soon as I get to like someone, I mean really like someone, you know what I mean, it all goes tits up!'

'Let's see what we see, eh, before we jump to conclusions again. Can't we go any faster?'

'Oh yes, Guv, a lot faster,' and she flattened the accelerator and the big car bucked and leapt ahead.

There was a ragbag of cars parked outside Portobello Towers. Some working, some not, some taxed, some not, some owned, and no doubt some stolen, but they weren't interested in that.

'Do you see David Baker's car anywhere?'

She glanced around.

'No, Guv, he drives a flash company thing. It's not here.'

'Corla said she saw the man walking across the square, maybe he came on foot.'

'Could be.'

Gibbons and Jenny arrived, Jenny driving, as she mouthed through the glass, 'Stuck in traffic.'

Walter nodded. Karen's mobile rang.

They both thought it might be Mrs West.

Karen glanced at the screen and gasped.

'What's up?'

'It's him, Guv.'

'David Baker?'

Karen nodded and took the call.

'Hi, sugar,' he said. 'Are you alright?'

'I'm fine,' said Karen, sharing a look with Walter. 'What can I do for you, Mr Baker?'

'Well, I got to my first appointment a little early, and I was just thinking about you, and I thought how nice it would be to hear your sweet voice, and talk to you for five minutes, so here I am...'

'And where are you, exactly?'

272

He glanced up at the old grey building before him.

'I'm in Crewe, outside Cheshire Oats and Muesli PLC, a very romantic spot, I don't think. Got an appointment in ten minutes....'

'You're in Crewe?'

'Yeah, that's what I said, why?'

Karen turned to Walter and said under her breath, 'How far is Crewe from here?'

'About twenty-five miles,' said Walter.

'So if my David is twenty-five miles away, who the hell's the guy Corla saw crossing the square?'

'IF he's in Crewe,' said Walter, getting out of the car. 'It's about time we discovered what the hell's going on here!'

'I'll ring you back!' said Karen, cutting DB off, and jumping out of the car, feeling a lot better about things. She slammed the door, beeped it locked, and hurried after the others. They were closing in on the large dark timber doors that led into the bowels of Portobello Towers.

Chapter Thirty-Six

Gibbons pumped the lift button. Damn all happened.

'They're off,' said Walter. 'Corla told me.'

'Bugger!' said Gibbons, glancing at the stairs.

'Gibbons and Karen, go on ahead,' said Walter. 'And be careful. Jenny, you keep me company.'

'Which floor?' said Gibbons.

'Eight. Number 35.'

'Bugger!' said Gibbons again.

'Language, Darren,' said Walter, shaking his head. 'It's not necessary.'

'Sorry, Guv,' and Gibbons and Karen began the long jog up 128 stairs towards the eighth floor.

The man had beaten them to it by a good twenty minutes. When he arrived on the eighth floor, he found it deserted. The door to flat 35 was open and blowing in the draught Portobello Towers was renowned for.

He eased the door open and crept inside.

Someone had left in a hurry, almost as if they had been tipped off. They couldn't have gone far. There were three half full mugs of coffee on the small table. Still warm. The kettle in the kitchen was hot to the touch. The place smelt of baby food. It would have been better if there had been just the one cup, but no matter. It wouldn't stop him. He thought of settling down and making a coffee, and waiting to see if they returned. But he wasn't a waiting around kind of guy. Always thought it better to take positive action, to be proactive in all things.

He returned to the sitting room and gazed around.

Pushed in against one wall was an old-fashioned glass display cabinet, and in the unit were a selection of round glass paperweights, blue and green and aquamarine. Everyone knew they were heavy and made perfect missiles. He opened the doors and picked up two and slipped them in his jacket pockets. Grabbed another two, and kept them in hand.

He stepped out of the flat and paused at the top of the stairs. Footsteps from below echoed through the common parts, coming higher. A man and a woman's, one light, one heavy, fit people, coming on, silent, not pausing for breath. He could empathise with that, it had been heavy exercise to reach the eighth floor.

He crouched and stared down the stairwell. He couldn't see them completely, just shadows, and occasional glimpses of hardworking elbows, and fleeting feet, powering the ascent. He could hear them puffing and blowing, the man leading the way, though not by much. He stood tall and thought he'd slow them down. Pulled back his arm and brought it forward, fast and true, and sent the first blue missile hurtling down the stairwell.

It crashed into the black plastic covered metal banister, right beside Gibbons, and exploded into fifty pieces of jagged glass.

'Bugger!' said Gibbons, for a third time.

He paused and shook his head. There were shards of coloured glass on his jacket sleeve. He shook them away and checked he wasn't hit. He seemed okay, and glanced down six or seven steps.

Karen was there, lying on her back, across the stairs, one arm dangling through the metal balustrade. There was blood on her face. Gibbons glanced up the stairwell, checking for further incoming fire. He couldn't see or hear anything, no movement; no sign of anyone still up there, as if they had seen their chance, and had scurried away.

'Buggering-hell!' said Gibbons, retreating to Karen. 'Are you okay?'

Her nose bled from a nicking flesh wound. He gave her his handkerchief, reached across and tugged in her protruding hand

and arm from the edge of the staircase, in to safety, out of sight, and as he did that, for five seconds he showed himself. It was enough.

Karen whispered, 'Go and get the bastard!'

Two floors up, the man saw his opportunity, glimpsed the head, and let go a second missile. Heavy cobalt Bristol blue glass full of pretty swirly bubbles hurtled through the air, propelled by gravity, and a muscular bicep, running straight and true, like an airborne torpedo. It thudded into Gibbons, striking him a heavy blow, hitting him at the junction of the top of the neck and bottom of the head, right side, where it bounced off and fell straight on down, passing a puffing Walter and Jenny, coming up two floors below, on its way to ground zero.

'What the hell was that?' said Walter.

Jenny shook her head and yelled upwards, 'Karen, Darren, are you okay?'

Gibbons crumpled in a heap on a still prone Karen, and didn't move. She wriggled free and turned him on his back.

'I'm okay,' she yelled, though not convincingly, and a minute later Jenny arrived at her side.

'You're bleeding!' she said, glancing at Karen's face.

Karen wiped her nose and cheek. The handkerchief was soaked scarlet. It was surprising how much blood can gush from a small flesh wound to the ears, nose and face.

'I'm okay,' she said. 'But I'm not sure about Gibbons,' and they glanced down at the man. He was out cold.

Walter arrived, blowing hard, taking a moment out, bending over to clutch his knees. Andrea Dennehey's words flashed into his brain. *I thought you lot had to keep in shape.* He stood up, hurried to Gibbons and said, 'How is he?'

'He'll live, I think,' said Jenny. 'But he needs checking over, could be concussed.'

Walter glanced at Karen's bloodied face.

'Are you okay? You look a mess.'

'Thanks, Guv. Just a flesh thing, looks much worse than it is.'

276

'I'll take your word for that,' and Walter nodded and said, 'Call an ambulance for Gibbons,' who was showing signs of coming round, 'And call for backup, and where the hell is Hector?'

Jenny shrugged her shoulders on the Hector thing and pulled out her mobile. Walter did too and rang Hector. He picked up immediately and said, 'Hi?'

'Where the hell are you?'

'Hi, Guv. I'm in Portobello Towers.'

'Whereabouts?'

'I saw some people on the ground floor. They told me of a little used rear traders' staircase. I thought I'd try that, seemed a likely getaway route if anyone wanted to use it and slip away.'

'Good work! How far up are you?'

'Fourth floor.'

'Okay, see you on the eighth, and look out! The bastard's lobbing down missiles, Gibbons and Karen have both been hit.'

'What? Badly?'

'No. They'll live. See you soon.'

'You got it, Guv.'

Walter sucked in air.

He convinced himself he was enjoying a second wind.

Karen said, 'Coloured glass paperweights, remember?'

'Only too well, in that cabinet. Jenny, you stay here and look after Karen and Gibbons. Wait for the ambo people.'

'I'm alright, Guv,' insisted Karen.

'You're not!' said Walter. 'Look at the state of you!' Brooking no argument. Blood was running again. It didn't look good.

The man above let go another missile. It had been a precious collectable once. Vivid aquamarine. It crashed into the edge of the stone step close by and exploded. Everyone threw up their hands and arms to protect themselves from incoming glass, and what little of it came their way thudded into the arm of Walter's heavy overcoat. A further missile followed, but missed everything, and hurtled straight on down. Up above, they heard a man's footsteps running away, going higher.

277

'Hector and I will deal with this character,' said Walter, striding out towards the next step. 'Keep undercover, in case,' and they watched the Guv grab the black banister and haul himself upwards like an irritated snorting bull.

Karen tapped Gibbons' cheek.

'Wakey-wakey, boy.'

Gibbons' alarmed eyes opened with a start.

'Shit!' he said. 'What hit me?'

The girls giggled.

'Glass paperweight.'

'Felt more like a cruise missile.'

'Lie still,' said Jenny. 'Ambulance on the way.'

'I'm okay,' he said, and Gibbons tried to stand.

He didn't get half way.

'No, you are not!' said Jenny. 'Just lie still.'

'Who do you think it is?' asked Jenny. 'Up above?'

'I think it's the Mirror man,' said Karen.

'So do I, I always have.'

'I think it's Speight,' said Gibbons, 'put money on it.'

'One thing's for sure,' said Karen, 'it can't be Flanagan, he's in the cells, and it can't be David Baker either, he's in Crewe,' if he was telling the truth.

'David who?' said Gibbons, wondering what he'd missed.

Karen changed the subject.

'I'll look after Gibbons, Jenny, you go on up and help the Guv. You're more good there.'

She nodded and said, 'Sure, Sarge,' and took a run at the staircase, and disappeared up them, Karen's voice chasing after her. 'Be careful!'

Downstairs, sirens could be heard. Backup, ambulance, maybe both, but it was a comforting noise, nonetheless.

Up above, Walter made it to the eighth floor. He was breathing heavy, but what man approaching sixty wouldn't be? Not that many. He made his way along the corridor towards number 35. Hector popped out of a narrow door at the far end of the corridor. He was breathing hard too, but not so much.

'Am I glad to see you,' said Walter.

Hector nodded and said, 'Did you see him?'

'Nope, but I heard him, and I saw the damage he did with his glass missiles.'

The door to number 35 was swaying to and fro. Walter eased it open and crept inside. Hector followed. There was no one in there, no happy nieces, no gurgling great-nephew. There was a glass display cabinet with half the prize exhibits missing, and half drunk coffee on the table, faintly warm.

'Looks like they cleared out,' said Walter, retreating outside. 'She was frightened, was Corla, maybe made a wise move.'

Hector nodded and said, 'I think he's gone higher.'

Walter nodded and said, 'Agreed. You go on, I'll follow,' and Hector hit the stairs running, but before Walter could follow, the door to another flat opened a tad. Eyes peered out, and the door opened further. Corla appeared and whispered, 'In here, Walter.'

Walter hurried inside and Corla shut the door.

They were all there, Corla and the nieces, and Chantelle's toddler, Ben. The door to one bedroom was wide open and inside, two young men were busy, headphones on, tape and CD decks all over the place, computers by the dozen, big small and modern and alive, and Walter heard a jingle being played, *Dee Bee Cee – the continuing sound of free pirate radio,* and one of the lads said, 'We are interrupting this programme to bring you a special news report. The man known as the baseball bat murderer is being chased as we speak by police through Portobello Towers. More news as we get it, but for now, steer clear of Portobello.'

One young man came to the door and checked out the suspicious-looking stranger, and pushed the door closed.

Corla said, 'Ignore them. They're good boys. Have you caught him yet?'

'Not yet, but we will, I think he's gone up on the roof.'

Corla nodded and said, 'He's here to kill me. You know that, don't you?'

'He's not going to kill anyone. I'm going after him,' and Walter headed for the door, Corla following.

'Be careful,' she said. 'He's mad and he's dangerous.'

'I know that. We have two officers down.'

She let him out and closed and locked the door.

Up top, Hector had reached the top floor. There was a small narrow fire escape door with a metal bar across, half way up. He pressed the bar, and the door flipped open with a soft clang. He went through, and up six breeze-block steps to the left, and he was out on the roof.

There was not much there, just a flat pitched roof with a single small building on it, looked like a big square box, located above the on-strike lifts. Probably contained all the elevator gubbins. A minute later the Guv joined him on the roof.

Walter glanced around, surveying the scene. It was a great view up there, and for once despite being one of the murkiest Novembers on record, it was a clear day. He could see for miles, the River Dee winding its way through the old city, and North Wales beyond, the snow-capped mountains of Snowdonia away in the distance, but he wasn't there to admire the view.

Away to the right was a suspicious looking radio transmitter aerial, a lashed up effort on the corner of the building, held together with black electrician's tape, no doubt pumping our Dee Bee Cee's exciting exclusive. The only other thing on the roof was the small boxy building.

'Have you looked behind that?' asked Walter, pointing.

Hector shook his head.

'Do it now!'

Hector nodded and ran to the building, went behind it, and disappeared from view for a matter of seconds, as if he was visiting the dark side of the moon, and reappeared, shaking his head.

He returned to Walter, and said, 'What now?'

Walter gazed at the small building, his mind running on overtime.

'On the top of it, Hector. Check out the top.'

Hector grinned and muttered, 'You could be right,' and he took a run at the building, and jumped at it, his right foot hitting it half way up, his hands reaching high, grasping for the top, as he grabbed the roof, and heaved himself up, athletically, not a problem for a six foot fit man like Hector Browne.

He jogged into the centre of the small add-on building and turned and grinned back down at Walter, and said, 'Nothing here, Guv. Not a thing!'

Walter nodded too and said, 'Come on down.'

Hector turned around and held onto the side of the topmost roof and kicked off and jumped down backwards, as easy as an Olympic gymnast dismounting the bars.

Jenny reached the top floor, breathing hard through physical effort. She saw the open door that led up onto the roof, but another narrow door at the far end of the corridor caught her eye. It was blowing to and fro and something about it didn't look right.

She ran along the corridor and pulled the door open and looked around. It was the traders' staircase, and she paused and listened. She could hear muffled voices somewhere down below, male voices, and the echoing sound of steps on the concrete stairs. Were they coming up or going down? It was hard to tell.

She shouted down the stairs, 'Guv?'

A quick reply hurtled back, 'Bugger off!'

Jenny didn't recognise the voice and started down the stairs, running, so much easier going down than coming up. She yelled, 'Stop! Police!' and caught them within three floors. Two late teenage boys, close cropped hair, not a surplus ounce of weight on them, insolent attitude, but nothing Jenny hadn't seen and heard and dealt with a hundred times before.

'What are you doing here?' she asked.

'We're going to work. What are you doing here?'

'Where do you work?'

'On the carwash on the Greyhound estate.'

'Have you seen anyone else, a six foot tall dark haired man, or a big black guy?'

'Nope and nope. Is that it?'

Jenny nodded and muttered, 'That's it,' and she turned and hurried back up the stairs.

One of them said, 'She's a frigging nutcase!' And they laughed aloud and hurried on down.

Up on the roof Hector said, 'What now?'

'If he's not on the lift shaft roof, and he's not behind the building, the only other place he could have gone is in one of the flats, or over the side.'

'Brave man if he has,' said Hector.

'You take north and west, I'll take south and east,' said Walter, heading for the eastern edge. 'And be careful.'

Hector nodded and headed for the north side.

Walter stood as close to the edge as he dared and peered over. There was no wall or fence of any kind on the edge, nothing to stop anyone falling off. About four feet down, all the way round, was a black metal net, narrow gauge, small holes in the netting, sticking out maybe three feet, designed as some kind of safety feature, probably there to stop anything raining down on the unsuspecting public below. Objects like sticks and stones maybe, dropped there by nesting or squabbling gulls, and over time blown towards and over the edge. It was debatable whether that net could catch and hold a human, and certainly not a human determined to go that way… all the way down.

But for someone to climb down there, and over and beyond the net, and back into the side of the building, that appeared almost impossible to Walter. Maybe an ultra-strong ultra-fit gymnast

282

might make it, but beyond the net there was precious little in the way of handgrips or footholds, or so it seemed to Walter, and he couldn't see how anyone could do it.

Walter retreated into the centre of the main roof and said, 'East and South clear.'

Hector came back, nodding, saying, 'North and West clear too.'

'If someone's gone over the side they've got more balls than I have,' said Walter.

'Me too, I couldn't do it.'

Walter scratched his chin.

Hector said, 'Looks like he's got away, Guv.'

'No,' said Walter. 'He's still here. I can feel it.'

Chapter Thirty-Seven

Hector pulled a face and switched his weight from one foot to the other, and said, 'I'm not with you. I don't follow. How do you mean?'

'I think you do, Hector. I only have one question: Why?'

Hector pursed his lips and pulled a grim face, looked downcast and shrugged his shoulders and said, 'How did you know?'

'I didn't, not until a moment ago. It's the old thing. Take away all possibilities, and the only one left is the correct one, and that set me thinking.'

'About what?'

'It was the fingerprint thing that didn't fit. There was always something too convenient about it, and just the one too. No other trace of Flanagan ever being in Belinda Cooper's place, and you were the only one pushing for him to be the guilty party, and it was you who went to Flanagan's place with Gibbons, and my guess is that while Gibbons kept him talking, you made your way into the kitchen and picked up a handy item, a small glass, maybe, and pocketed it, hoping there might be a print on it, and you got lucky, because there was.'

Hector sniffed and stared Walter's way.

Walter continued. 'It isn't easy to lift a print and re-lay it in a different location. But with your expertise, and the things we have taught you, you managed to do it pretty well. Nice touch to put it inside the bedside table drawer, by the way. That took things to a whole new level, intimacy wise. And then there was the ID parade that you managed to avoid by fixing up a dental appointment, no doubt at the last minute. You probably told them you had terrible toothache, and you did that because you'd discovered Corla could and would ID you if she set eyes on you, just as she did this morning on your way here. And you came here to kill her, didn't you? Well, didn't you?'

Hector sniffed a cold laugh but didn't answer.

Walter spoke again.

'It was a moment ago, when you athletically leapt on that roof, a six foot slim man, leaping up there, and all along we have been looking for a six foot slim man who could look after himself, with dark hair and eyes, just like yours, Hector. And you still haven't answered my question: Why?'

It looked like he wasn't going to speak, but he did.

'Do you remember that Sunday in the Maaz Khan case when I persuaded everyone to work overtime? It was the day I'd set aside to give my lady, Sweet Georgia Browne, a full weekend's CPA.'

'Concentrated Personal Attention,' said Walter. 'I remember it well, what of it?'

'Well, she never forgave me for that, me messing her around, and about ten days later, Heather Holmes, that's her real name, gave me the elbow.'

'Is that what this is all about? Being rejected by a woman?'

'No, Guv, not quite. It's far more complicated than that.'

'Explain yourself!'

'She was everything to me. An exceptional person. Everyone else by comparison was irrelevant, and afterwards she refused to see me, changed her phone numbers and email address, and I couldn't contact her. I really flipped. I never knew you could feel like that about anyone, kind of numb.
And I was so damned angry. I can't explain it. I stopped eating, couldn't sleep at night, but kept falling asleep at work. It was eating me up, gnawing away at my guts.

'And one night I was out getting drunk, and I got talking to this guy who told me about this good-time girl who had a caravan down by the river, and how she'd do anything for fifty quid, and he really did mean anything. I thought maybe if I went down there somehow it might bring my Heather back.'

285

'By killing her, you mean? Eleanor?'

Hector nodded. 'Yeah, that was the deal. I didn't want anything else. I went tooled up with petrol and matches, and by then my brain was scrambled. I wasn't thinking straight.'

'Go on.'

'She was a real strange kid, that Ellie Wright.'

'How do you mean?'

'As I was doing it, throttling her, do you know what she did?'

'I can't imagine. What?'

'She reached up and kissed me, Guv. Can you believe that? She kissed her killer, as if in thanks, as if she wanted me to kill her all along.'

Walter snorted his disbelief and said, 'And Belinda Cooper? What did she do to deserve to die?'

'That was completely different.'

'In what way?'

'I only wanted to frighten her. I wanted to spread panic through the city. I wanted to see what you would do, and I figured if I was right there with you I'd always be one step ahead.'

'You did that all right, spread panic and fear.'

'You don't understand, Guv.'

'Explain!'

'She came at me, real crazy. Tried to kill me, tried to turn the tables. It was always going to end badly.'

Walter sighed and stared across into Hector's gaunt face. He'd turned a shade of November dirty white. Some days in November in England everything is dirty black, or dirty white. Seemed like that, right there.

'You almost killed two of your fellow officers.'

'I'm sorry about that. They're not seriously injured, are they?'

'They'll live, no thanks to you. You need help, man.'

'It's too late for that, Guv.'

'No, it isn't!'

But even as Walter spoke he saw Hector's future. The remainder of his life behind bars in a place where he would be a marked man, a sitting duck, shunned, and a big trophy to be hunted down by every sick and evil individual the State had decided to incarcerate. Sooner or later they would get to him, they both knew that. Crooked police officers went through hell in prison, and who was to say they didn't deserve it? But a police officer who had turned into a killer, that was something else, a rare and heinous thing, and all on Walter's watch. No doubt the stinking stains would flood across the records of everyone involved.

The door to the roof opened again and Jenny and Corla stepped out and stared across at the two men. The guys' body language looked wrong; as if it were all over, when it wasn't.

'Guv?' said Jenny. 'Everything okay?'

'You!' yelled Corla, pointing and glaring at Hector. 'It's him! He's the killer!'

Jenny glanced at Hector and Walter in turn.

Walter let go the tiniest of confirming nods.

Jenny grimaced in disbelief and shook her head.

'Come on, Hector,' said Walter. 'We need to go and get this sorted,' and he slipped a pair of cuffs from his coat pocket.

'I'm so sorry, Walter.'

Hector had never used his boss's Christian name before.

Walter nodded and stepped towards him.

Hector brushed Walter's hand aside.

'You've been great, Guv. I love the bones of you.'

'It's time to show some real courage, DC Browne.'

'It's all drained from me, Guv. Slipped away forever, forgive me, will you?'

He brushed past Walter and ran towards the edge.

Jenny read the situation well. She'd guessed what Hector might do, and leapt into action. She ran towards him, trying to head him off, but realised she wouldn't get there in time. She leapt full length like a rugby fullback tackling a flying winger, reaching out for the ankles, hoping to bring him down before the white line.

Hector half expected something of the kind. At the last second he hurdled Jenny's outstretched arms and grasping fingers, kicking her hands in the process, fracturing two digits. He was strong, incredibly strong, much stronger than he looked, and dainty feminine fingers were never going to stop a healthy hurtling man.

Walter and Corla watched Hector clear Jenny, and dive over the edge, missing the black netting with ease, and like an Acapulco cliff diver, he soared through the air, and was gone.

Walter, Jenny and Corla rushed to the edge in time to see Hector plummeting earthwards, towards his end, ever faster through the chilly November air, content with his life choice of violent death.

'Look out!' screamed Walter to those below.

Some people looked up and saw thirteen stones of masculine human muscle and bones hurtling down towards them. Huge terrified eyes stared up at disbelieving eyes glaring down.

The former DC Hector Browne crashed into the worn tarmac with a sickening thud. The body bounced, though not by much, for that's what it was, a dead body, where once not long ago, it had been a fine young man, and a promising police officer, who in recent days had twisted and turned into a ruthless and merciless killer. What is it they say? Even a dead cat bounces, as do mentally ill policemen. They'd seen the proof.

'Why?' said Jenny, holding her damaged hand to her side.

'Rejection,' said Walter.

'That's a pathetic excuse!' scowled Corla.

'Of course it is!' agreed Walter. 'But that's the reason.'

'He must have been an incredibly weak man,' muttered Corla.

'He was,' said Walter. 'Weak in mind, strong in body.'

He glanced across at the women. Jenny's hand was almost twice its normal size. 'What's happened to Karen and Darren?'

'Gone with the medics.'

'And that's where you're going too. Come on, let's get you some treatment.'

'I'm glad he's dead,' said Corla.

She was the only one who was.

Corla sniffed the freshening wind and mumbled, 'I feel free at last. Totally free, and I can sleep easy.'

Walter and Jenny shared a look, as they all made their way back to the stairs.

Chapter Thirty-Eight

Caw! Caw! Caw! The rooks were doing what rooks do, seeing in the dawn. It was just gone 7.30am on the first day of December. There was a thick crunching frost on the grass, and it was beginning to snow.

Old gravestones and headstones and different sized blackened and mossy stone crosses lined the frosty lawn, standing out at weird angles. None of Hector's family and friends chose to attend the garden of remembrance.

Maybe it was too early for them, maybe they were too ashamed, perhaps they simply didn't care. It's forever surprising how many people in the twenty-first century suffer unattended funerals. You can have a hundred thousand friends on social media and still be alone at the graveside.

Walter was there, as was Mrs West, and the close-knit members of the team, three of them looking like walking wounded. Darren's neck-brace was still on, and would be for a couple of weeks. Jenny's arm was in a sling, though it was the fingers that were damaged and mending, while Karen had downsized the plaster on her nose and cheek, as the cut slowly healed and vanished. They'd all receive bravery commendations, especially Jenny, and well deserved too.

In truth, it wasn't a funeral at all.

There were no limousines and no service and no programme, and no favourite songs, no prayers and no happy memories of a cherished person, now departed, not even a vicar mumbling words. The Chief Constable had suggested the ashes be sprinkled over the lawned garden anonymously, and the sooner the better, and with as little fuss as possible, and that explained the time, and the place.

None of the team wanted that, no one there, hence their attendance. They stood in a short line on the path overlooking the grey frosted lawn, Walter, Darren, Karen, Jenny, and Mrs West. Walter holding before him a small urn of ashes. Feminine footsteps could be heard approaching, echoing along the path in the cold still air, and that set the rooks off again.

The humans turned to look.

Corla Revelation nodded a slight morning greeting as she approached. She looked smart too in a good quality long black coat, black hat set at a jaunty angle, and matching shiny shoes.

'Who the hell told her the time and date?' muttered an irritated Mrs West.

'Not me,' said Walter.

'Nor me,' said Jenny.

'As if,' said Karen.

Darren snorted and shook his head.

'Hello, Corla,' said Walter, as she joined them. 'How did you know the time and place?'

'Really, Walter. Do you still doubt my powers and gifts?'

'You mean, you saw the time and place in your mind?'

'I'm here, aren't I? What more proof do you need?'

She smiled up at Walter and took her place beside him.

Mrs West had no time for such nonsense.

She said, 'Top brass have suggested no service and no prayers for the deceased for the shame he brought on the Force. I suggest a minute's silence for contemplation and reflection. After that, Walter, if you would be so kind as to do the honours.'

'Ma'am,' he said, flicking his wrist and checking his overlarge watch, as the second hand set off.

The minute took an age.

It began to snow harder, large dainty flakes slowly falling from the dark grey sky, blanketing the lawn, whitening everything in seconds, settling on shoulders like giant dandruff. The rooks started up again. Caw! Caw! Maybe in protest at the heavier snow, or the mixed bunch of people below, out earlier than usual, on their garden of remembrance.

And then it was over, and Walter stepped a pace forward onto the whitened grass and removed the top from the casket, and turned and handed the lid to Darren. Walter glanced at each of them in turn. Mrs West nodded him on, anxious to be finished and out of there. Walter turned back to the front and shook ashes from the urn. A dollop fell before them onto the snow. He shook again. A larger amount spilt out, just as a squall came through and picked up the tiny grey cloud, and dispersed it across the frosty and lightly dusted lawn. Another shake, and the casket was empty. Hector Browne had vanished.

They stared down at the strange smudge in the snow, the last sign that Detective Constable Hector Browne had ever existed. By noon, the winter sun would be strong enough to burn off the frost and snow, and the smudge would slip into the cold, dank turf, and vanish.

'Okay,' said Mrs West, lightly clapping her gloved hands. 'That's everything, best foot forward,' and she stepped out, Karen beside her, making small talk, heading back toward the cars. Darren and Jenny exchanged glances and fell in behind. Corla linked Walter's arm and said, 'Hope you don't mind escorting me.'

'Of course not. Why did you come?'

'I read in the press of all the good things he did. I guess I felt a little guilty.'

'About what?'

'About saying I was glad he was dead. I no longer think and feel that, just sad and sorry he did the things he did.'

'We all feel that way, but never forget this; he murdered two women in cold blood, that's the important thing to remember. They and their families is where the sympathy should lie.'

'And he'd have murdered me too if he could.'

Walter nodded and muttered, 'Quite possibly.'

Corla shivered and said, 'There's something else I wanted to mention.'

'Oh?'

'I hope you don't think this an inappropriate moment.'

'Go on.'

'Do I still qualify for the reward?'

'Ah, maybe not the right time to discuss that.'

'Yes, you're right, of course. Will you ring me sometime, let me know what you think?'

Walter nodded and said, 'Sure, I'll ring you,' and he glanced back over his shoulder at the smudge in the snow. The rooks were there, looking busy, pecking and investigating, maybe sensing a juicy breakfast. They'd be disappointed. The smudge was dissipating. Hector Browne had departed.

Back at the cars, Mrs West, Karen and Darren jumped into the first one, as Walter offered Corla a lift back into town.

She smiled and nodded and said, 'That would be great.'

'I'll drive,' he said, glancing at Jenny's sling.

'Thanks, Guv,' she said, easing into the back, and the cars rolled away. Hector Browne's life was over, though he would always be remembered, but for the wrong reasons.

A couple of days later Walter checked out the reward thing. As far as he was concerned he would have been happy for Corla to receive something, for she did set them on the way to closing the case. But the man who put up the cash, one Gareth Williams, solicitor of the parish, pointed out there had been no successful prosecution, and he didn't deem it appropriate any payment be made. Knowing the man, Walter wasn't surprised, and it fell to him to break the news.

He picked up the phone and prodded in Corla's number.

'Can't say as I am surprised,' she said, before adding, 'I can put curses on people, you know.'

'Not on me, I hope.'

'No, Walter, not on you. Never.'

'While I'm here, there is one other matter.'

293

'Yes?' she said, unable to keep a note of expectancy from her voice.

'I can't turn my eyes away from illegal broadcasting emanating from Portobello Towers.'

'That's nothing to do with me.'

'Maybe not, but pass on some well-meant advice. I am bound to forward what I know to the appropriate authorities.'

'You'll never stop them, not completely.'

'That's as maybe, but they can expect high-powered visitors, and soon.'

'Thanks for the tip. Anything else you want to ask me?'

'Not right now.'

'Fair enough. Stay in touch, Walter.'

'Sure,' he said. 'I will,' and gently set the phone down.

At lunchtime he left the office and jumped a cab for Easton Road. The same yellow Cayton was parked outside number 56. He made his way upstairs and rang the bell to 3A. Mary Warner opened up with a smile. It was pastel green day. She looked kind of cute.

'Hello again,' she said. 'What can I do for you?'

'I was passing, and I thought you might like to know our enquiries about the other matter have been completed.'

'Derek's in the clear, is he?'

'Of course he is, he was never really involved.'

'I know that, Mr Darriteau. I do read the papers and watch TV.'

'Yes, I'm sure, I just thought you'd like to know.'

Mary grinned and said, 'Would you like a coffee?'

'Another time, maybe. It looks like you were on the way out.'

'I was, just nipping into town.'

'Any chance you could offer an overworked policeman a lift?'

'I might.'

'Good,' he said, suddenly lost for words.

'Such a terrible business.'

'Yes, appalling.'

'It must have been frightful for you, one of your own colleagues involved like that, such a shock, I imagine.'

'It was, I haven't quite come to terms with it.'

Mary bobbed her head and said, 'I'll get my things, raincoat and stuff.'

'Sure,' he said, kicking his heels on the cold landing outside. He didn't have to wait long. A minute later she joined him, locked the flat door, and in another minute they were downstairs, and she was beeping the cute Cayton open, and they both climbed in.

On the short trip to town he blurted out, 'Do you like music?'

'I love music. Why?'

'There's a choral concert on at the Cathedral, Mozart, I think it is, 8pm tomorrow. I was wondering if you'd like to go.'

'I'd love to go.'

'Great! I'll call for you, 7.30, if that's okay?'

'That's fine. It's a date.'

'Just one thing.'

'Yes?'

'Can we go in your car?'

'Of course,' and she laughed and said, 'you're not banned, are you, from driving?'

Walter guffawed.

'Course not. It's just I'm a car-less person at present.'

'Not a problem, I adore driving.'

She dropped him in town, and he hurried back to the office to see Mrs West, to take up her offer of free tickets, before she gave them to someone else.

David Baker arrived at Karen's apartment at 8pm. She'd pulled out all the stops and had bought expensive wine, organic steaks, and avocado, and had gone to the trouble of making her own unique version of Baked Alaska.

Earlier, she'd found a quiet hour and a half to have her fine blonde hair washed and styled and gently trimmed, and back at the flat she'd slipped into that little black dress again, and looked stunning.

Maybe tonight I'll find out how much he really likes me, she pondered, unable to keep an expectant and excited grin from invading her fair face. The bell rang from downstairs. She jumped to it and sprang the door open, and a minute later he entered her flat, and by heaven he looked good. Tall, dark and handsome, and he looked fitter too, as if he had been secretly working out, as if he was trying to impress her, and how cool was that? *Try harder.* Her earlier suggestion came back into her mind. Maybe he was, trying harder, it sure looked that way.

He was carrying a large bouquet of red roses.

'For me?' she said, reaching out for them.

'I guess,' he said, as she took them and set them to one side, for they both had more important things in mind. He reached out, tugged her to him, and kissed her expectant lips, a mere brushing welcoming kiss that morphed into a hard, heavy and passionate one. She hadn't been kissed like that since the days of Rodney, and maybe David Baker was an even better kisser than Rodders; and that was a pleasant surprise.

She let him kiss her again, as if to check it was as wonderful as she'd imagined, and it was, and how brilliant it was to be able to relax, and lose oneself without worry or fear.

This time she could rest easy in knowing she wasn't in the arms of a dangerous man, while kissing, and being kissed by a killer. Probably.

David's Notes

Thank you for buying and reading my book and I hope you enjoyed it. When you have a spare few minutes, I'd appreciate a brief review on any of the main book sales websites. That would be very kind of you. A single paragraph would suffice. It does help me.

As always, all mistakes in this book are mine and mine alone. My friends and I work hard in eradicating the little blighters, but occasionally little beasties and bugs slip through. I hope they didn't detract from your enjoyment. We kill them whenever we can!

If you'd like to read more of Walter Darriteau and the team, you can do that today. Please check out "The Legal & the Illicit", "The Death Broker", "Five Dead Rooks", "Old Cold Bones", and "Falling", the 2021 new release, all out and available for a modest sum!

Next year, there will be an all-new Walter Darriteau murder/mystery story released, God willing, and he's very excited about that, as am I, so do look out for that. Please check out my website www.davidcarterbooks.co.uk for the latest news and reviews on that, and my other books too. You can contact me via the website on any matter.

Thanks again for supporting independent writers and publishers. I appreciate it. Without you, we wouldn't exist. Have a great day, and don't have nightmares,

David Carter.

*****

Sign up for my occasional FREE Newsletter
and get yourself
"The Death Broker" completely FREE!
Here's the link for that:

http://eepurl.com/czen0T

Please follow me on Twitter
@TheBookBloke

9/22

Printed in Great Britain
by Amazon

84967157R00173